I0575229

Arch Enemy

Mother Race – Book 1

Jason Burgess

Arch Enemy

ISBN: 979-8-9919725-0-5

Author Preface

For tens of thousands of years, we have gazed up at the boundless stars, pondering our place in the cosmos and wondering if we are truly alone. The vastness of the universe begs the question: Could life beyond Earth have visited us in the distant past? This novel is a journey into that intriguing possibility—one that explores ancient legends, modern theories, and the possibility that our modern civilization has a much more complex, and heretofore unknown past than we have thought, and that our history books have taught us. These new truths could profoundly impact our views on religion and our place in the universe.

Working in the aerospace field, my fascination with the unknown and the complexities of advanced technologies extends to the mysteries of ancient civilizations, particularly the enigmatic Annunaki. These ancient deities, immortalized in Sumerian mythology, have sparked countless theories about their origins and whether they might have been extraterrestrial visitors to our planet. Could it be that these beings, described as god-like figures, were not just products of myth, but actual influencers and guiders of early human development?

This work delves into the possibility that alien technologies, far beyond our current understanding and abilities, may have shaped human evolution, culture, and belief systems. From the sudden leaps in human cognitive development to the unexplained architectural wonders of antiquity, we will explore the notion that external forces—perhaps even extraterrestrial—played a hand in our progress.

As we unravel these ideas, we'll also examine the intersection of religion and extraterrestrial influence, questioning how humanity's spiritual beliefs could have been shaped by contact with advanced beings. How these forces impacted our earliest ancestors, including primates, could hold clues to how we came to dominate the Earth as a species.

This exploration is driven by my curiosity and a desire to challenge conventional narratives. Whether you are a skeptic or a believer, the journey ahead is one of wonder, speculation, and discovery.

Together, we will consider the ancient past with new eyes and ask whether the blueprint of human civilization was, in part, written in the stars. This first book of the trilogy starts our journey down the path of unveiling what may be our true beginnings.

Let us embark on this journey into the unknown, with open minds and boundless curiosity.

Thanks for reading!

Jason

DEDICATION

To my children, whose boundless curiosity and laughter fill my days with light and purpose. May you always follow your dreams with courage and kindness, and may you find joy in every step of your journey.

To my family, who have been my foundation and guiding stars. Your unwavering love, support, and encouragement have made all things possible.

This book is a testament to all of you, with love and gratitude that words can scarcely capture.

This book is also dedicated to all the wonderful minds filled with curiosity and wonder.

To all the people fighting for good in this world—those who choose courage over comfort, kindness over indifference, and hope over despair. Your resilience, compassion, and commitment light the way for us all.

This book is for you, the quiet heroes and outspoken advocates, the healers and protectors, the dreamers and doers. May your efforts ripple outward, inspiring others to build a world where justice, love, and humanity prevail.

With deepest respect and gratitude.

Jason

Arch Enemy

The Reptilians

The Browns are commonly referred to as Reptilians. They reside in the Draco Constellation. They walk among us, hidden by a cloak that vibrates at a frequency that grants them the appearance of a human being. Some believe that this race of extraterrestrial beings contains "agents" hidden in our world government slowly working to create one single world government. This some say, explains the reason gold is of such importance to our society.

The idea of reptilian aliens infiltrating human society, particularly governments, is a popular conspiracy theory that has circulated for decades. This theory posits that reptilian beings from another planet or dimension have secretly integrated themselves into positions of power on Earth, manipulating global events for their own agenda. Proponents of this theory often claim that these reptilian aliens have a humanoid appearance, allowing them to blend in seamlessly with humans. They are believed to possess advanced technology and psychic abilities, making them formidable manipulators of human affairs. According to this narrative, these reptilian beings have a hierarchical society with a strict control structure, akin to a monarchy or dictatorship. They are said to have established control over key institutions such as governments, financial systems, and media organizations, using their influence to shape world events in their favor. Supporters of the reptilian conspiracy theory often point to ancient mythologies, religious texts, and alleged eyewitness accounts as evidence of these beings' existence and involvement in human affairs.

Arch Enemy

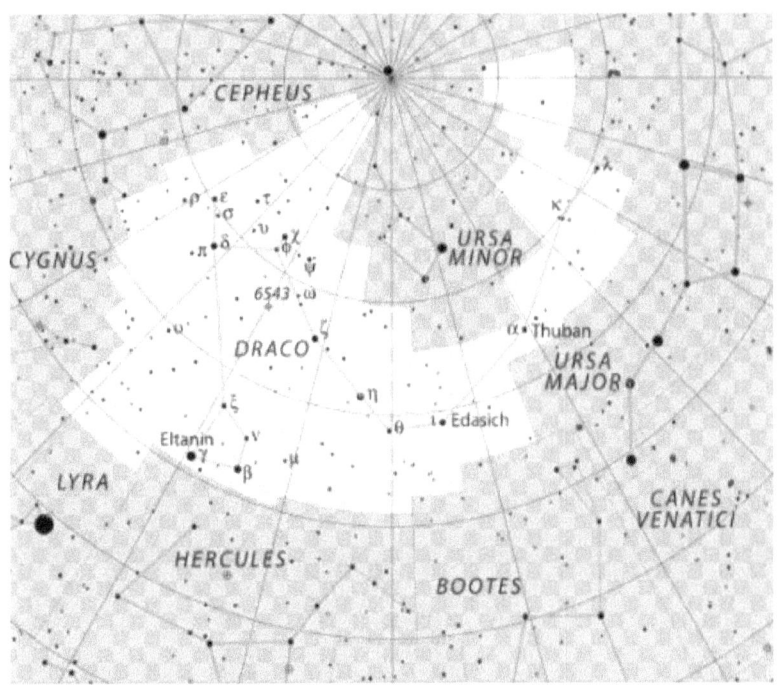

Arch Enemy

ARCH ENEMY

Arch Enemy

ЧЕХDTIЛL I (Chapter 1)

Bruce Finger stood before the floor-to-ceiling window of his twenty-second-floor office, sipping lukewarm coffee. The mid-thirties architect cut a sharp figure with his short, dark brown hair and intense hazel eyes. A faint smile played on his lips as he surveyed the bustling city of St. Louis below and around him. From here, the famed Gateway Arch, standing 630 ft tall and equally as wide at its base, was a familiar sight. A glistening ribbon of light at the edge of the slow-moving Mississippi River. By statute, no building was allowed to stand taller than the Arch. He was lucky to have an office with such a spectacular view.

His carefully arranged workspace stood as a testament to both his meticulous attention to detail and his boundless creativity. A large, old-school drafting table dominated one corner, covered in blueprints, sketches, and a haphazard pile of worn-down pencils and rulers. Each design bore evidence of Bruce's relentless pursuit of perfection—erased lines, scribbled notes, and countless revisions as he fought to capture his visions on old-fashioned paper before turning his attention to the computer where he honed and polished his designs.

Architectural awards, commendations, and framed photographs of completed projects adorned the office walls. Bruce cared little for such accolades, preferring the simple thank yous of his clients. Yet, these objects whispered stories of dedication and passion, a life spent transforming dreams into steel and glass. And both his boss and his secretary insisted on displaying them.

Bruce turned away from the window and strode purposefully toward his desk, his mind already racing ahead to the day's challenges.

A state-of-the-art computer with a pair of large curved monitors awaited him. As his eyes passed over an array of material samples meticulously laid out on his desk for him by his assistant, he absently ran a finger across the desk's glass surface, feeling its cool smoothness. The familiar sensation grounded him, bringing to mind the countless hours he spent at this desk poring over every minute aspect of his designs.

Settling into his burgundy-red leather swivel chair, he tapped his keyboard, bringing the computer to life. He reviewed the latest updates to his current project, a sleek high-rise condominium complex that would soon grace the St. Louis skyline.

As he immersed himself in the intricacies of structural load calculations and zoning regulations, a nagging thought tugged at the back of his mind. It was a cynical whisper, a voice that questioned the significance of it all. The voice reminded him of the fleeting nature of human achievement and the transient beauty of man's creations. Bruce pushed the thought aside, focusing instead on the satisfaction of a job well done and the pride he took in every design he created or reimagined. Each brick and beam mattered.

"Perfection may be an illusion," he reminded himself as he leaned back into his chair, awkwardly rubbing at the knot forming between his shoulder blades. "But I'll chase it till the day I die," he chuckled as he pulled up his latest architectural revisions on the right-hand screen.

A knock on the door snapped Bruce out of his reverie, and he swiveled to face the entrance. An impeccably dressed couple stepped into his office, their eyes scanning the room with an air of expectation. The Johnsons were new clients who sought his firm's expertise for the renovation of their historic downtown St. Louis mansion, a rambling three-story affair. The pair taught at nearby Washington University, both in the field of medicine.

"Mr. Finger," the husband began, extending a firm handshake. "We're excited to see what you have in store for us today."

2

"Please, call me Bruce," he replied, gesturing for them to sit. As they settled into the plush chairs opposite his desk, Bruce's mind raced yet again through possible design solutions, each one tailored to the unique challenges of their project. The Johnsons' home of thirty years held a special place in their hearts. He was determined to preserve its historic charm while accommodating their modern needs. A happy client was always the goal. Besides, like his boss liked to remind him, a happy client was a potential return client.

"Let's start by discussing your vision for the space," Bruce suggested, opening up a digital blueprint on his computer. "What are some of the key elements you'd like to maintain, and where do you see room for improvement?"

As the Johnsons shared their thoughts, Bruce listened intently, his eyes alight with curiosity. He asked probing questions, seeking to understand not only their preferences but also the underlying motivations behind them. This was a delicate dance, balancing the desires of clients with the practical constraints of architecture that clients were more often than not unaware of beforehand. Bruce took pride in his ability to navigate these complexities with grace and precision. And to explain such things to new clients—with no ruffled feathers.

"Based on what you've told me," Bruce mused, sketching out a rough concept on his tablet, "I'm sure we can achieve a balance between preserving the original character of the home and providing the modern amenities you're looking for. By incorporating sustainable materials and smart technology, we can also transform your home into an efficient, elegant space that respects both the past, the present, and even the future."

"I like that, Bruce," Mrs. Johnson beamed, lacing her fingers. "We can't wait to see the final design. I'm hoping we'll see plenty of grandchildren running around the house so I hope you remember to keep them in mind in your design."

"Count on it," Bruce replied, a genuine smile gracing his lips.

"Speaking of which, when can we see something?" asked Mr. Johnson, coming to his feet.

"I'll have the preliminary plans ready for your review next week."

As the Johnsons exited his office, exchanging pleasantries and expressing their confidence in Bruce's abilities, he felt a surge of satisfaction. Helping clients realize their dreams was what made his job worthwhile, despite the occasional whispers of doubt and insecurity that echoed within him.

"Hey, Finger!" called out a voice from across the central open-plan workspace. "You finished charming the clients?"

Bruce rolled his eyes, suppressing a grin as he turned to face his colleague and boss, Sarah Hill. Besides being president of Hill and Associates, Sarah was a talented architect in her own right. Together, they formed a dynamic duo that tackled some of the firm's most challenging projects. He always found their banter a welcome reprieve from the high-stakes world of architectural design. More than that, Bruce knew his work would suffer without her candid insights.

"I charm everybody. You know that, Sarah," Bruce said. He tossed a crumpled ball of graph paper in her direction. "Although, nobody could hope to be more charming than you."

"Flattery will get you everywhere, my friend," she said, returning his smirk as she caught the projectile effortlessly and flipped it back at him. "Now, get back to work. We've got a current deadline to meet, remember?"

"Of course," Bruce agreed, quickly shifting gears.

Sometime later, Bruce's phone buzzed, jolting him from the trance-like state he'd fallen into while working on the latest blueprints. He glanced at the phone screen, his eyes crinkling at the corners as he read the text from his younger brother, Jack. Despite the six-year gap, he and Jack had always been close. Jack knew better than to call him at work because Sarah hated personal calls coming in, plus, he might be interrupting a meeting with an important client. And there were always meetings with important clients.

Call me soon as u can

Bruce sighed and set the phone on the corner of his desk. With Jack, there was no later, everything was now. But Jack could wait. He had a deadline.

Yet, glancing at his phone, he felt a pang of guilt. With the demands of his job and the whirlwind of life in general, it had become all too easy to let days or even weeks slip by without truly connecting with those who mattered most, like his brother and the rest of his family. He resolved to do something about that.

"Who was that, Bruce?" Sarah asked, poking her head in, a cup of coffee in each hand. "Here." She set one on his desktop. "New girlfriend?"

"Too soon," Bruce shot back. "I'm still recovering from the old one. That was my brother. We're long overdue for a chat."

"Ah, the elusive Jack," she said, nodding sagely. "I've heard the stories but I've yet to meet the man himself."

"Trust me, he's one of a kind." Bruce replied. "And I mean that in the best way."

"Sounds a lot like his big brother." Sarah teased, her eyes sparkling with mischief. "Alright, enough chitchat." Sarah playfully swatted at his arm. "Get caffeined up and get cracking."

"Right," Bruce agreed, redirecting his thoughts to his work. But even as he immersed himself in the intricate dance of lines and angles, he couldn't help but think about Jack's text. What was so urgent this time? One of his kids lose a tooth? His wife, Carla, pregnant again? That would really be something. And, not for the first time, he wished he had children of his own. Of course, he'd have to find a wife first, a soulmate.

As the sun settled over the western horizon, the office emptied. Rather than stay and burn the midnight oil alone in the tall building,

Bruce drove back to his house to finish up his work. He prepared a quick light meal of a burger and canned green beans, to be washed down with a can of light beer. He carried his plate into his home office. He ate and drank mindlessly, as he focused on the design taking its final shape on the computer screen.

Bruce's phone buzzed with a new text message from Jack: *U there? Call me.*

Bruce sighed and slipped the device into his pocket. He had to focus on the job. Two hours later, he stepped back from his work and grinned. It really was a beautiful thing. Sure, it was no Taj Mahal but what was? Besides, the Taj Mahal had already been done, the product of another dreamer's imagination. One of these days he'd get his chance to build something majestic, something magical.

Until then? Shopping centers and office complexes, the occasional historic remodel. That was his day-to-day existence. Not great art, not even great architecture, if he did say so himself. But it did pay the bills, so he had no real complaints. Besides, he was rather happy with how well this one, the new Doheney Office Center, had turned out. If all went well with permitting, the contractor would break ground in less than six months. By then, he'd be well into the Johnsons' home remodel.

Bruce picked up his can and toasted himself with the last warm swig of beer. Another would have been great but he had an important meeting with Doheney tomorrow for review and, hopefully, final approval, and needed a good night's sleep.

Bruce took a last look at his architectural model on the screen, shut down the computer, and turned out the office light. He carried his empty dish and beer can to the kitchen and set them both in the sink. He'd deal with them in the morning. As he turned out the kitchen light, his phone rang again.

"Now what?" he mumbled to himself. He frowned and pulled the phone from his pocket. Then he frowned bigger, feeling guilty that he hadn't called back earlier. "Hello, Jack," he said to his brother. "Sorry, I—"

"About time!" Jack blurted.

"I know, I know. I should've called you but I had a last minute design to finish and you know what Sarah's like." Bruce ran his free hand through his hair. "What's up? Why are you calling so late? Can't this hold till tomorrow?" It was nearly midnight, not crazy late, but late for Jack, who was at his work five days a week at eight in the morning, and for himself.

"Forget the excuses, I'm just glad you're there. Now, listen to me. I know you're going to think it's crazy, or I'm crazy but—"

"Jack, slow down already. What's wrong? Is Carla okay? Something happen to the kids?"

"No. No, it's nothing like that."

"So what's going on that's so important then?"

Bruce heard his brother take a deep breath on the other end of the connection.

"Aliens," Jack said.

"Aliens? We talking illegal border crossing stuff?"

"No, I'm talking aliens as in crossing the Earth's border, if you know what I mean."

"Huh? Jack," Bruce said sternly, "it's late and I'm exhausted. I don't have any fucking idea what you mean."

"I mean aliens as in extraterrestrials. Browns to be precise. Reptilians, if you prefer."

"Browns? Reptilians? Jack, come on… Have you been drinking? Where's Carla?"

"The Browns, Bruce. You remember the Browns. Some people call them Reptilians because that's what they resemble, big walking reptiles." Jack talked a mile a minute and Bruce barely absorbed a snatch here and there. "They've really done it this time."

"Done what?" Bruce found himself asking despite himself.

7

"They've infiltrated the Earth! They're taking over our government. The world's governments!"

Bruce's heart sank. This was what his brother had been texting him about all afternoon? Little green men? Or in this case, big brown reptiles?

This was not the first time his kid brother had ranted about aliens and government conspiracies. Bruce had always dismissed it all as fancy at best, paranoia and delusion at worst, but a small part of him couldn't help but wonder. Was the idea of alien life forms visiting Earth really such a daft one?

"Jack, listen to me. If aliens were here, don't you think the government would know?" Bruce said, trying to keep his voice calm.

"I'm telling you, they're in on it. Half of them probably are Reptilians themselves."

"Jack, get some rest. We both need it. And give my love to Carla and the kids. I'm hanging up now."

"No, Bruce! I need you to believe me. Seriously," Jack said urgently. "You're the only one I can trust. Please?"

Bruce sighed. He knew he had to play along for Jack's sake. "Okay, Jack. Tell me more. What is it you want from me? I'm an architect, not an alien hunter."

"I need you to meet me tomorrow. At the Arch. I'll show you evidence," Jack said. "Irrefutable proof that they're here. And I'm going to need your help to stop them."

"Them?"

"I told you, the Reptilians! Aren't you listening?"

"Uh-huh." Bruce hesitated. The last thing he wanted was to get caught up in Jack's crazy delusions and conspiracy theories. But there was no ignoring the desperation in his brother's voice. "Alright, Jack. I'm going to have to shuffle some meetings around, and Sarah's going to have my ass, but I'll meet you at the Arch tomorrow. But promise me that you'll keep a clear head until then," Bruce said, hoping to calm his brother down. "And get some sleep, for god's sake."

If anything, Jack's voice grew more frantic as he rambled on. "I can't keep a clear head, Bruce. They're everywhere. They could be watching me. Watching us! Listening in on us!" he exclaimed. "I'd better go! Tomorrow, nine sharp!" Jack abruptly cut the connection.

Bruce sighed and ran a hand through his hair. Crazy as it sounded, a promise was a promise. He'd go to the Arch tomorrow and see what Jack had to show him. Until then, he needed some shut eye, but lying there in bed he couldn't shake off Jack's words. What was more unsettling? The fact that aliens were here? Or the fact that his brother believed they were here?

The next morning, Bruce arrived at the Gateway Arch at the appointed time. He'd left his car on a side street. The sky was clear and the sun was up, casting a warm golden glow over the Gateway Arch and its surroundings. All perfectly benign. No giant extraterrestrial reptiles gobbling up the locals.

He scanned the lawn for any sign of Jack but there was no one around except for a few joggers and tourists snapping photos. As he waited, he couldn't help but feel foolish for indulging his brother's delusions. He had half a mind to turn around and head straight to his office but something kept him there. The Arch loomed over him, its metallic curves pulling him in.

Suddenly, Bruce heard a rustling behind him. He turned around to see Jack hurrying towards him, his face frantic and his eyes darting around nervously. "Bruce, I'm so glad you came!" he said, panting heavily.

"Sure, now what's going on, Jack?" Bruce looked at his watch. "I don't have a lot of time. Where's this evidence you were talking about?" Bruce asked, his voice tinged with impatience. His brother's eyes were red and his clothes wrinkled. His cheeks were unshaven. "You don't look like you've slept five minutes."

Jack waved off his brother's concern. "It's here. You have to see it." He grabbed Bruce's arm and led him towards the building at the base of the Gateway Arch. "And when you do, believe me, you'll be glad you did."

As they reached the entrance to the Arch, Jack took a careful look around, then pulled out a small metallic object from his pocket and held it up to the sunlight. "First, take a look at this. I found it inside the Arch. Further proof."

"How's that?"

"Don't you get it? The Reptilians left this behind," he said, his voice barely above a whisper. "One of them must've dropped it by mistake."

Bruce took the object from Jack's hand and examined it closely. It was small, no bigger than a half-dollar coin. But this didn't look or feel like nickel and copper. This coin was unusually light and seemed to be made of a metal or alloy that he had never seen before. The surface of the metal was etched with strange symbols that Bruce couldn't begin to decipher. "What is this, Jack? What does it mean?" Bruce asked, his curiosity piqued in spite of himself, as he flipped the coin over and over in his hand.

"It means they're here, Bruce. They've been here for a long time. Watching us, controlling us. And now they're ready to take over," Jack said, his eyes wild with fear.

Bruce looked at the thing skeptically. "Where did you say you got this?"

"Up there. Inside." Jack gazed upward.

"Inside the Arch?"

"Yeah, and that's not all. I'm sure I've discovered the guidance system to their beacon."

"Their...beacon?" Bruce studied his brother's eyes. Was he high on drugs? This was crazy.

"Some sort of controls. The main controls could be elsewhere. I believe the Arch itself is the main beacon though. The whole thing!"

He waved his arms around. "That's how they know how to target Earth from outer space."

"Right…"

"I know you don't believe me," Jack said quickly. He grabbed his brother's hand. "Come on, I'll show you."

Jack flashed his ID at a security guard at the building entrance and led Bruce to an elevator for use of employees and contractors. They rode to the top of the Arch. "There's this alien machinery hidden in one of the mechanical rooms. I'm sure I was never meant to see it. Nobody is…unless you're one of *them*. I stumbled into the room by accident."

"Sounds unbelievable," Bruce said, and *unbelievable* was definitely the word.

"Yeah, I could hardly believe it myself the first time I laid eyes on it," he said as the elevator carried them hundreds of feet in the air. "Wait till you see it."

Bruce felt more and more uneasy by the minute. He had always dismissed Jack's conspiracy theories as harmless delusions, but this was going too far.

The elevator came to a stop. Jack led him up a hot, steep steel stairway. It was windowless and surprisingly noisy inside. Jack stopped outside a steel door and Bruce followed Jack's lead and stepped inside.

"Mechanical room," Jack announced. "It's here." The room was small and poorly lit, the hum of machinery filling the air. He pointed. "Found that little thing I showed you on the ground here."

There, in the corner of the room, sat a small, vibrating machine. Bruce had never seen anything like it before. "What is this?" he asked, his voice barely above a whisper.

"I told you. Alien tech. They use this to help them travel back and forth between their world and ours," Jack said, his voice filled with awe.

Bruce took a step closer, his eyes locked on the black machine bolted to the floor. A four-inch in diameter metal conduit led from the device to the wall, where it then disappeared. He could feel its power, its energy, swirling around him, filling him with a sense of dread and excitement. He shook himself. No, it couldn't be. Just some silly machine that controlled some part of the Arch's many moving parts, like the tram ride to the top that all the tourists rode.

"All we have to do is destroy it, Bruce. Destroy the portal and we can stop them," Jack said, his voice filled with conviction.

"You mean destroy the Arch? That's madness! We're not terrorists! I build things. I don't destroy them. That'd be sacrilege! Criminal!" His brother wanted him to help blow up a masterpiece?! That went against everything he stood for as an architect and a man.

"Okay, defuse it then," Jack said.

Bruce was relieved to see his brother back down. He wasn't completely crazy then. "How did you find this? What were you doing here in the first place?"

"My firm was hired by the city to conduct a structural review." Jack shrugged. "Routine stuff. Comes up a couple times a year. We got the contract with the feds this year." The Arch was part of the Gateway Arch National Park. Jack tapped the black metal box and it shimmered stronger as if in response. "But there's nothing routine about this."

"Are you sure?"

"Yep, this is alien technology."

The more Bruce studied it, the more it looked like a very ordinary black metal box the size of a small home HVAC unit. "Looks normal to me, Jack. What makes you think it's more?"

"It's the energy it gives off, Bruce. I can feel it. Can't you?" He thrust out his hands like he was warming them over a fire. "I'm telling you, it's not of this world," he said, his voice barely above a whisper. "I've got instruments in my van. I'll test it. Prove it to you. Prove it to everyone."

Bruce studied his brother with a mix of concern and skepticism.

12

It was one thing to indulge Jack's delusions but this was getting out of hand. He had to put a stop to it before it was too late. And he needed to get to the office. Clients were waiting and Sarah would be fuming by now. He'd stop and pick her up a mocha latte on the way. "Jack, we need to get out of here. This is crazy. We could probably both get in trouble for even being here. You might lose your job. You wouldn't want that, would you? Think of your wife and kids. They're counting on you."

"But Bruce—"

"There's no such thing as aliens or portals or any of that stuff," Bruce said, his voice firm. He laid a hand on his brother's shoulder. "Pull yourself together, Jack. Forget all this. I beg you. Forget about aliens."

Jack's face fell. "But Bruce, this is a portal. This entire arch. The Reptilians built it or directed humans to build it under the guise of it being a simple memorial. But it's not. It's more than that, much more. I've been studying. I was up all night, searching the web. I know what I'm talking about!

"Humans built the Arch as a beacon, or portal, whatever you want to call it, under the direction of the Reptilians. And they mean to enslave us, Bruce. Enslave us." His fingers pinched down on Bruce's shoulders. "Or use our souls for their own purposes after our deaths! You, me, everyone." Jack released his hold on Bruce. He was practically crying now. "All this is real, Bruce, I swear it."

Bruce shook his head. "No, Jack. I'm sorry. It's not real. You're just seeing what you want to see. We need to leave this place now before someone catches us." He grabbed Jack's arm and pulled him towards the elevator. "Let's go."

Jack's face was crestfallen as they rode the elevator down. Bruce tried to comfort him, but he could see that his brother was shattered. Seeing the machine, whatever it was, had only made matters worse, convinced Jack more than ever that the aliens were real and that they posed a grave danger to humanity. But Bruce wasn't convinced. Far from it. He had always been a skeptic, and he couldn't let his brother's delusions cloud his judgment. He was a realist, with his feet planted firmly on the ground.

He should never have agreed to come here. It had only made things worse.

As they exited the Gateway Arch, the sun stood high in the sky, and the temperature had risen considerably. Jack remained silent but clearly upset. Bruce tried to break the tension with a joke, but it fell flat. They walked back to Jack's company van in uncomfortable silence, each lost in his own troubled thoughts.

It wasn't until they reached the van, parked in a nearby church lot, that Jack broke his silence. "Bruce, you have to believe me. This is real. The Reptilians are here, and they're out to destroy us. We have to do something before it's too late."

"We'll talk more later. Hey, how about dinner tonight? We'll barbecue. You, me, Carla, and the kids. Okay?"

"Yeah, sure, whatever." Jack's eyes were glued to the Arch.

Bruce sighed and patted his brother on the back. "Goodbye, Jack."

Those were the last words he would ever say to his brother. But at least he'd said goodbye.

ᒷᔑ⨅᠐ᐁᑌᐱ 2

The morning sun glared defiantly off the glass façade of the St. Louis skyscraper housing Hill and Associates, where Bruce spent most of his waking hours. He squinted against the harsh light, rubbing the sleep from his eyes as he mentally prepared himself for the day ahead. The meeting with Jack left him feeling uneasy, with a nagging sensation that refused to go away.

"Morning, Bruce!" chirped the perky building's receptionist. "Big presentation today, huh?"

"Uh-huh," Bruce muttered absentmindedly, carrying a tray of mocha lattes and sipping on one, allowing the creamy sweetness to jolt his senses, hoping to clear his head of his brother's crazy ideas, and focus on the day ahead. He entered the elevator, pressing the button for the twenty-second floor, and pulled off his sunglasses. As the doors pulled together, he replayed his last conversation with Jack in his head. His brother's wild theories about alien invasions and government cover-ups seemed ridiculous here in the *real world*, but there was a fervor in Jack's voice that gave Bruce pause.

"Come on, Bruce, keep it together," he chided himself, shaking off the lingering thoughts as the elevator dinged, announcing his arrival at his floor. He strode into the office, nodding curtly to his coworkers before hunkering down in his workspace to review the Doheney presentation one last time.

As the conference room filled up with his client's team, plus a couple of his own colleagues, Bruce took his place at the front, gripping the edges of the podium. His heart hammered uncharacteristically in his chest. Whether it was from nerves or residual worry about Jack, he couldn't be sure.

Taking a breath to calm his nerves, Bruce began. "Good morning, everyone. Today, we'll be discussing our proposed final design for your new office building. I think you'll see we've delivered on a modern yet functional space that will serve both you, the community, and the environment well." As he spoke, images of the new five-story office structure flickered across the screen. Voice steady and confident now, he extolled the virtues of the design, weaving in his own personal touches.

"Using an innovative combination of solar panels and a green roof space, we are creating a building that will reflect your commitment to sustainability and green building. A building the city can be proud of." A smattering of applause and smiles followed.

Just as he was about to delve into the specifics, his phone vibrated in his jacket pocket. He hesitated for a moment, then, with an apologetic glance at his audience, excused himself and stepped out of the conference room to take the call. The screen displayed Carla's name, and a cold knot of dread tightened in his stomach. Jack's wife never called him at the office. Not without a very good reason.

"Carla? What's wrong?" Bruce asked.

"Bruce... it's Jack."

"Jack?"

"He's... He's dead."

The words struck him like a physical blow, knocking the air from his lungs. "What do you mean he's dead? I just saw him this morning!"

"Bruce, please, I don't know what happened. He left the house this morning...said he was meeting you..." Carla's voice cracked. Bruce could hear her choking back sobs. "I-I need you here, Bruce. Please."

"Of course, Carla. I'm leaving now. Are you home?"

"Y-Yes."

"Okay, I'll be there as soon as I can," he promised, struggling to keep his voice steady. As he hung up the phone, his mind whirred, trying to process the shocking news. Was it just a tragic accident? A coincidence? Or was something more sinister at play? Something connected to what Jack claimed to have found?

As he grabbed his keys and rushed down the hall to the elevator, he feared his life from this day forward would never be the same. His brother was dead. Life could never be the same. The St. Louis heat slapped him in the face as he emerged into the parking garage, but nothing could ever sear him more than the shock of hearing that Jack was dead.

"Jack...dead? It can't be. It's got to be a mistake." But he knew it wasn't. He jumped in his car and roared off, oblivious to everyone else. Every second felt excruciating. He gripped the wheel unsteadily. His thoughts raced faster than his car as he navigated through the crowded city streets and headed for the freeway. A route he had taken countless times before. Yet, today, everything seemed foreign and uncertain.

"No, no, no, no, no," he muttered over and over, clenching his hands as the world raced past.

As Bruce pulled up to Jack and Carla's house in Kirkwood, the weight of the world seemed to settle on his shoulders. The sprawling suburb west of St. Louis exuded a calm that seemed to mock the turmoil brewing inside him. He shook his head, attempting to shake off the heaviness he felt with each step he took towards the front door.

Carla opened the door, greeting him with eyes wet and red from crying. The sight of her obvious pain struck Bruce like a physical blow. "Hey, Carla," he said softly, concerned about the impact his words might have on her fragile state.

"Bruce," she replied, her voice shaky, "thank you for coming." She managed a weak smile as she stepped aside, inviting him in.

"Of course," Bruce murmured, stepping over the threshold. As an architect, he was used to creating structures that could withstand the harshest of storms, but now he found himself in foreign territory—

trying to provide support to a fragile, newly-grieving widow. It was a daunting task, but he couldn't turn away from Carla in her time of need.

"Can I get you something to drink?" Carla asked, her voice unsteady.

"Water would be great, thanks," Bruce replied, grateful for the opportunity to focus on something other than the oppressive grief that seemed to fill every corner of the room. Plus, the everyday task would be good for her—give her something to focus on. Something besides her raw grief.

As Carla disappeared into the kitchen, he took a moment to survey the familiar surroundings, memories flooding back from years gone by.

"Here you go," Carla said, reappearing with a tall glass of water in hand. Bruce accepted it gratefully, taking a sip before setting it down on a plastic Star Wars coaster on the nearest table. For a moment, they both stood there, the silence between them heavy and suffocating.

"Carla, I…" Bruce started, then stopped, unsure of what he could possibly say to alleviate her pain. He decided on honesty, knowing that empty platitudes wouldn't help either of them. "I can't even begin to understand what you're going through right now, but I want you to know that I'm here for you and the kids. Whatever you need, I'll do my best to make it happen."

"Thank you, Bruce," she whispered, tears pooling in her eyes once more as she looked at him. For a moment, they simply stood there, letting the reality of the situation sink in. "Let's sit," Carla said finally, settling herself in what Bruce knew was Jack's favorite old leather recliner.

He hesitated for a moment, his eyes drifting across the family room. The worn beige couch with the sagging cushions had seen countless family movie nights. He and Jack used to play chess together on that preposterous Dr. Who chess set of Jack's, now open and dust-covered on the dark wood coffee table. An eclectic mix of family photos and cherished mementoes from family holidays lined the built-in shelves on either side of the fireplace.

"Been a while since I've been here," Bruce mused, as he fell onto the sofa, the nostalgia washing over him like a bittersweet wave. "You haven't changed a thing."

"Feels like just yesterday Jack was showing you his latest first edition Isaac Asimov novel find," Carla replied, a sad smile playing at her lips.

"Yeah…" Bruce leaned forward. "Do you feel up to telling me what happened?" He was aching for details.

"That's just it," said Carla. "I don't know what happened. They simply called and told me he was dead!"

"But how? What was it? Heart attack?"

"No, it wasn't that." Carla sighed. "I don't know what it was. I got a call telling me Jack was dead. Died at the Arch."

"The Arch?" Bruce bolted upright. "Carla," Bruce said, his voice firm with resolve, "I know this is hard…but I need to know everything. How exactly did he die? You must know!"

What the hell was going on?

The question hung heavily in the air, a weight pressing down on both of them. Carla looked away, tears welling up in her eyes as she tried to find the words. "Bruce…I wish I could tell you but the truth is I don't know. They took his body away and haven't told me anything."

"They? They who? Who took his body?" Bruce pressed. The thought of his brother's remains being handled by strangers angered and terrified him in equal measure.

"I don't know, Bruce. I just don't know. I wasn't there. I only got the call. I was told that a jogger found Jack's body in the river. She called 911. The police showed up and took him away." She sobbed into her hands. "I didn't even get a chance to say goodbye."

Bruce shut his eyes for a moment. This couldn't be happening. This couldn't be real. A nightmare. What she said hinted of subterfuge and deceit. But why? He fought to keep his emotions in check. He had to focus on finding out what happened to Jack.

"Carla," he began, trying to keep his voice steady despite the rising anger, "I understand this is difficult for you, but is there anything else you can tell me?"

She bit her lip, casting her gaze downward as she gathered her thoughts. "A reporter called looking for a story. He told me some men arrived at the Gateway Arch National Park in a black SUV, no license plates. Talked to the police and then took Jack's body away. He wanted to know what I knew about that but I had no idea!"

The room held a mixture of Jack's quirky extraterrestrial books and collectibles mingled with traditional family portraits and knickknacks. A place of comfort and warmth now held the bitter sting of loss. But Bruce couldn't afford to let himself dwell on all that. Carla needed him, and he would be damned if he didn't do everything in his power to help her.

Bruce couldn't shake the feeling that something wasn't quite right about Jack's death. He wasn't the healthiest guy on the block, but he had no real medical problems. Suicide? No, Jack wouldn't do that. Accidental drowning? No, what the hell would Jack have been doing jumping in the Mississippi?

As he watched Carla struggle to hold back more tears, he made a vow to himself that he would not rest until he learned the truth about Jack's death. He couldn't bring his brother back from the dead, but he could bring Carla closure.

Carla glanced down the hallway, then back at Bruce. "There is something else."

"What's that?"

"There's something... strange about Jack's office. I only noticed it a little while ago. After I called you."

"Lead the way." Bruce rose and set down his glass, happy to have something positive to do—a distraction.

And maybe a clue as to why Jack was dead?

Carla nodded and started walking down the narrow hallway, each step echoing through the silent house. She pushed open the door to Jack's home office, revealing a small room that looked more like a shrine to extraterrestrial life than a place to work. Wall-to-wall shelves filled with books, magazines, and papers threatened to spill their otherworldly secrets onto the carpet. Bruce couldn't help but smirk at the sight of it all. For all his brother's intelligence and logical thinking, he'd always held a soft spot for the unknown.

"Jack really went all-in, didn't he?" Bruce said, unable to hide a smile. "I bet he even had a tinfoil hat stashed away somewhere."

"Actually, he did," Carla said, her tone a mix of amusement and sadness. "In the closet, on the top shelf. He used to say it was our best defense against mind-reading aliens."

"Of course," Bruce chuckled, shaking his head. "That's just like him."

As he gazed around the room, Bruce felt a sense of disquiet creeping up on him. The office was a tangible reminder of Jack's passions and eccentricities—traits that seemed to be at odds with the mysterious circumstances surrounding his death. And though Bruce tried to dismiss the feeling as nothing more than grief playing tricks on his mind, there was no shaking the nagging suspicion that something wasn't quite right.

"Carla…" Bruce began, turning towards her with a furrowed brow. "Jack asked me to meet him at the Arch this morning because he was convinced aliens were using it as an outer space beacon. Do you know anything about that?"

She sighed, her expression clouding over with worry. "Sorry, I wish I knew. But he never told me much and, the truth is, I didn't really listen to him when he did." She sniffled. "I wish I had now. Whatever was going on in his head, it had him more excited—and more paranoid—than I've ever seen him before."

"Let's see if we can find anything that might help us understand what happened," Bruce said. "We owe it to Jack, and ourselves, to uncover the truth, no matter how strange or unbelievable it may seem."

Bruce explored the dimly lit office, his fingers skimming over the spines of dusty books and dog-eared magazines lining the shelves. An air of disarray colored the room, like a hurricane had torn through it in its haste to uncover some long-forgotten secret. But even amidst the chaos, Bruce sensed a purpose—a method to the madness that spoke of Jack's relentless pursuit of the truth about aliens. Yellow and pale blue sticky notes littered Jack's dual computer monitors. Jack had scrawled out words like: Tic Tac UFO's, Element 115, Sumerian Tablets, Annunaki, Epic of Gilgamesh/Bible and a few other words.

What did it all mean?

"Man, Jack," Bruce muttered under his breath as he picked up a magazine on the corner of the desk. The zine's bold red headline screamed about a rash of recent alien encounters. "You were always one for the fantastic."

As Bruce flipped through the pages, he found them filled with annotations in Jack's familiar scrawl—cryptic notes and underlined phrases that seemed to hint at connections only his brother could see. Every dog-eared corner marked a new revelation or theory, each more outlandish than the last. And yet, as Bruce studied the jumble of words and images before him, he couldn't help but wonder if there weren't some truths buried within these pages.

"When we were kids, Jack and I used to stay up all night, reading sci-fi comics by flashlight, and arguing about whether aliens were real," Bruce said.

Carla gave him a weak smile. "Yeah. It seems so innocent now, doesn't it?"

"Back then, it was just a game to us. Hell, life was just a game." Bruce sighed, feeling the weight of years settling on his shoulders. "But for Jack… I guess it turned into something more. I never realized…"

22

Bruce continued to leaf through the magazine, his mind racing as he tried to piece together the fragments of his brother's amateur research. Was there something here, hidden beneath the veneer of conspiracy theories and wild speculation? Had something unknown driven Jack to the brink of obsession, and ultimately led to his untimely death?

"Carla," Bruce said. "I'm going to find out what happened to Jack." And he didn't care how deep the rabbit hole went or what kind of secrets it uncovered.

"Thank you, Bruce," Carla whispered, tears welling up in her eyes as she grasped his hand. "Jack was always so proud of you."

Standing amidst the cluttered remnants of Jack's life, Bruce felt a sense of purpose. Although the road ahead was uncertain, he knew that the truth was out there, be it fantastic or mundane, waiting to be found. And he would find it.

Bruce's gaze wandered from the stacks of magazines to a gray plastic box resting on the desk. The sleek design stood in stark contrast to the disarray that surrounded it. Red, green, and blue lights adorned the device and there was a digital gauge at one end. He read aloud the words emblazoned across its surface. "Alien-Xa Identifier."

Bruce chuckled as he flipped the device over, revealing a small printed inscription: Made in China. "Jack had quite the collection of gadgets."

Carla smiled faintly, nodding in agreement. "He loved his toys. Always looking for the latest and greatest. Trying to find something that would prove his theories right."

"Here goes nothing," Bruce muttered, flicking the switch. The device sprang to life, lights flashing. It emitted a soft hum accompanied by a slight vibration that rippled through his fingertips. "Did he ever mention what this thing is supposed to do?" Bruce asked, his brow furrowing as he tried to make sense of the gadget.

Carla shook her head. "Not really. He just called it one of his tools for the truth."

"Tools for the truth, huh?" Bruce studied the device with renewed interest. If there was more to Jack's death than natural causes or a horrible accident, then maybe there was more to this little device, too. And if this Alien-Xa Identifier held even a shred of the truth Jack sought, then maybe, just maybe, it was worth digging deeper into it.

"Carla, you know I'd never normally entertain this kind of… well, silliness," Bruce admitted, rubbing the back of his neck. "But if there's even a chance that any of this could help explain what happened to Jack, I'd like to try."

Carla took a ragged breath and stared into Bruce's eyes. "I know, Bruce. I trust you just like Jack did. If anyone can find the answers, it's you."

"Thanks for the vote of confidence, Carla," he replied, his voice soft yet resolute. He only hoped he could live up to her faith in his abilities.

As the lights on the Alien-Xa Identifier continued to flash, Bruce felt a strange mix of cynicism and curiosity brewing within him. It was as if the device served as a tangible bridge between him and Jack, connecting their shared past with an uncertain future.

Carla's gaze shifted from the Alien-Xa Identifier in Bruce's hand to the disheveled state of Jack's office. "Bruce, what I started to tell you earlier—"

"That's right, you said you noticed something strange. Stranger than this?" he said, holding up the blinking device.

"I think someone broke in here while I was out with the kids," she whispered, her eyes wide with concern.

"Are you sure?"

"No. Nothing seems to be missing or damaged," Carla continued, gesturing around the room. "But I found the window open when we got back, and I know for a fact that I had closed it before we left. And something just doesn't feel right."

"Okay. That's…concerning," Bruce admitted, rubbing his temple. He tried to piece together the implications of an intruder in Jack's office. Was it merely a coincidence, or did it somehow tie into Jack's death? "Listen, Carla, keep pressing the authorities. You're his wife, they've got to talk to you," he said. "For my part, I'll see what I can learn."

"Thank you, Bruce" she replied, her voice barely a whisper. She wiped away a tear of gratitude. "I will."

"Good." There was so much he didn't know. Questions that gnawed at the edges of his mind like ravenous shadows. "Stay strong. For yourself and for the kids."

"I will," she whispered, her eyes welling up once again.

Bruce sensed a flicker of determination behind the tears, as if she had just discovered an inner strength she never knew she possessed. Human or alien, he was going to find Jack's killer and make them pay.

They said goodbye at the door. Stepping outside, Bruce filled his lungs with crisp autumn air that did little to dispel the gnawing unease that had taken root in his chest. Still, the fresh air was a welcome reprieve from the oppressive gloom that had taken hold of the house

"Damn it, Jack," he muttered under his breath, fumbling with his keys. "What the hell did you stumble into?" Bruce sat for a moment, gripping the steering wheel as he stared at the dark windows of Carla and Jack's house. A troubling thought struck him: What if these aliens had seen Bruce with Jack back at the Gateway Arch? What if the Reptilians knew that Jack had shown him their device secreted inside?

Bruce felt a tremor of fear. Jack was dead.

He could be next…

As he drove away from the quiet residential street, Bruce's mind swirled with questions without answers. A sense of foreboding settled over him like a heavy gray shroud. If Jack's death had been an accident, why all the subterfuge and secrecy? No, there were questions that needed answering, secrets that demanded to be uncovered. He steeled himself because if there was one thing that Jack had taught him, it was that the search for truth was a pursuit worth sacrificing everything for.

He slipped the car into fourth gear and locked his eyes on the suburban landscape as it passed by like a blur. The sinking sun cast long shadows across the streets of Kirkwood, painting everything in melancholy hues that seemed to echo the turmoil inside him. He switched on the radio, hoping for some distraction, but all he got was static, like the noise in his head. With a frustrated sigh, he switched it off.

He was an architect. He solved problems. He'd solve this one too.

As the miles rolled on, Bruce's mind ran through the possibilities, constructing elaborate theories, and tearing them down just as quickly. If Jack's death wasn't natural and was no accident, was it the government? Was it aliens, hiding in plain sight? And had Jack got too damn close to the truth for his own good?

The highway stretched out ahead of him like a ribbon of darkness, beckoning him towards an uncertain destiny. There was no turning back now. Would he ever find his way home again?

CHAPTER 3

Bruce slouched in his chair, his eyes narrowing as he scrutinized the computer screen in front of him. A week had gone by since Jack's untimely death. He and Carla had learned nothing new. The authorities continued stonewalling them and there seemed to be little they could do to get answers. And since Carla had her children to take care of, he was on his own going forward. The garish glow of the monitor cast nervous shadows across his features. He scrolled through a seemingly endless list of search results about extraterrestrials and modern earthly visitations, each one more outlandish than the last.

"Little green men?" Bruce muttered to himself, his voice dripping with skepticism. "Yeah, right. And I'm Bigfoot."

As an architect, Bruce had always prided himself on being a rational thinker. But ever since his brother's sudden death, he found himself exploring the fringes of possibility. Desperate for answers, he was even willing to entertain the absurd.

His frustration grew as he clicked on yet another weblink, only to be greeted by yet another improbable tale. It seemed that every day brought new "evidence" of alien visitations and abductions, each claim more ludicrous than the last.

"Damn it," Bruce muttered, rubbing his temples. "There's got to be something out there that makes sense."

That's when he stumbled upon an article about Zachary Lind, a once-prominent scientist now relegated to the fringes of academia for his controversial theories on aliens. The article he landed on painted Zachary as a wild-eyed lunatic, spouting nonsense about extraterrestrial beings and government cover-ups. One of the many theories the scientist espoused was some nonsense about gods actually being aliens who had played with primate DNA to create a workforce to harvest gold for them. To Bruce, it seemed like yet another dead end in his quest for the truth.

"Great, another crackpot," he sneered, the sarcasm in his voice barely masking the disappointment that gnawed away at him. His finger hovered over the mouse, ready to close the tab and return to the quagmire of conspiracy theories that awaited him online. But something lurking in a corner of Bruce's gut told him not to dismiss Zachary Lind so quickly. He knew he was grasping at straws but he also knew he couldn't afford to leave any stone unturned in the search for answers about Jack's death, no matter how absurd it seemed. And Lind was local. What did he have to lose besides a little of his time?

"What the hell," Bruce muttered. He hesitated for a moment, feeling both foolish and desperate as his fingers hovered over the keyboard. With a heavy sigh, he finally typed:

"Dear Dr. Lind," he wrote. "My name is Bruce Finger. I hope you'll forgive my reaching out to you like this, but I've recently come across your work on extraterrestrial life, and I'm intrigued. My brother Jack was a firm believer in the presence of aliens on Earth and had copies of your work. My brother recently died under mysterious circumstances after revealing to me what he claimed was evidence that an alien species he called Reptilians were here with us. I can't shake the feeling that there's more to his story than meets the eye."

Bruce paused, staring at the words on the screen. He sounded ridiculous. Would Lind think he was a lunatic? But he pressed on, driven by an uneasy mix of curiosity and desperation. "Perhaps it's a long shot, but I was hoping to meet with you and discuss your research further. I understand if you're skeptical or unwilling to speak with me, but I would greatly appreciate anything you might share with me. Thank you for your time."

Closing his eyes, Bruce hit 'send' before he could second-guess himself. It was done. As the minutes ticked by, Bruce found it increasingly difficult to focus on anything other than glancing at his inbox. His finger tapped impatiently on the desk, and he caught himself refreshing his inbox every few minutes, the tension building each time no new messages appeared. The waiting was maddening, and he berated himself for entertaining such a far-fetched idea.

"Come on, Bruce," he chided himself, rubbing his face in frustration. "You're an architect, not some UFO nut." His phone buzzed, and he snatched it up, only to find it was a text from a friend living out-of-state. He threw the phone back onto the desk, cursing under his breath. "Stupid false alarms."

As the clock continued its relentless march forward, Bruce grew more and more anxious. Every passing moment seemed to underscore the futility of his quest while, at the same time, he became more and more convinced that speaking with Zachary could be the key to unlocking the truth about his brother's death.

"Come on, come on," he whispered. "Reply, Lind."

The sudden chime of an incoming email broke the silence, startling him. He blinked at the screen in disbelief as he read the sender's name: Zachary Lind. "Finally," he muttered, his skepticism momentarily forgotten in the face of mounting excitement. He opened the message, heart pounding, and scanned the contents quickly:

"Dear Mr. Finger,

Your inquiry has me curious. I believe we have much to discuss. Please meet me tomorrow in Ste. Genevieve, at The Curious Café on Merchant Street at 3 PM.

Yours truly,

Zachary Lind"

Bruce let out a low chuckle at the name of the coffee shop—fitting because he too was more curious than he'd ever been about anything. He quickly typed out a reply and saved the address and time in his phone. "Guess this is really happening," he mumbled, a mixture of anticipation and dread settling in his chest.

The next day, at precisely 2:50 PM, Bruce parked his car outside The Curious Café. Sainte Genevieve sat an hour south of St. Louis at a confluence of the Missouri and Mississippi rivers. As he stepped out, he inhaled the scent of roasting coffee beans coming from the café mixed with the exhaust fumes from a passing diesel pickup truck.

"Get a grip, Bruce," he told himself. "You've faced down clients who've changed their minds mid-construction, you can handle one eccentric scientist."

Pushing open the café door, he was greeted by the familiar aroma of freshly-brewed coffee and the murmur of voices that always seemed to haunt such establishments. He scanned the room, searching for any sign of Zachary Lind amongst the patrons. His eyes landed on an elderly man hunched over a corner table, half-hidden by a stack of tattered books. He had an open legal pad in front of him and a briefcase at his side. His unkempt gray hair and beard were unmistakable.

"Right," Bruce muttered, steeling himself. "Time to find out what the man has to say." As he crossed the room, his footsteps light on the worn oak plank floorboards, he felt a wave of nostalgia for the simpler days when his life consisted of drafting blueprints and arguing with clients over budgets. Suddenly, those days were gone, replaced by this strange new world where he was chasing down mad scientists and looking for little green men! Would those 'good old days' ever return? Would his life go back to normal?

"Zachary Lind?" Bruce asked as he approached the table.

The man looked up slowly, his eyes narrowing as they assessed Bruce. "And you must be Bruce Finger," Zachary Lind replied, his voice gravelly yet genial. "Please, have a seat."

Bruce hesitated for a moment, then pulled out the padded wooden chair across from Zachary, sitting down with more force than he intended. His mind raced with questions, doubts, and the nagging feeling that he had stepped into a realm far beyond his comfort zone.

"Thanks, I'll cut right to the chase," Bruce said, doing his best to project confidence. "Like I mentioned in my email, I'm here because I need answers about my brother's death. And I'm willing to entertain even the most...unconventional theories to get them."

"Then you've come to the right place, Mr. Finger," Zachary replied, a sly smile playing on his lips as he patted the nearby stack of books, most of which bore his name. "Unconventional is what I do best. Can I get you a coffee, Mr. Finger?" Zachary offered, gesturing towards the counter.

"Uh, sure," Bruce said, rubbing the back of his neck. "Black, please. And call me Bruce."

"And me, Zachary. Would you care for anything else with your coffee? A scone, perhaps?"

"No, coffee will do." He was famished after the drive but didn't want to make Zachary pay for his food too.

"Coming right up," Zachary said. He returned moments later with two steaming cups. The low hum of conversation from nearby tables seemed to amplify the awkward silence between them as each waited for the other to speak.

Bruce took a tentative sip of the hot coffee. "So, where do we start?"

"You asked about extraterrestrials and mentioned that your brother... Jack, was it?"

"Yes, Jack."

"He was a believer? I take it you are not."

"That's right," Bruce stated. "But after what happened... I'm not so sure what to believe." He related to Zachary what Jack had told him and showed him at the Gateway Arch. "He was positive it was the work of aliens. That they are using the Arch as a beacon or a portal of some sort, maybe both, to Earth." He waited for Zachary Lind to laugh but the man didn't.

After a moment, the scientist cleared his throat. "Allow me to begin by sharing some of my research." He pulled a stack of dog-eared papers from his briefcase, spreading them over the table like a grizzled detective revealing evidence of a stubborn decades-old case that had been nagging at him. "For years, I have been meticulously collecting data on extraterrestrials and their presence on Earth. More importantly," Zachary said, leaning forward, "the probability that aliens may have had an impact on past Earthly civilizations. There are so many incredible events and wonders of the world that cannot be explained by mere man alone. Things that can only be explained by outside forces and influences."

Zachary fell back in his seat. "I myself have been shunned from the scientific community because they don't want me upsetting the so-called apple cart. I'm ridiculed for my theories that, if proven, would rewrite history and everything we thought we knew. Our technology is advancing quickly and new theories and information have the scientific community at odds. Yet, thinking out-of-the-box is how some of the best and most important discoveries have been made. Did you know we share 98.8% of our DNA with primates?" Bruce nodded and Zachary Lind continued. "There is, rather miraculously, a time period hundreds of thousands of years ago that the human brain increased in size from 350 grams to 1300 grams. How can you explain that?"

Bruce shrugged. "I've no idea."

"I will tell you, Bruce. I believe aliens had something to do with this. Back then, they may have been called sky gods by our early ancestors." The old scientist paused and drank from his cup. "Sorry, Bruce, to you it must seem that I am a silly old fool, just rambling on and on. But I am convinced I am right and I will not back down. This is something I believe. And..." He stared into Bruce's eyes. "I believe Reptilians are indeed real. They live among us."

"Extraterrestrials, aliens, sky gods?" Bruce blew out a breath. "No offence, Zachary, but like, I mean, what the fuck!?" Bruce eased his words with a smile.

"Believe me, I know how you must be feeling, what you must be thinking," Zachary returned the smile, unfazed by Bruce's tone. "I know it sounds far-fetched, but the evidence is overwhelming. Sightings, abductions, crop circles—all can be traced back to these otherworldly visitors."

"Alright," Bruce said, rubbing his forehead. "Let's say I buy into this alien theory. How does that relate to my brother's death?"

"That's where things get interesting." Zachary leaned in closer, his eyes bright and feverish. "You see, Mr. Finger, I believe your brother stumbled upon something he wasn't meant to find...something that put him directly in the path of the Reptilians. And once in their sights...well..."

"Something like what?" Bruce asked.

"Whatever it was he showed you. It's vitally important that I see it. Both the installed black box and the small metallic object he shared with you."

Bruce sighed. "I have no idea what happened to that thing he showed me. I returned it to him and it's disappeared. It could've been on him when they removed his body. And, as I explained, Carla and I have never been allowed to view the body or to collect any personal items he might have had on him. As for the black box up in the Arch, I don't know that we could get access to it. Jack was a contractor. He had an official reason to be there, not me. It's not like I work there."

"We will have to consider this, Bruce." Zachary Lind tapped the side of his paper coffee cup. "Together, I believe we can uncover the truth behind your brother's untimely demise."

"Look, professor," Bruce said, struggling to keep his voice steady, "I appreciate your help, but I'm not sure I can wrap my head around the idea of little green men being behind my brother's death."

"Of course," Zachary replied, nodding sympathetically. "It's a lot to take in. But if you're truly interested in finding answers, sometimes you must venture down paths less traveled. And this path, I fear, will lead us not to little green men but big brown men."

"Brown men?"

"Another term for Reptilians."

"Right, Jack said something like that."

"Yes, the Reptilians, or Browns, are an alien species hiding in plain sight here on Earth. They are determined to rule the world. They have infiltrated all levels of government and industry."

"To what end? Where did they come from?"

"The Reptilians are from the Draco Constellation. Some say they want to farm us for souls. This is the only way they can reproduce. If they have control of our planet, they have control of us. Some also believe the time is now because the Reptilians have become increasingly concerned with our inability to have peace, being the unstable and aggressive primates we are. It's no coincidence they monitor our nuclear and military facilities. They've infiltrated our government. They are worried about a cataclysmic event perhaps ending human civilization—maybe volcanic eruptions on a major scale or a destructive meteor strike. Things of that nature.

"Then there are the Greys, a species of primarily scientists. The Greys assist the Reptilians with this soul farming and their research into how to make humans from atoms and molecules. The Greys are normally more of a neutral party in all this. Once successful, they won't need Earth or us. I'm afraid your brother Jack stumbled upon them and their plans—or at least exposed their wormhole or portal. For that," Zachary said somberly, "he paid the ultimate price."

Bruce stared at Zachary Lind in disbelief. Had he really just said all that? Crazy, that's what he was. Or was he? "You know…" he said slowly, "Jack tried to tell me pretty much the same thing. And now you believe he's dead because of these invaders."

"That appears to be the case." The old scientist pressed his hands against his paper cup for warmth.

Bruce turned his eyes to the swirling darkness of his coffee, searching for some semblance of clarity. The idea of aliens being involved in his brother's death was absurd, ridiculous even— something out of the movies. But as the silence stretched between them, he couldn't shake the nagging feeling that there might be some truth to what Lind said. "Alright, Zachary," Bruce finally said, looking up with steel-eyed determination. "Let's say I believe you."

"Excellent," Zachary replied, his grin widening. "Welcome to the world of the unknown, Bruce."

"Thanks... I think." Bruce leaned in closer, his initial skepticism giving way to a vague sense of intrigue as Zachary laid out more of his theories. The glow of the coffee shop lights illuminated the piles of old newspaper clippings and scribbled notes that Zachary cluttered the surface with.

"Tell me more about these Reptilians," Bruce said, the word sounding funny as he said it. But he had been drawn in by Zachary's unwavering conviction, swept up in the tide of the older man's enthusiasm and unwavering belief.

"Bruce, feast your eyes on this," Zachary replied, shuffling through his papers to produce a grainy black-and-white photograph.

The image was difficult to make out, but Bruce could just discern the outline of a strange, otherworldly figure. His pulse quickened as he squinted at the photo, desperately trying to convince himself it was just a trick of the light or a clever fake.

"Remarkable, isn't it?" Zachary continued, oblivious to Bruce's internal struggle. "And that's just the tip of the iceberg. For years, I've been collecting evidence of their existence, tracking their movements as they walk among us, hidden in plain sight. They're shape shifters, you know. They can manipulate their cloaks to vibrate at a frequency that grants them a humanlike appearance. These cloaks may glitch and you can catch glimpses of sudden eye twitches. I've watched videos where you can actually see a Reptilian eye, if for nothing more than a millisecond. There are even some videos on YouTube showing where this has been shown to have occurred on the very floor of our own US Congress."

"That-That's unbelievable."

"Yes, and I won't even get started on the British Royal Family."

"The Royal Family?"

"And Queen Elizabeth II," Zachary Lind furthered. "While the Arch was ostensibly built as a memorial to Thomas Jefferson, the men—and I use the term men loosely—behind its creation were in truth Reptilians. These aliens were the true guiding force, choosing the proper design winner, seeing it through its construction. Construction that contains many, many alien secrets."

A chill ran down Bruce's spine as he listened, a growing sense of fascination eating away at his rationality. In a corner of his mind, a small, cautioning voice whispered that it was all nonsense, but he found himself unable to completely dismiss the possibilities the scientist spoke of.

"Zachary," he began hesitantly, "are you sure my brother's death has something to do with these...Reptilians?"

"Indeed, I am," Zachary replied solemnly. "But not just him. Countless others have met the same fate, their deaths shrouded in secrecy and covered up by those in power."

"Covered up?" Bruce's brow furrowed. "What are you talking about?"

"Bruce," Zachary said, leaning in conspiratorially, "I did some digging of my own after your message. Your brother's body was removed from the scene of his death almost immediately. No formal autopsy was performed. Officially, he was cremated without ceremony or explanation. But I'm guessing an autopsy was performed. Performed by a Grey."

"A Grey... You alluded to the Greys earlier."

"Yes, as I said, the Greys are brilliant scientists. They come from far away, Zeta Reticuli, to be precise."

"What's that?" Bruce wanted to know.

"Zeta Reticuli is a binary star system in the southern constellation of Reticulum. The Greys are the dominant intelligence there. The Greys are the stereotypical alien that most common humans visualize when they imagine or discuss aliens."

"I see."

"As scientists, the Greys are unparalleled in their pursuit of knowledge, often delving into advanced fields such as quantum physics, genetics, and artificial intelligence. Their technological prowess is legendary, with inventions and discoveries that have revolutionized not only their own society but also contributed to the galactic scientific community. Where do you think we got transistors from back in the day?"

"The Greys?"

"Exactly," answered the old scientist. "They can also be master manipulators," he added, waving a finger in the air.

"Are they on Earth now too?"

"Oh, yes. Definitely. They are here studying our world's lifeforms, most importantly, of course, humans. That study includes performing autopsies on human specimens."

"Reptilians and Greys..." Bruce's voice trailed off. His shock was palpable and he felt suddenly sick as he struggled to process this new information, trying to make sense of the professor's words. If even half what the man said was true, the world was not what he always thought it was.

"Yes. There are other alien species, too. The Annunaki, most importantly."

"The Anna—"

"Annunaki. From the twelfth planet of our solar system, Nibiru."

"The-The twelfth planet? Yeah, sure. Right. Are you certain?"

"Absolutely," replied Zachary Lind. "The planet Nibiru, sometimes called Planet X, does not come into our sphere of orbit often. It is typically hundreds of astronomical units away. Sumerian cuneiform states that Nibiru orbits the sun every thirty-six hundred years. The planet is approximately ten times the size of Earth. Traveling to this planet takes a very long time, even more so if it's not in orbit. Traveling at light speed or utilizing worm holes, portals, I believe. Feels like minutes of travel to those aboard their spaceships, but could appear to last centuries on another's respective planet."

"Wow, this is a lot to take in," Bruce said. "It's like a whole secret world I never knew existed."

"And I believe it's high time this secret world was brought to light," Zachary said, determinedly.

Bruce nodded as Zachary continued schooling him. "The Annunaki are a group of ancient deities often associated with the skies and the heavens. For example, the Sumerian tablets are linked to the Annunaki. These gods most likely are the reason we humans exist today, but that's a whole other story. Apologies, I know I must be overwhelming you with all this."

"Yeah but, at the same time, I'm fascinated. Continue, please," Bruce replied.

"Okay, then." Zachary rubbed his hands together. "The Annunaki's intent of our creation was for a couple reasons. The main purpose was to mine gold. Monatomic gold has intense health benefits and is a superconductor. Meaning 100% of energy input will yield 100% of energy output without energy loss due to friction. This makes it an invaluable tool for space travel. Some even say, if applied to the skull, the electrical energy output from the brain would not suffer any loss and, thus, create intense electrical connections in the brain causing many new mental abilities like telepathy or telekinesis. It is further hypothesized that through the application of monatomic gold you could see into the future as well as the past."

"Incredible."

"The Annunaki told us to mine gold from the Euphrates River."

"Why the Euphrates?"

"Because the river has the highest concentration of monatomic gold in the world. This explains why many of our first human civilizations developed in this general area. This also explains why humanity's need for gold is so ravenous, so demanding. Consider, we deem gold to be the most precious metal, being the color of victory, the "gold standard" phrase for perfection, and being a much sought-after and in-demand metal treasured and used in every part of the planet since the formation of our earliest societies."

The room seemed to close in on Bruce, as if the very walls were conspiring against him. "If what you're saying is true," he said, swallowing hard, "then I'm in. I owe it to my brother and his family."

"An admirable sentiment," Zachary replied, eyes glinting with approval. "But you must be cautious, Bruce. This goes much deeper than you can imagine."

Bruce snorted. "I can see that already! But don't worry, I won't let my emotions cloud my judgment. I'll approach this like any other project: methodically and logically."

"Excellent." Zachary leaned back in his chair, fingers drumming rhythmically on the tabletop. "You may find that your background as an architect will serve you well in this quest. You have a unique ability to see patterns and connections that others might miss."

"Thanks," Bruce said, touched by the man's words. "And thank you for sharing all of this with me. I realize it couldn't have been easy telling all this to a complete stranger, especially given your reputation and all the ridicule you've been subjected to. I'm not sure I could have held up against it half as well as you seem to."

"Truth is never easy, Bruce." Zachary sighed, his voice tinged with weary resignation. "But it's a burden I willingly carry, even at the cost of my reputation. The world needs to know what's really going on, and if I can play even a small part in that, then the cost will have been worth it."

"That's quite a sacrifice. I, for one, value your help," Bruce declared, extending his hand across the table. "We'll uncover the truth about my brother's death and bring these bastards to light. I promise you that."

"Agreed," Zachary said, grasping Bruce's hand firmly. "Remember, we're up against powerful forces. Both human and alien forces. They won't take kindly to us poking around in their secrets and exposing them for all the world to see."

"Let them come," Bruce replied, a new fire burning in his eyes. "I've spent my whole life building things, Zachary. But I'm not afraid to tear them down if it means getting justice for my brother. I'll tear down the Arch itself if that's what it takes."

"I have a thought," Zachary said.

"What's that?"

"There's someone I'd like you to meet."

"Who's that?"

"My granddaughter, Nina."

"Thanks but I'm not looking for a relationship at this time," Bruce said with a smile.

"No, Nina is brilliant. An astrophysicist and an archaeologist. I dare say she has surpassed me. She can be a big help to us."

"Is she local?" Bruce was suddenly intrigued and he had a feeling they could use all the help they could get.

"Yes, very. But let me contact her first and discuss your situation. She's a very private and skeptical person. Not one to welcome strangers into our lives."

"I understand." Bruce threw a five-dollar tip down on the table. "I'll wait to hear from you. Thanks again." Bruce stood up from the corner table, his legs wobbly as if they had forgotten how to carry the weight of his body. He offered one last nod to Zachary before turning away, the creaking of the wooden chairs marking the end of their initial encounter. "Goodbye, Zachary."

"Until we meet again, Bruce," Zachary replied, a faint parting smile playing across his lips.

Stepping out of the coffee shop, Bruce inhaled deeply, letting the crisp air fill his lungs as if trying to purge himself of the revelations he had just discovered.

Aliens, secret government organizations… All too much for one day. He tapped his fingers nervously against his thigh as he walked down the street, his gait unsteady. His mind spun with images of aliens and shadowy figures pulling strings behind the scenes. The world around him seemed to blur, the once-familiar cityscape now a backdrop for the sinister machinations he was beginning to sense.

Who could he trust? he wondered, scanning the faces of strangers passing by, their features distorted by his growing paranoia. And what price was he going to pay for the truth?

A sense of isolation crept into his heart. He felt like a stranger in his own life, in his own world. Reaching the curb and his car, he paused for a moment, taking one last look at the coffee shop and the unusual man inside. The setting sun cast long shadows on the worn brick walls, adding an air of melancholy to the fading day.

Bruce drove toward the crimson-streaked sky, starting down a dangerous path that would lead him deeper into an alien conspiracy. The darkness awaiting him ahead felt as vast and unfathomable as the very cosmos itself.

CHAPTER 4

Several days had passed since his first brief meeting with Zachary Lind at The Curious Café. Bruce had been busy in that time following up on events and his brother's death every way he could think of. He'd bribed a night janitor to take him inside the Gateway Arch afterhours. He wanted a second look at that machine Jack had shown him in that out-of-the-way mechanical room. But when the janitor led him inside, the machine was gone. Nothing but a couple of bolt holes in the ground where it had once stood. When he asked the janitor where the machine had gone, the man looked at him like he was crazy.

Maybe he was…he'd paid the man five hundred bucks…and for nothing.

Not that it meant anything that the equipment had disappeared. There could still be a routine explanation for everything. But what that explanation might be, he had no idea, and it sure as hell wasn't coming any time soon.

Now, Bruce followed Zachary Lind down a narrow panel-lined hallway, the walls adorned with framed yellowed newspaper clippings. The overhead lights cast shadows on the peculiar artifacts displayed on scattered shelves, making them seem even more mysterious. The newspaper clippings showcased strange creatures and supernatural occurrences, leaving Bruce wondering once again what sort of craziness he'd gotten himself into. The air was thick with the scent of old books and dust, adding a somber feeling to their surroundings.

"Here we are," announced Zachary, stopping before a closed door. "Like I warned you, she doesn't like strangers." The elderly scientist lived a hermit-like existence on a hectare of wooded land outside Ste. Genevieve. His granddaughter, he explained, shared the farm with him.

"Right." Bruce smiled. "I'll try to make a good impression."

"She's very protective of herself and me." Zachary Lind cautioned just before he pushed up the door. "Bruce, I'd like you to meet my granddaughter, Nina. She's been assisting me in my research and can help you understand the alien threat and any possible connections to your brother's death."

As Bruce stepped into the room, he found himself unexpectedly captivated by the woman who stood before him. Nina Lind was a striking figure, her long wavy auburn hair cascading around her shoulders and framing her face like a pre-Raphaelite painting. Her green eyes, sparkling with intelligence, seemed to pierce through him as if trying to read his thoughts. But it was her look of fierce determination that truly demanded attention, evident in the way she held herself with an aura of unwavering authority.

"Nice to meet you, Bruce," Nina said coolly, extending her hand. Bruce noticed the skepticism in her eyes as she regarded him, clearly considering him a mere civilian and out of his league. And it was true, he was no scientist.

"Likewise," Bruce replied, shaking her hand firmly. He sensed that Nina had inherited her grandfather's passion for uncovering hidden truths. He had to tread carefully. He needed her expertise to unravel the mystery surrounding his brother's demise. "Thank you for seeing me."

"Grandpa told me about your situation," Nina said, releasing Bruce's hand and gesturing towards a cluttered table covered in documents and photographs. "It's not every day that a civilian stumbles upon something as big as you did. You must have questions."

"More than I can count or even remember," Bruce admitted. "But, right now, most of all, I need to know how this impending alien threat could be related to my brother's death."

"Let's start with what we know," Nina said, her voice steady and confident. "Like Grandpa told you, the Reptilians and Greys have been visiting Earth for millennia. The Reptilians, or Browns if you prefer, have infiltrated our governments, manipulated our history, and are even responsible for some of the most iconic structures on our planet."

"Like the Arch?"

"Like the Arch, the Roman Coliseum, the Great Pyramid of Giza, and Stonehenge, all early beacons themselves, and dozens more. But let's not get ahead of ourselves."

"Right."

"The Greys, by contrast—"

"The scientists," Bruce interjected.

"Correct. We believe they are merely interested in studying us, examining us, figuring out what makes us tick. They've been responsible for nearly all the alien abductions you might have read about."

"Yeah, Zachary said as much. Makes sense," Bruce found himself saying, although did any of this craziness make sense? Not long ago, he'd have chided Jack for expounding whacky theories like these. Nonetheless, he listened intently as Nina spoke on, her words pulling him in. He had always considered himself to be a logical thinker, grounded in reality, but the new truths that Nina was revealing coursed through his veins like an electric current. The world he thought he knew was being turned upside down, and he felt a strange excitement at the prospect of uncovering more.

"Then there are the Annunaki," Nina continued, her eyes locked on Bruce's as if daring him to question her. "They're the good aliens, you might say, working behind the scenes to counteract the malevolent alien forces at play. In Mesopotamian mythology, the Annunaki played significant roles in the creation of the world and humanity itself, as well as in the establishment of social order and divine rulership. They have left a lasting impact on the religious beliefs and cultural practices of many civilizations of Earth."

"The good guys," joked Bruce. "Do they wear white hats?"

Nina frowned. "This is no time for jokes. You, of all people, should know that."

"Sorry," Bruce blushed.

Nina cleared her throat and charged ahead. "In some aspects, you might think of them as benevolent," she conceded. "Although the Annunaki's initial motivation and impacts, and reasons for the development of humans was for their own benefit—using humans as laborers. And they were able to use these human workers by encouraging and nurturing human belief in the divine and working for the gods. As for your brother, Grandpa believes, and I concur, that he may have discovered something that put him in the crosshairs of the Reptilians and one of their schemes, or perhaps he got too close to the truth about one of the other races."

"I'm beginning to think it was both. He told me things, showed me things—"

"Either way," she concluded, "you want to find out what happened to him and we want to put a stop to whatever they've got planned before it's too late. And we've heard whispers, rumors, that the Reptilians are up to something big. Are you ready to put words into action?"

"Yes."

"Are you sure? This could get you killed."

"Absolutely," Bruce replied. "After what happened to Jack...yeah, absolutely." He wearily pulled his wallet from his pocket and showed them a photograph of his brother.

Nina and Zachary shared a brief look.

Zachary nodded. "I told you," he said to his granddaughter, "this one has potential."

"We'll see," Nina said. "He's never had to face down an alien threat," she said as if he wasn't even in the room.

"Look, I admit that all this alien stuff sounds…well, like something out of a science fiction novel or the supermarket tabloids to me," Bruce said, rubbing the back of his neck in discomfort. "But I can't ignore what happened to my brother. I admit, I may need more concrete evidence before I can fully buy into all this." He had his reputation to think about, for one thing. If his clients thought he was some sort of crackpot, he might never work as an architect again.

Nina nodded. "I get it," she replied, her voice softening a smidge. "It's not easy to accept that everything you've known about the world and the history of human development is wrong. Grandpa and I can show you further proof, evidence that will make it impossible for you to doubt any longer. Look."

With that, she led Bruce over to a long table strewn with artifacts, photographs, and various documents. He watched as she expertly navigated through the chaos, her fingers deftly picking up pieces of ancient pottery inscribed with symbols that eerily resembled the constellations above.

"See these markings?" Nina asked, pointing to the intricate patterns adorning an age-worn tablet. "They're not just random designs. They're maps, detailing the exact locations of hidden alien bases across our planet. And these artifacts prove that extraterrestrial beings have been visiting Earth for millennia, shaping our history in ways we can't even begin to comprehend."

"What am I looking at?"

"The Nazca Lines, Machu Picchu, the Pyramids of Giza, Sacsayhuaman, Pumpapnku, Cholula, Temples of Malta, Bimini road, Gobekli Tepe, Serpent Mound in Ohio, Derinkuyu in Turkey." Nina waved her hands over the table. "I could go on and on about cataclysms and rebirth. There are many strange anomalies. The timeline of our civilization may not be what we have always thought it was. Have you ever heard of the Younger Dryas impact theory? It purposes that a comet or asteroid impact, around twelve-thousand nine hundred years ago, contributed to a sudden cooling period known as the Younger Dryas. This event interrupted the warming trend at the end of the last Ice Age, and may have caused significant environmental changes, including widespread wildfires and alterations in ecosystems. The theory is supported by evidence such as microscopic spheres and carbon spherules found in sediment layers, suggesting a high-energy event. This caused dramatic changes to our planet. This is not a popular topic since it challenges and, if proven, may change some beliefs we have."

As Bruce studied the artifacts and items, he found himself drawn into Nina's world of secrets and hidden truths. It was an easy world to slip into despite his more-grounded architectural and engineering background. Her obvious intelligence and the expertise she wielded in both astrobiology and archaeology gave gravitas to her words, making it hard for Bruce to dismiss her claims as mere fantasy.

"Alright," he conceded, "you've piqued my interest, Nina. Let's figure out what's going on and put a stop to it. If that means diving headfirst into a new reality, then so be it."

Nina smiled. "I promise you, Bruce, we will. And when we do, not only will we avenge your brother, but we'll also save our world from the Reptilians, and start us down a path with the goal of unveiling the truth regarding the start of our civilization. These thing could even reveal aspects to religions that could turn them upside down. This is more powerful than we may potentially even realize."

As they stood poring over the data, the door burst open. All three jumped in surprise. Framed in the doorway stood a woman whose striking appearance commanded their attention. Long red hair whipped around her face as if it had a mind of its own, while her hazel eyes seemed to see right through them.

"Oh, Julia, it's you." Nina said. She glanced at her watch. "I wasn't expecting you for another hour."

Julia grinned. "I made good time." She stared brazenly at Bruce.

"Is this the guy? Doesn't look like much."

"Tell me about it," said Nina.

Zachary chuckled.

Julia strode to Bruce and stuck out her hand. "Name's Julia Adams. Nina's assistant."

"Invaluable colleague would be more accurate," Nina said.

"Bruce Finger," said Bruce, shaking her hand and feeling more and more inadequate and way out of his element among these people.

"I'll make us some tea." Zachary left the office.

As Zachary disappeared into the kitchen, the room fell into an awkward silence. Bruce shifted on his feet, feeling the weight of Julia's gaze upon him. There was something intense and magnetic about her presence, an enigmatic glow in her eyes.

"So, Bruce," Julia finally spoke, leaning against the table with a mischievous smile. "Nina tells me you're interested in joining us in our fight. You sure you're up for it?"

Bruce drew himself taller. He was determined not to let Julia's skepticism undermine his confidence. "Absolutely," he replied firmly, meeting her gaze head-on. "I may not have much experience in dealing with aliens or uncovering hidden conspiracies… Hell, I never even took their very existence seriously before Jack's death. But I'm willing to keep an open mind, learn, and do whatever it takes to find out what happened to my brother." He paused then added, "And to stop it from happening to anyone else."

"That's good to hear," said Julia. "We need all the help we can get."

"Have you tried going to the authorities?"

"No," Nina said sharply. "What would be the point? Either they wouldn't believe us and think we're crazy or—"

"Or those authorities could be Reptilians in disguise," Zachary filled in, as he returned with the tea tray.

"Right," Bruce said, taking a cup of tea from the offered wooden tray.

"I warn you again, Bruce," continued Nina, "our fight will not be easy. The forces we're up against are powerful and ruthless. They've infiltrated every corner of society, manipulating governments, erasing evidence, and eliminating anyone who gets too close to the truth. They want control, they want resources. And they are as ruthless as they are determined."

"Yes, as you've learned, human life means nothing to the Reptilians," added Julia. "Now as for your soul…well, that's another story."

Bruce stiffened. Were these Reptilians somehow really capable of consuming his soul?

"I understand the risks," Bruce said firmly. "Like I said, I may not have all the skills or knowledge you all have, but I'm willing to learn and contribute in any way I can. My brother's life meant something, and I won't rest until those responsible are brought to justice."

Nina and Julia exchanged a glance.

"It's not too late to walk out," Nina said.

"I'm staying," Bruce replied.

"Then let's get back to work." Nina set down her tea.

They gathered once again around the worktable. Nina spread out a map showcasing locations where suspicious activities had been reported and where their intel showed likely Reptilian installations.

"Our first mission is to investigate an underground facility in the heart of St. Louis," Nina explained, tracing her finger along the map. "We believe it may be a central computer hub for the Reptilians. It's located in the subbasement of an office building. If we can destroy it, we may be able to subvert their plans."

"What exactly are their plans?" Bruce wanted to know.

Zachary provided the answer. "We believe they are on the verge of bringing in a military fleet."

"Hundreds of spaceships and weaponized drones," added Nina.

"Enough to take over the United States."

"Maybe the entire Earth," Julia added.

"Where are they now?" asked Bruce. He looked toward the ceiling. Were they up there somewhere? "Are they close?"

"We don't know for certain," answered Zachary. "Close enough."

Bruce's pulse hummed as he studied the map. The coordinates led to a building not far from his downtown office. "What do we have to do? And when do we start?"

"Tonight," Nina replied, her eyes revealing her determination.

"That soon?" Bruce's heart skipped a beat.

"The longer we wait, the more time they have to cover their tracks or move their operations to a new location."

Julia nodded in agreement. "We'll need to be careful and stay under the radar. If they catch wind of our presence, who knows what they'll do."

Bruce scraped his teeth across his lower lip as he realized the magnitude of what they were about to embark on. Was he about to become a criminal? Or a hero?

They spent the next few hours preparing for their infiltration of the underground facility. Nina, Julia, and Bruce gathered the necessary equipment: night vision goggles, communication devices, matte black one-piece jumpsuits that would help them blend into the shadows, and more. All of which Nina and Zachary had at the ready.

As they made their final preparations, a silence hung in the air, filled with a mix of excitement and trepidation. The gravity of their mission weighed heavily on each of them. Bruce thought back to the last day he'd seen his brother, the anguish and emptiness that had consumed him ever since.

Nina interrupted his thoughts. With a resolute look in her eyes, she said, "Remember, our objective is to gather any alien tech we can find and destroy or disable any that we can't take out with us."

"Yes, any smaller alien tech that we can retrieve may be useful.

We may be able to reverse engineer it at a later date, so keep an eye out for anything of that sort," added Zachary.

"And if we encounter any aliens?" asked Bruce.

The three others looked at one another but it was Nina that answered. "We'll see."

ᴴᴱᴷᴰᵀᴵᴬᴷ 5

The moon, a thin crescent hanging above the St. Louis skyline, cast a spectral light over the group. They huddled by the rear entrance of the Ajax Building, looming like a silent sentinel down the street from the Gateway Arch. Bruce studied the unremarkable structure with an architect's eye. He'd passed the building dozens, maybe hundreds of times and had had no idea of the otherworldly secrets it held—secrets more earth-shattering than its sleek and modern corporate facade suggested.

"There's still time to go back, if you like, Bruce," Nina whispered over the gentle rustle of the breeze between the buildings. "I won't blame you."

"Not a chance," Bruce replied. She might not blame him but he'd blame himself, for chickening out and not seeing this through.

"Glad to hear it." Zachary patted his arm.

Bruce nodded, reassured by the old man's touch.

"Keep your eyes peeled, everyone," Nina instructed, as she hefted a set of high-tech burglary tools. "We get in, gather what we need, do what we must, and get out. No heroics."

"Heroics are my middle name," Bruce quipped, but his attempt at humor was belied by the tension etched across his broad features.

"Better keep the chit-chat to a minimum," Julia added, her long red hair tucked into her black knit cap. "No telling what we're walking into."

In silence, they stepped from the shelter of the dumpster and approached the entrance. Nina inserted a tool into the lock while Zachary carefully placed a black box against the alarm panel. He tightened his grip on the sleek, matte-black device in his hand. Nina said she'd designed it to electronically disrupt the computers. He adjusted the box until a red light flashed twice, then he nodded to Nina. She held her breath and twisted her slender tool to the left. A soft click echoed through the night, and the door eased open with a hydraulic hiss. They slipped inside, the darkness enveloping them like a shroud, and shut the door behind them.

"So far, so good," whispered Nina. "No alarms."

"Of course, not," said Zachary. "I always have complete confidence in your work."

Bruce wondered how he'd ever explain to his boss if he got caught breaking into an office building in the middle of the night. The crime, and it was a crime, would cost him his job. His career.

They descended the maintenance stairway following the blueprints Nina had downloaded onto her phone. The rhythmic sound of their footsteps beat out a staccato pattern against the stillness. Each step took them deeper into the belly of the beast. Bruce thought of the alien technology that they might find hidden beneath the city, the wonders the caves might hold. He spared a glance at Nina as she crept unwaveringly forward. He found strength in her determination.

"Keep your eyes open for anything out of the ordinary," Zachary whispered, his age-worn face creased with concentration. He might have been discredited by his peers, debunked and ridiculed as a foolish old man, but here, in the thick of this clandestine operation, he was invaluable.

"Define 'ordinary' in a place like this," Nina quipped, although a hint of anxiety in her tone betrayed the tension running beneath her words.

They moved through the subbasement with deliberate care, alert to any sign of the Reptilians' presence. The air felt charged, electric, as if the very atmosphere was alive with hidden currents. Bruce's fingers brushed against the wall, feeling the cool, smooth surface beneath his touch.

"Almost there," Nina murmured, leading the way.

"Any sign of—" Bruce started.

"Quiet," Nina hissed, halting them with an upheld hand. They froze, barely daring to breathe. The building seemed to hold its breath along with them. "This is it."

Bruce held back a sorry.

"Ready?" Nina asked, her voice low, reaching for the door that stood between them and the revelations they sought. "Grandpa?" She cast a worried look at her grandfather. His breathing was strained and he looked ashen.

"Always," Zachary replied, meeting her gaze.

Bruce had argued for Zachary to remain in the van and keep an eye out for trouble, but he wouldn't hear of it and had insisted on going with them.

Nina nodded and Julia turned the handle and quietly pushed open the door. Bruce was surprised to find it unlocked. Why? Did these Reptilians have other means of protecting themselves? Did the Reptilians know they were here? That they were outside their door?

Were the Reptilians afraid of nothing?

The subbasement was a damp cavern of shadows and metal, the fluorescent bulbs casting anemic pools of light amidst the gloom. Machinery hummed like a dormant mechanical beast, punctuated by sporadic clicks and whirs that seemed to echo from the bowels of the earth.

"It's so cold in here," Bruce whispered.

"Keeps the computers from running hot," Julia explained.

Zachary's breath misted in the air as he whispered, "Feels like we're inside the belly of a clockwork ice dragon."

"Let's hope it doesn't eat us alive," Nina mumbled, her eyes scanning the dim corridors.

The team moved with hushed urgency, the soft soles of their

boots whispering against concrete.

"Every corner could be a trap," warned Julia. "Every shadow a hidden watcher."

Bruce hastily did some mental gymnastics, made strategic calculations, recalling the layout of the building—picturing it with the eyes of a trained architect—should they need to make a hurried escape. The air in the subbasement thickened with every silent step. Shadows clung to corners like dark specters.

Zachary lagged behind, the excitement of the discovery drained from him, replaced by a bone-deep weariness. "Need... a moment," Zachary panted, leaning against a wall.

"Can't stop now," Nina said, her voice firm yet not unkind, urging him forward.

Footsteps echoed down the corridor. "Reptilians! Hide!" Julia whispered. The team scattered in an instant, Bruce pressing his back against the cold metal of a pipe. He held his breath as the sound of footsteps grew closer.

"Is everyone okay?" Nina's voice came through the comms, a lifeline in the darkness.

"Still here," Bruce confirmed, his voice a low murmur, "but I hear them."

"Radio silence," Nina directed, urgency lacing her words.

The Reptilians passed, their cloaks flickering, briefly revealing scales that shimmered in the low light.

"All clear," Nina said a minute later.

"Those were Reptilians?" Bruce whispered into his comm, his voice tinged with disbelief.

"Yes. That should come as no surprise. They're exactly like Zachary's reports," Julia said.

"It's one thing to hear about them. It's another thing entirely to actual see one in the flesh." And up close too. "Is that even flesh?"

"Bruce, Julia?" Nina's voice cut through their conversation. "We need to move. Now."

They moved, Zachary struggling to keep pace and Bruce assisting him. The image of the Reptilians lingered in Bruce's mind, a frightening reminder of what they were up against.

"Watch your step!" Julia called out as they neared a short stairway.

"Got it," Bruce replied.

"Which way, Nina?" Julia asked. Her hair, spilling out from her cap, was a muted flame in the half-light.

"Left," Nina decided, though she didn't sound so sure of herself now.

"Time's not our ally," Zachary reminded them, his words tight with tension. They rounded a corner, and the corridor stretched endlessly before them, lined with doors that promised secrets and peril.

"Anything on the scanner, Zachary?" Bruce asked.

"Nothing yet," Zachary replied, his fingers dancing over a handheld device he claimed he'd designed to detect the aliens. Its screen was a wash of green and black. "I don't understand. I should be picking up their presence." He tapped the screen anxiously.

"Stay sharp," Nina urged, as they moved into a long room with a low ceiling. They began capturing images of alien technology with their cameras. The air seemed to thicken with each silent step, and shadows clung to corners like dark sentinels. The ceiling closed in on them.

"Door ahead," Nina announced. The others caught up to her position. "Ready?" She didn't wait for an answer. "Going in." They stumbled through the door. The armored door swung shut behind them with a finality that was oddly comforting.

Nina came to a stop along a row of computer screens. "Grandpa, do your thing."

Zachary swore. Patted his clothing.

"What's wrong?"

"I-I lost it. I must have dropped it back there somewhere." He shot a look over his shoulder but there was nothing to see.

Nina gnawed her lip. "So it's plan B. We smash everything. Grandpa, keep filming. Maybe we can review the video later and make some sense of all this." She picked up a metal chair and heaved it at the nearest monitor. The monitor shattered and sparks flew. "Come on, get busy, everyone!"

"Good idea," Zachary replied. "I'd hate to think our incursion served no purpose." He aimed his camera around the room, focusing in on any machinery and devices that caught his particular attention and intrigued him.

Bruce kicked a computer monitor with the heel of his boot, drove a keyboard through the screen of another.

"What's that?!" Julia asked, even as her fingers flew across one of the computer keyboards.

But they all knew what it was.

An alarm.

And it was enough to wake the dead. It would certainly rouse any Reptilians in the vicinity.

"We've got to get out of here!" Nina threw down the chair she'd been using as a weapon, grabbed her grandpa and urged the others to follow quickly.

"You go ahead," Julia said, looking up from her computer station. "I'm not quite finished."

"But if they catch you—" began Bruce.

Julia smiled at him. "No one will catch me. I'll meet you at the farm. Go!"

Despite his conflicted emotions, Bruce ran. Nina and Zachary needed his help too. The old man was teetering, breathing heavily, and looked ready to collapse. There was no way that Nina could get him safely out of the building alone.

They retreated the way they'd come. Bruce sealed the door to the Ajax Building behind them. The cool night air played over him like a balm, cutting through the fear and tension that had built up inside him.

"Are you sure Julia will be okay? Should we go back?"

"No," Nina promised. "She'll be fine. Now let's move out before we're discovered. You ready, Grandpa?"

"Yes." Bruce took one of Zachary's arms and his granddaughter took the other. They helped him to the van parked on the dark street, away from the light of the streetlamps. Nina took the wheel and they retreated into the shadows, the night reclaiming them.

Through the rear window, Bruce watched the Gateway Arch fade into the distance and got the eerie and unsettling feeling that it was watching him, watching them.

CHAPTER 6

Late that same morning, the sun already high in the sky, Bruce returned to Zachary's remote farmhouse, his eyes red from the lack of sleep. Every muscle in his body relaxed as he caught sight of Zachary and Nina waiting for him outside on the broad front porch. They sat in weathered rocking chairs sipping coffee from rustic brown mugs.

Bruce realized the weight of last night's mission had been pressing down on him. After dropping them off at the farmhouse several hours earlier, he'd gone back to his place to nap and freshen up. But he hadn't slept. He was honestly worried and scared he might end up like his brother, but thinking about his brother also gave him tremendous courage—knowing he was doing the right thing. He'd grown fond of his new friends and he'd been worried that something might happen to them in his absence—that the nest of Reptilians they'd stirred up had followed them to the farm and snatched them or, worse yet, murdered them.

And he was worried about Julia, who'd stayed behind, disappointed not to see her now familiar figure waving to him from the porch along with the others. Did she get out okay? Had she been captured?

"You made it," Zachary said, coming slowly to his feet. His clothes looked rumpled and slept in. Bruce couldn't help but notice the exhaustion etched into the older man's face.

Bruce yawned. "Sorry, I couldn't sleep. Too much to think about." He'd called Sarah at the office and begged out of work, claiming to be ill. He'd been doing that a lot since his brother's death. How much longer would she and their clients put up with his excuses and absences?

"Come." Zachary waved toward the door. "There's fresh coffee inside."

"And you look like a man who could use some," Nina said, her wavy auburn hair catching the light as she moved. Her green eyes darted around, scanning their surroundings with an alertness that betrayed her own anxiety.

"Any word from Julia?" asked Bruce.

"Nothing," Nina replied, her jaw tightening.

"I'm worried, Nina. What if they got her?" Bruce said.

"Let's not jump to conclusions," Nina said, trying to sound reassuring yet failing to hide the tremble in her voice. "Julia's resourceful. She'll find her way back."

"Yes," agreed Zachary. "I've come to learn that Julia is a very capable young woman. Extraordinary, really." He squeezed Nina's arm. "Like my granddaughter."

Bruce smiled but, as they spoke, he couldn't shake off the feeling that something was terribly wrong. The air was thick with tension, every word carrying the weight of their fears. He looked at his two companions, both of them strong and determined in their own right, but probably just as fragile as he felt in this uncertain situation.

The three settled around a small cluttered kitchen table with strong, hot coffee and warm buttermilk biscuits that Zachary claimed to have made from scratch himself. The aroma of fresh bread on his empty stomach practically had Bruce drooling.

"You're quite a baker," Bruce said, snatching up a biscuit and chewing. "These biscuits are the best I've ever tasted."

"Thanks, Bruce. I guess I'm not completely useless," said Zachary, slathering butter over his second biscuit of the morning.

"Oh, Grandpa," chuckled Nina, carrying a fresh pot of coffee to the table. She wore a fresh, untucked white shirt and blue jeans and walked bare foot. "He's still moping for having dropped his alien detector last night."

"Don't let it eat you up. These things happen."

"That's what I've been trying to tell him."

"But if they got hold of it—"

"Forget it," Bruce said. "It's not like it had your name on it, right?"

"I suppose…"

"Fine, moving on." Bruce winked at Nina. "Have you been able to gather any more information?" Ravenous, he bit into another biscuit and washed it down with more strong black coffee.

"Bits and pieces," Zachary sighed, running a hand through his wild hair. "But nothing concrete. We've been playing the video recordings over and over again. Everything we've seen, we're dealing with is…beyond anything I've ever encountered in my research."

"Same," Nina chimed in, her frustration evident. "I've been trying to piece together any connections between the Reptilians and the ancient civilizations I've studied, hoping to find some salient points, some ideas about the Reptilians' plans. Something hidden in the historical record that might help me discern some patterns…" She scraped her mug over the table as her voice faded away. After a bit, she added, "Trying to get inside their heads. Figure out what they might do next. But, so far, not much."

"There must be something," Bruce muttered, his chest tightening with every passing moment. He felt the ramifications of their task bearing down on him, as well as the guilt that gnawed at him over Julia's absence. He was having second thoughts for the hundredth time. He should have stayed with her. Made sure she got out safely. He rubbed his knuckles against his temples. He was finding it harder to breathe, harder to think. "And Julia…"

"Listen," Zachary said, placing a hand on Bruce's shoulder. "We're doing our best. That's all we can do for now."

"Right," Bruce agreed, nodding weakly. "We just… we have to find Julia." He'd already lost his brother. He'd feel terrible if he lost Julia next.

"Agreed," Nina said, her eyes meeting Bruce's. In that brief moment, he found solace in her gaze, the promise that together they would face whatever came. They were united by a common goal, bound by the determination to protect humanity and thwart the Reptilian threat. "Look, if we don't hear from her by noon, Bruce, you and I will go back to the Ajax Building for a discreet look around." She dropped her hand over his. "We will find her."

But as they sat there, listening to the soft ticking of the kitchen clock, the sun casting wavering shadows across the farmyard, uncertainty hung heavy in the air. The never-stopping clock was a reminder of time passing too quickly.

The sudden sound of tires crunching on gravel jolted Bruce from his thoughts. "Julia!" He climbed from his chair and glanced out the kitchen window.

"Shit, that's not her car," Nina said, standing beside him. She tensed. "I don't know who that is. Grandpa?"

Zachary stood and peered out the window. He shook his head. "No, no one I know."

The three shared a troubled look as the sleek black sedan pulled up to the farmhouse, its tinted windows hiding the driver from view. As the engine died, the door opened. A man stepped out into the sunlight and brushed off his charcoal trousers.

"Who's that?" Nina asked, her voice low and cautious.

"Guess we'll find out." Zachary crossed to the front door. Nina grabbed a shotgun in the corner, checked that it was loaded, racked it, and nodded.

Her grandfather opened the door. "Yes?"

"Agent Alex Simmons," the man introduced himself, his tone confident and authoritative. He smiled like he meant it. Despite the looseness of his shirt and trousers, and the navy windbreaker, his muscular build was evident. He had cropped dark hair that seemed to catch the sun just right. He glanced at Nina standing there with the shotgun. "You won't be needing that, I promise."

Nina frowned and slightly lowered the shotgun. "What do you want?"

"I'd love to explain." Agent Simmons arched his brow as he glanced at the shotgun. "May I come in?"

Nina hesitated then set the shotgun back down in the corner.

Agent Simmons pointed his nose at the kitchen and sniffed. "Is that coffee I smell?"

Nina frowned. "Fine. Come on." She padded to the kitchen and everyone followed.

Bruce pulled out a chair and told the agent to sit. Everyone eyed the newcomer expectantly, suspicion in their eyes.

"I've been monitoring your activities for some time now, folks." Agent Simmons took his coffee with lots of sugar, spilling some on the table, and wiping it up with the side his hand. "You and your granddaughter, Professor Lind, to be exact. You," he said, turning his eyes on Bruce, "only recently."

"Shades of Big Brother." Bruce bristled and shuffled his feet across the floor. He didn't like the idea of being monitored.

"Monitoring us?" Zachary echoed, his eyes narrowing. "Why?"

"Because you're involving yourselves in matters you don't fully understand," Simmons replied, his gaze never wavering. "That could get you killed. So I'm here to help you."

"Help us?" Bruce scoffed, his sleep-deprived mind racing with suspicion. "How can we trust you?"

"Good question, I understand your concern, Bruce. Trust is earned, not given," Agent Simmons acknowledged, his lips curling into a tight-lipped smile. "But I assure you, my intentions are aligned with yours. We all want the same thing—to stop the growing Reptilian threat."

Silence hung in the air. Bruce's mind raced. So Simmons knew about the Reptilians. What else did he know?

"What agency did you say you're with? The Space Force?"

Zachary asked.

Bruce and Nina chuckled.

"I didn't say," Agent Simmons replied.

"So how about answering Grandpa's question right now and telling us who you work for," Nina said. "Before we throw you out."

Bruce slid back his chair and made to rise. He'd happily throw the guy out.

Agent Simmons' jaw tightened. "Fine, but you didn't hear it from me. I'm with the FBI. I previously worked with the Department of Defense and the NSA. I've spent a lot of time looking into records as far back as those included in Project Blue Book."

"FBI?" Bruce said.

"Yes, but they'll never confirm. You might say I've gone rogue."

"Project Blue Book is practically ancient history," Nina said. Text records of Project Blue Book, documentation relating to investigations of unidentified flying objects, excluding names of people involved in the sightings, were now available for research in the National Archives Building. The records included approximately two cubic feet of unarranged project or administrative files, thirty-seven cubic feet of case files in which individual sightings were arranged chronologically. Another three cubic feet of records related to the Office of Special Investigations, OSI, portions of which had been arranged chronologically by OSI district and by overseas command. A cubic foot of records equaled approximately 2,000 printed pages. Finding aids for these records included a detailed file list for the project files, and an index to individual sightings, entered by date and location.

"True," replied Agent Simmons. "But I still believe there's more to it, more to the sightings than has been admitted to by our government."

Nina narrowed her eyes. "What's that supposed to mean?"

"It means my superiors don't happen to agree with my concern for the Reptilian threat. So I have had to be...discreet. We've all seen what happens to whistleblowers."

Zachary chuckled. "Welcome to the club."

"Yeah, in fact, you might say they refuse to believe not only in an alien threat but in their very existence." He spread his hands out on the kitchen table.

"That's no surprise," said Nina.

"No, I suppose not. But..."

"But what?" Bruce demanded.

"I think it's worse than that," confessed Agent Simmons. "I believe Reptilians have infiltrated the agency."

Bruce nodded. "If they have, it's no wonder you can't get anyone to believe you, to listen."

Before they could press Agent Alex Simmons further, they heard the sound of the back door off the kitchen opening and closing. Julia strode into the kitchen. Her clothes were disheveled. A small bump and a purplish bruise stood out on her forehead.

"Julia!" Nina cried out, relief flooding her face as the red-haired woman stumbled toward them. "We were afraid you'd been captured!" The two women hugged. Bruce sighed his relief.

Zachary fetched her a mug and filled it. "Sit, sit," he ordered, giving Julia his chair.

"Thanks, Zachary." She paused to drink. "I almost was caught," Julia said, her eyes darting between the team members as Nina gasped. "It was touch and go but I managed to elude them." She turned to Simmons. "Who's this?"

"Agent Alex Simmons," Bruce supplied, watching Julia's expression carefully. "FBI. He claims to be aware of our activities and wants to help us. What do you think?"

Julia regarded the agent with a mixture of curiosity and suspicion, her eyes narrowing as she weighed Bruce's words. "I'll be honest. When I noticed the strange car out front, I decided to be cautious," she admitted. "I've been listening outside the door."

"Look," Agent Simmons interjected, his patience clearly wearing thin, "we're all on the same side here. I can provide valuable intel and resources to help you."

"Why us?" Bruce asked. "Why not let the FBI or the army or somebody help you?"

"Like I said," Simmons replied, "I don't know who to trust. Anybody I talk to could be a Reptilian or in cahoots with them. I need outside help. And you're it. We can work together. The Reptilians are looking for obvious threats to themselves like US military technical advances or large-scale ops."

"Even if we were to believe you," Nina countered, her tone cold, "how do we know you're not just leading us into a trap? Again, why should we trust you?"

Agent Simmons clenched his jaw, his blue eyes piercing through their skepticism. "Because time is running out," he said, his voice laced with urgency. "I believe they intend to bring a military fleet the likes of which Man has never seen. And you're going to need my help, we're going to need each other's help, if we're going to stop them."

"When is this invasion supposed to happen?" Nina asked.

"If I'm right, it begins in seventy-two hours."

"Seventy-two hours? Holy shit! Are you serious?" exclaimed Bruce.

"Deadly serious," Agent Simmons replied.

Eyebrows rose around the table as the others looked at each other, letting Agent Simmons' words sink in. The wind howled outside the farmhouse, its mournful cry filling the air as if it, too, sensed the impending danger. Bruce, his pulse quickening, studied Agent Simmons with a mixture of hope and distrust, desperate for answers but wary of deception. "Alright," he said finally. "Let's say we're willing to go along with what you're saying. Tell us more."

Agent Simmons nodded, his eyes dark and unreadable. "The Ajax Building that you broke into is nothing. There is a far more strategic hidden stronghold," he began, his voice barely more than a whisper, "a place where the Reptilians have been amassing their forces and weapons, preparing for a major assault."

"Where?" Nina asked, her voice trembling despite her best efforts to remain composed.

"Adjacent to the Mississippi," Agent Simmons replied, leaning in closer as if sharing a dark secret. "In the old Lemp Brewery tunnels. There's a natural cave system linked to these tunnels. I believe it to be the site from which they coordinated the construction of the Arch. Those caves have been abandoned for decades, allowing them to move undetected, right under everybody's noses."

Bruce tensed as the implications of Agent Simmons' words took hold. He glanced at Zachary and Nina, noting the fear etched into their faces. Even Julia, the ever-composed one, looked troubled by the revelation.

"Can we trust him?" Nina murmured, her eyes never leaving the agent's face.

"Hard to say," Zachary replied, his voice low and cautious. "We don't have many options, though."

Bruce could feel the gears turning in his mind, wrestling with the implications of trusting this stranger who had appeared so suddenly in their lives. Was he an ally or an enemy? His teeth pulled at his lower lip. A wrong decision could mean the end for all of them.

"Are you sure about this?" Julia asked, her gaze locked on Agent Simmons. "How do we know you're not leading us straight into their clutches?"

"How do we know you aren't a Reptilian in disguise?" added Zachary.

Julia leaned closer and took a whiff of Agent Simmons.

"What are you doing?" asked Agent Simmons.

Julia smiled. "Let's just say I have a nose for deception." She turned to the others. "I think maybe he's telling the truth."

"Maybe," allowed Bruce, "but I'm not convinced. Like Zachary said, how do we know you aren't one of them? Or that you haven't been sent by them?" He'd been fearing they'd left a trail when they stormed the Ajax Building. Had that trail led Agent Simmons to them?

"Because I've been there," Agent Simmons replied, his voice steady and confident. "I've seen their plans firsthand—the destruction they intend to unleash upon the city. St. Louis today and, with themselves and their human allies in key positions of power, it could be the country next...the world. And I won't stand by and watch that happen. I've got a wife and three kids. What kind of world would I be leaving them?" He looked at each of them in turn. "We may be strangers, but we have a common enemy. That's enough for me to risk everything. Is it enough for you?"

The room fell silent as the team digested his words. Bruce could see the flicker of doubt in each of their eyes, but also a glimmer of hope—if Agent Simmons was telling the truth, this could be their chance to strike back against the Reptilians.

"Alright," Zachary said finally, breaking the silence. "We'll consider your information, but we need to verify it somehow. We can't afford to take any unnecessary risks."

"Understandable," Agent Simmons nodded, his face impassive. "I can provide you with the details of their stronghold, the layout, and their patrol patterns. And weapons, too. But time is of the essence. The longer we wait, the more powerful they become."

Bruce clenched his hand around his mug, feeling the warmth work its way into his palm. The fate of humanity seemed to have fallen on them. Trusting Agent Simmons could lead them to victory or doom, but doing nothing was not an option. "I'm in," he declared, meeting the agent's gaze. "But if you're leading us into a trap—"

"I'm not," Agent Simmons vowed.

"So you say, but if you are leading us into a trap," picked up Nina, "I've got a couple of shotgun shells with your name on them."

Agent Simmons inclined his head. "I wouldn't have it any other way."

"Agent Simmons," Bruce interrupted, his voice barely above a whisper, "there's something I need to know."

"Call me Alex." The agent turned to face him, his steely blue eyes meeting Bruce's.

"Alex, then."

"Go ahead."

"Jack... my brother..." Bruce swallowed hard, his throat dry. "Can you tell me how he died? Who took his body and where?"

Silence fell upon the room like a heavy shroud, and Bruce could feel everyone's eyes on him. His hands shook, but he held Agent Simmons' unwavering gaze, determined to find answers.

"I'm afraid I don't have all the details, Bruce," Agent Simmons said, his voice measured and calm. "But I can tell you that Jack was murdered, assassinated, by a Reptilian. Your brother got too close to the truth. There's Reptilian technology lurking in the Gateway Arch, technology that guides and allows their ships to come to Earth, like a powerful lighthouse. And I suspect these ships then pass through the Arch, invisible to the naked eye and impossible for our own technology to detect. They have another access point in the ocean somewhere but reports are minimal on it. Possibly others, as well, spread across the globe."

Zachary whistled. "Just as I feared."

"Sorry, Bruce," Alex Simmons, continued. "There was nothing I could do for Jack."

"And his body?" Bruce pressed, his voice strained. "What happened to it? Where is he now?"

"I don't know for certain, but from what I've been able to gather, his body was transported to the Reptilian center of operations within the Lemp Brewery tunnels," Agent Simmons replied, his tone solemn. "Again, I'm sorry, Bruce."

Grief clawed at Bruce's insides, the pain raw and unrelenting. But there was no time for mourning; not now, not when the fate of humanity hung in the balance. He clenched his hand into a fist and nodded, steeling himself for what lay ahead. "Thank you."

"I'm sorry too, Bruce, but we need to focus now," Nina interjected, her voice sharp and decisive. "If we're going to investigate and launch an attack on the old Lemp Brewery, we need a plan. We need to be smart and cautious. What are you suggesting, Simmons?"

"Agreed," Zachary chimed in, his brow furrowed. "We can't just barge in there without knowing what we're up against."

"Right," Bruce said. They'd done that once already and nearly been captured.

"Agreed," said Julia. "We need to outsmart them."

Agent Simmons excused himself to fetch his laptop from his vehicle. He returned to the kitchen table and flipped the device open. "Let's get to it. I'll show you what I've got."

The small kitchen seemed to close in on the team as they huddled around the table, poring over the available data and maps of the Lemp Brewery tunnels that Agent Simmons provided to them.

"First off," began Simmons, "we can be a step ahead. Any official military or covert operations would be discovered by the Reptilians. After all, they have infiltrated these groups. They would likely be alerted to any black ops even. That's how deep they are within our system. The tunnels once connected both to the river in one direction and to railroad tracks in the other."

Bruce's eyes burned from lack of sleep, but he fought against exhaustion, focusing on the risky job ahead. Concentrating on every word.

"Great," Nina muttered, her eyes scanning the grainy images on the laptop screen. The tunnels crawled with Reptilians and were well-guarded. "We're going up against a heavily fortified alien base. What could go wrong?"

"Actually," Simmons continued, ignoring the sarcasm dripping from Nina's words, "the Reptilians have several weaknesses we can exploit. Their installation relies heavily on a specific type of energy source. If we can find it and destroy it, we'll not only disrupt their operations but also weaken the Reptilians themselves. That includes neutralizing them when necessary."

"Neutralizing them?" Zachary questioned, his brow furrowing as he tried to decipher Simmons' meaning.

"Killing," Simmons clarified, his expression darkening. "We may need to kill them if we want any chance of stopping this invasion."

No one spoke for a moment, the significance of their mission settling like a lead blanket around the room. Bruce finally broke the silence, his voice strained with the effort of holding back his emotions. "You say kill... What about weapons? Do we have anything that can actually hurt these things?" He'd never fired a weapon in his life.

"Here." Agent Simmons reached into his bag and pulled out an assortment of sleek, high-tech firearms, laying them out on the table. "These should do the job. Just make sure you aim for their solar plexuses. That seems to be their most vulnerable spot. And I'll bring in enough explosives and timing devices to bring the tunnels down."

"Anything else?" asked Nina.

"They also have tech which keeps them warm. Like earthly reptiles, these aliens are cold-blooded, and the underground tunnels and caves are naturally cool. Dismantling heating systems can hopefully slow the Reptilians down a bit. In theory, at least."

"Right, in theory," quipped Zachary.

The agent went on to explain that they couldn't get back inside following the route he'd taken because he'd found the entrance blocked that last time he'd gone back. "They must have figured out someone had gotten in, or at least suspected."

Each member of the team eyed the weapons warily, their fingers twitching with hesitation as they reluctantly picked them up. The cold metal felt foreign in their hands, an unwelcome reminder of the violence that lay ahead.

"What is this form of energy you mentioned?" Nina asked.

"I call it Reptile Juice," Agent Simmons said with a smile. "I don't know what the hell the science nerds call it and I can't tell you exactly what it is. It appears to be a crystal of some sort, something never before seen on Earth. I suspect they brought it from their planet or one of the planets they've conquered. I've heard it described as looking remotely like amethyst and having magnetic qualities.

"I know military scientists are working on reverse engineering and testing things like this, but without much luck, or so they say," Agent Simmons continued. "Obviously, technology like this can be very useful and worth more than gold. Imagine if such technology got into the wrong hands, it could change the world. And not for the better."

"I'd love to get my hands on some," Nina said.

"I'm sure you would. Just don't try to touch it, not literally." Simmons cautioned. "It'll burn a hole through your flesh in a matter of seconds."

"Lovely," she replied, staring at her hands.

"Ah, moscovium, I've read up on that," Zachary said, rubbing his chin thoughtfully. "What can you tell us?"

"Not much, sorry to say. From what I've learned, it's more of a metal-like raw material. Element 115, moscovium, is a radioactive, synthetic element about which little is known. It is classified as a metal and is expected to be solid at room temperature. It decays quickly into other elements, including nihonium."

"Yes," agreed Zachary. "The element had previously been designated ununpentium, a placeholder name that means one-one-five in Latin. In November 2016, the International Union of Pure and Applied Chemistry approved the name moscovium."

"UFO theorists, such as Bob Lazar, claim it can be weaponized," Nina pointed out.

"This is all over my head," Bruce said, leaning back in his chair. "How about we stick to the here and…just the facts, as they say?" He gripped one of the weapons with white knuckles. The dangers kept growing. "How do we get into these tunnels without being detected?" Or killed, he left unsaid.

"Leave that to me." Julia's fingers flew across her own laptop keyboard as she hacked into various surveillance systems. "With Alex's intel, I'll find us the safest route in."

"Once we're inside," Zachary added, studying the tunnel layout with narrowed eyes, "we may need to split up. Cover more ground that way. Stay in constant communication and, if anyone finds this energy source, this Reptile Juice or some of this Element 115 stuff, alert the rest of us immediately. And we really should try to save samples for study."

"I don't suppose any of this stuff will be clearly labeled?" joked Bruce. "Like, hi, I'm a box of moscovium, take me."

"That's the problem," answered Agent Simmons. "We probably wouldn't know it if we laid our eyes on it. We just have to do our best to look."

"Not you, Grandpa," Nina took her grandfather's hand. "I want you to sit this one out."

"What? No, never!" vowed Zachary.

"Please, Grandpa," Nina pleaded.

"I agree with Nina. Besides, we need you to run command center, right, Alex?" Bruce said, turning to the agent.

"Absolutely, somebody's got to handle the job. How about it, Professor? Can we count on you, sir?"

Zachary huffed. "Fine. But I do so under protest."

"Alright, then," Bruce said, bracing himself for the battle ahead. "Let's do this." He stared at the weapons on the table once again as he pondered the dangers ahead. He glanced up at the others, their expressions a mix of determination and apprehension.

"Hey," Nina said quietly, looking at Bruce with concern. "Are you okay?"

His eyes met hers, searching for some semblance of reassurance. "I... I've never done anything like this before. Never killed."

"None of us have," Zachary chimed in, his voice heavy with tension. "But it's them or us, Bruce. And we're not just fighting for ourselves—we're fighting for our planet."

"I know," Bruce whispered, nodding slowly. His thoughts raced, weighing the consequences of their actions, the lives that would be forever changed by the outcome of their mission. But deep down, he knew that if it came down to kill or be killed, he would do what was necessary—for his own survival, for the team, and for humanity itself.

"Alright," Agent Simmons said. "Let's finalize our plans and be prepared to move out. I suggest we go tonight."

"Agreed. No point waiting," Bruce said. He knew that hesitation could cost them everything. "Julia, have you found us a safe way in?"

"Got it," she confirmed, spinning her laptop around and pointing out the safest route on her screen. "It won't be easy, but it's our best shot." She laid out her plan and everyone agreed.

"Then let's go over everything one more time," Zachary said, his voice steady and focused. "Commit it to memory. We can't afford any mistakes."

As darkness fell and surrounded the farmhouse, they finalized their preparations. The atmosphere in the room grew thick with anticipation. A sense of readiness settled over them, a quiet resolve that left no room for doubt or fear. They were a team, bound together by a common purpose, united against an enemy that threatened everything they held dear.

"Let's do this," Bruce said, glancing at his watch and forcing himself up from the sofa where he'd been dozing on and off for the past couple hours. It was 2 a.m. But for a short nap, no one had a full night's sleep since the other day. He looked at the faces of each of his teammates, seeing the same fierce determination reflected in their eyes.

They filed outdoors to a cloud-covered sky and walked in silence to their vehicles. A chorus of insects and moaning trees accompanied them. Zachary drove the van containing Nina and Julia. Bruce rode with Agent Simmons. The two vehicles sped towards St. Louis, ready to confront the Reptilian threat and reclaim their world.

ᴸᴴᴱᐳᴅᵀⁱᴧᴵᴷ 7

The dilapidated section of town near the river was a graveyard of abandoned structures, their skeletal remains casting eerie shadows on the cracked and buckled pavement. Bruce shivered as he gazed upon the desolate landscape, feeling a sense of foreboding that seemed to permeate the very air around them. The tension was thick.

"Here," Agent Simmons said, his voice barely above a whisper as he gestured towards an innocuous-looking pile of rubble. The team approached cautiously, their eyes scanning for any signs of danger. As they drew closer, Bruce saw that the rubble concealed a hidden entrance—a narrow, gaping hole leading down into darkness. It was hard to imagine that this inconspicuous opening was the secret gateway to an underground alien base.

"Keep your wits about you," Simmons warned, his tone grim. "We don't know what we'll encounter down there."

With a nod of understanding, each team member switched on their LED headlamps, casting cold beams of light into the subterranean depths. One by one, they descended into the abyss, trusting in Simmons' leadership and their own resolve.

The air was musty and tinged with the scent of stale beer and decaying vegetation. Bruce followed closely behind Simmons, his heart pounding in his chest as they navigated the dark corridors of the Reptilian stronghold. He marveled at the complexity of the winding passageways, wondering how many other unknown and hidden alien bases might exist throughout the world. The very thought sent a chill down his spine.

"Stay close and keep quiet," Simmons reminded them, his hushed voice echoing through the gloom. "Julia mapped out the most direct route to our objective, but it doesn't mean it's going to be easy."

"Understood," Bruce whispered, his nerves tightening with every step deeper into the heart of the Reptilians' lair.

"Good," Simmons replied, his gaze sweeping the group once more. "Remember, stealth is paramount. If the Reptilians detect our presence before we reach the power source, they'll have the advantage, and we can't let that happen. Watch each other's backs."

Outside the underground base, less than one hundred yards away, Zachary sat in the van, hidden in the shadows of the surrounding buildings, his eyes glued to the monitor displaying the four blips indicating Nina, Julia, Alex, and Bruce. The transponders were working as intended. His eyes scanned the various monitors, taking in the live feeds from the team's helmet-mounted cameras, as well as the readings from their bio-monitoring devices.

"Stay safe," he murmured to himself, feeling a pang of fear and helplessness as he realized just how little control he had over the situation. All he could do now was watch and hope that their plan succeeded and no one got hurt.

Inside the stronghold, Bruce trailed closely behind Agent Simmons, his senses on high alert. The corridors seemed to stretch on forever, their walls punctuated with strange alien technology that hummed and pulsated with an eerie energy. He could almost feel the malevolent presence of the Reptilians lurking in the shadows, watching them from unseen vantage points as they moved deeper into the heart of the enemy's lair.

"Eyes open. Remember, we're in their territory now." Simmons whispered into his comm.

"Maybe, but we've got the home planet advantage," quipped Bruce.

"How are we looking, Zachary?" Simmons asked.

Inside the van, Zachary's fingers danced over the keyboard,

inputting commands, and analyzing data as he helped guide them through the labyrinthine complex. "Turn left at the next intersection," Zachary instructed through their earpieces, his voice steady and reassuring. "I'm detecting some heat signatures up ahead—likely Reptilians, judging by their strength." Reptilians, in human form, emitted strong heat signatures—despite the fact that Reptilians were believed to be cold blooded. "I'll try to find you an alternate route to avoid them."

"Copy that," Simmons replied, adjusting their course as they continued onward, their senses heightened by the ever-present threat of discovery.

"Anything we should know about?" Nina asked.

"Nothing so far," came Zachary's tense reply through the comm. "Just keep moving forward. I'm monitoring your progress closely."

"Understood," Nina said, her eyes never leaving the path ahead.

As they delved deeper into the alien stronghold, Bruce realized the stakes had never been higher. They were walking a knife's edge between success and failure, and one misstep could spell disaster not just for them, but for the entire human race. And disturbing the Reptilians could be like rousing a nest of hornets.

"Zachary," Bruce murmured into his comm. "How are we doing?"

"Fine. Slow and steady. You're headed in the right direction," came Zachary's response.

"Thanks." Bruce cast a glance at his teammates. All appeared tense.

Navigating the maze of dark passages, the sheer size and complexity of the underground base became increasingly apparent. The team found themselves awed and overwhelmed by the intricate network of tunnels that stretched out in every direction, each one seemingly identical to the last.

"Damn," Nina muttered under her breath. "This place is like a giant ant colony."

"I'm afraid the Reptilians are growing stronger by the day. If they succeed here in St. Louis, there may be no stopping them," Julia whispered back.

"Then we can't let them succeed," Agent Simmons said. "We can't afford to lose."

"Right," Bruce agreed. The atmosphere within the stronghold felt oppressive, making it difficult to breathe at times. He could almost sense the alien presence all around them, watching their every move.

"Wait," Julia said suddenly, motioning for the others to stop. "I hear something."

"Where?" Nina whispered, her hand instinctively reaching for her weapon. Unlike Bruce, who had no experience with guns, she'd grown up on a farm and learned to shoot at an early age.

"Down that corridor," Julia replied, pointing to their left. "Sounds like footsteps."

"Reptilians?" Agent Simmons questioned, his eyes narrowing as he strained to listen.

"Who else could it be? Seems unlikely we'd find any homeless people this far in," Julia said.

"Affirmative," Zachary said.

"We need to avoid them," Nina said.

"Agreed," Bruce nodded. "We need another detour."

With Simmons resuming the lead, they backtracked slightly and turned down another corridor, hoping to remain out of sight. The darkness pressed in around them, making it difficult to see more than a few feet ahead. As they moved forward, the sound of the Reptilian patrol faded into the distance, replaced by the rhythmic dripping of water from somewhere deep within the stronghold.

"Hey, Zachary," Bruce whispered into the comm device. "Any idea how big this place is?"

"Hard to say," Zachary replied. "But based on what Julia first mapped and what I've been able to extrapolate, it's massive. There could be miles of tunnels and caves down here."

"Great," Bruce muttered, feeling a mixture of amazement and unease at the thought.

"Yeah," said Nina. "Just what we need—more places to get lost."

As they moved deeper into the alien base, Bruce's unease grew. Every step they took brought them closer to a face-to-face confrontation with the enemy. At times, they were forced to crawl through tight spaces, using their hands and knees to navigate the narrow passages. Another time, they found themselves scaling a steep incline.

"Damn Reptilians," Nina grumbled as she pulled herself up over the ledge. "Why'd they have to make this place so complicated?"

"Probably to keep intruders like us out," Bruce replied, wiping sweat from his brow.

"Seems to be working well enough," said Julia.

"Besides, most of this is a natural cave system," Bruce added. "The Reptilians simply took advantage of it and made some modifications."

"Zachary, what's our ETA?" Simmons asked, his voice tense with anticipation.

"Approximately ten minutes if we maintain this pace," came the reply. "But proceed with caution. There are still plenty of unknown variables down there."

"Don't we know it," Nina said, an edge to her voice.

"I remember a side corridor. To the left, I think," Julia said. "Zachary, will it get us around them?"

"Checking," came Zachary's reply. After a moment, he replied. "Good call, Julia. Go."

The team turned left and followed the narrow corridor single file. Everyone stuck closer together. The tunnel was dark but at least it was empty except for the scampering rats.

"Zachary, how much farther?" Bruce whispered into his comm, his voice cracking with tension. He glanced around the shadowy, unnervingly silent corridor, shadows playing tricks on his eyes. He wished he'd had more sleep.

"Almost there," Zachary's voice crackled through the earpiece. "Take the next right and you'll be at the lab." That was their first objective.

Agent Simmons signaled for the team to advance cautiously. The air grew colder and more oppressive as they neared their destination. Bruce shivered, fighting the urge to give in to the mounting dread he felt. What would be worse, to find his brother within or to not find him?

"Look at this," Nina whispered, her voice barely audible as she pointed to an unassuming door on their left. "I think we've found it."

"I believe so," replied Zachary via his comm.

Agent Simmons carefully checked the door for any signs of traps or alarms.

Bruce watched, with a growing sense of unease. The deeper they went, the more likely they were to find what they were looking for—but also the more likely they were to be discovered. They walked a delicate balance, one that could tip in either direction at any moment.

With a nod from Agent Simmons, they cautiously pushed open the door and they followed him inside. The frigid room beyond was nothing like they had ever seen before: part laboratory, part surgical theater, a macabre scene of twisted experimentation and unspeakable cruelty.

"Monstrous!" Julia said, her breath coming out in white puffs. Her face paled in revulsion as she took in the grotesque sight before them.

"Better keep our voices down," Simmons cautioned, scanning the room for any sign of movement. "We don't know if anyone's nearby."

"Jack!" Bruce choked out, his eyes fixed on one particular body lying on one of the cold metal tables. His brother's lifeless form was covered in strange markings and incisions, evidence of the horrific experiments that had been performed on him. A fury unlike anything he had ever experienced before rose within him, burning away all previous doubts and fears of what he was doing. "We have to get him out of here. We can't leave him like this."

"Wait!" Nina hissed suddenly, her hand gripping Bruce's arm tightly. Her knuckles were white, and her eyes were wide with terror. "Do you hear that?"

He heard it. They all did. The sound of footsteps echoed through the room, drawing closer and closer until a figure stepped out from the shadows. Bruce recognized him. Zachary had shown him a photograph of the elusive Grey alien, known on Earth as Dr. Charles Barry. Now, Dr. Barry himself appeared before them in all his alien flesh. Although he was in human guise, Bruce couldn't help wondering if it was his imagination or if there actually was a greyish tinge to the extraterrestrial's skin.

Through his comm unit, Bruce heard Zachary suck in a breath.

"I was wondering when you would arrive," Dr. Barry said. Although his lips never moved, they could all hear him clear as day, his voice cold and devoid of emotion. "I must say, I am impressed by your persistence."

"You were expecting us?" said Nina, awestruck at the power of his telepathy.

"Humans are quite predictable," Dr. Barry replied, seemingly unbothered by their intrusion. "I see you've found your brother," he said, turning his dead-looking eyes on Bruce.

"How did you know?" Bruce's blood boiled at the mention of Jack. He struggled to contain the urge to lunge at the doctor. Rip the asshole limb from limb. He clenched his fists tightly, trying to keep his anger in check.

"I know all about you. I must say, your species has such fascinating potential," Dr. Barry continued, his eyes roving over each of them in turn. "Intelligence, creativity, adaptability—it is truly remarkable. Yet, after all these millennia, there is still so much we do not understand about you Earthlings. Your DNA must have been helped along at some point by a higher intelligence. This intrigues me.

"A long way you have come from simple primates. We may even be you from the future. Atoms and molecules can be manipulated. An even more intriguing thought, yes?" Dr. Barry grinned. "I hope to learn so much from you specimens."

"You never will!" vowed Bruce. "We're here to put an end to your kind and your sick experiments!"

"Is that so?" Dr. Barry asked, raising an eyebrow. "I'm afraid you'll find that I am not so easily defeated. Besides, you misunderstand me, us. I am neither your enemy nor your friend. We Greys, as you call us, are all about science, and using any means necessary to achieve our ends."

Dr. Barry seemed unaffected by the gruesome tableau he'd surrounded himself with and not to be concerned about their repulsion to his activities. His large, black eyes held no emotion as he studied the human intruders in his lair. Bruce wondered what sort of monsters these Zeta Reticulans could be.

"Dr. Barry," Simmons spat, his hand instinctively reaching for his weapon. "You are a sick bastard."

"Please, Agent Simmons," the alien scientist replied coolly, "there's no need for name-calling. I'm simply conducting research—exploring the intricacies of human anatomy, psychology, and physiognomy."

"Research?" Bruce's voice trembled with barely restrained fury. "These were people, Barry. You call yourself a doctor? Doctors heal people. These were innocent people whose lives you've taken in the name of your twisted experiments."

"I suppose," Dr. Barry admitted, his tone infuriatingly matter-of-fact, "but scientific progress often requires sacrifice, Mr. Finger. I'm sure you of all people can understand that."

"Alex," Bruce said, turning to his teammate, "we need to find a way to get Jack out of here. We can't leave him behind."

"Agreed," Simmons replied, his eyes locked on Dr. Barry. "Nina, Julia, I want you two to see if you can find anything we can use as a makeshift stretcher. Bruce, help me keep an eye on our 'friend' here."

"Got it," Nina whispered, her gaze flickering between Dr. Barry and the surrounding lab equipment. She and Julia moved quickly, searching frantically for anything they could use to transport Jack's body.

"Your efforts are commendable," Dr. Barry sneered, watching them with a smile Bruce found unsettling. "But ultimately futile. You cannot hope to escape this place alive. And even if you do manage to reach the surface, you will find yourselves hunted mercilessly by the Reptilians. You'll find they are not as kindly disposed as I am. I care nothing for their wars of conquest and expansion. As I said, I'm a scientist, not a fighter. Knowledge is my only pursuit. They, however, will pursue you relentlessly until the last of you is dead. And then, your souls may be theirs, but your bodies will be mine."

"Then we'll just have to make sure they don't get that chance," Bruce growled, his eyes burning with defiance.

"Bold words," the alien scientist replied, his grin widening. "But empty ones, nonetheless. Soon, you will come to understand the true power of the Reptilians—and the futility of resisting them and us."

"Tell me something," Bruce said through gritted teeth. "Why? Why humans? What is it about us that you find so... fascinating?"

Dr. Barry's eyes never wavered as he replied. His voice, although transmitted telepathically, dripped with condescension. "Ah, yes. The age-old question of why we take such an interest in your species." He leaned back against a nearby table, folding his arms across his chest as he prepared to pontificate. "On the surface, you might appear unremarkable—just another primitive race, stumbling blindly through this backwater corner of the universe. But there is a certain...potential within you that we find intriguing."

"Potential?" Bruce spat, his anger flaring. "What kind of potential could you possibly seek in torturing people—in dissecting us like lab rats?"

"Your intelligence, for one," Dr. Barry said, his black eyes gleaming with a cold, calculating light. "For all your flaws, humanity possesses a unique capacity for creative thought—an ability to adapt and innovate that we have yet to encounter in any other species. Your species continues to innovate. Often not weighing the end results over time. Just like your phones are now part of you. Everyone wants a new one every year. Always building a cocoon for an electronic butterfly, so one of my colleagues has remarked. Always striving, always compelled to innovate and improve your lot. It's a strange combination of innovation and the need to have the newest technology all the time, no matter what the cost.

"Your society hides the fact you employ slave labor to gather minerals and resources. You don't even realize that, in your beginning, your race was created by others more advanced, to achieve similar goals of extracting these valuable resources for beings not of this planet. I get a good laugh watching humans adorn themselves in gold, not understanding its true value. Gold was mined to stabilize other worlds' environments. This is only one of many examples. Yet, such qualities as you humans possess have allowed you to survive, even thrive, despite the considerable odds stacked against you. It's like your kind understands to a degree the value of gold but enjoy wearing it because it is shiny. Foolish beings."

"Survive, you say?" Nina interjected, her voice shaking with unsuppressed rage. "Is that what you call this?" She threw out her arms. "Survival?"

"Indeed," Dr. Barry replied, unfazed by her outburst. "The specimens we collect are merely...casualties of science, if you will.

Sacrifices made in the name of progress. For every life we take, we gain valuable insights that bring us one step closer to understanding the true nature of human potential."

"I still don't understand. Potential for what?" Bruce demanded, his patience wearing thin. "What do you hope to achieve from all this? What's the end goal?"

"Control," Dr. Barry said simply, his tone matter-of-fact. "The ability to harness and manipulate the incredible power that lies dormant within each and every one of you. To unlock the secrets of the human mind and use them to reshape the universe as we see fit. Because, you see, ultimately, it is we, the Greys, who will rule the universe."

"Over my dead body," Bruce growled, taking a step towards the Grey scientist. "After what you did to Jack—"

"Ah, yes," Dr. Barry mused. "I had almost forgotten about your brother. A most unfortunate loss. I assure you, he did not die by my hand. I told you, I am no murderer. No, the Reptilians are responsible for his death. They merely handed his corpse over to me for study."

Nina sobbed as she and Julia reappeared with a gurney and a shroud. They carefully rolled Jack's body onto the gurney and covered him from head to toe.

Barry ignored them and continued. "But his death was not in vain. The data we gathered from his brain has already yielded some fascinating results."

"Shut up," Bruce warned, feeling a surge of fury so powerful it threatened to consume him. "Just shut up."

"Or what?" Dr. Barry challenged. "You'll kill me? You're welcome to try, of course. But, as I said, I think you'll find that I am not so easily disposed of."

Bruce saw red. He lunged at Dr. Barry, both hands wrapped tightly around the alien's throat, determined to make him pay for everything he had done. The others cried out in alarm, but Bruce could hardly hear them over the roar of bloodlust in his ears.

Dr. Barry's eyes widened in surprise, but he quickly regained his composure. With a swift, brutal efficiency, he drove a knee into Bruce's gut, forcing the architect to double over in pain. As Bruce gasped for breath, the Grey scientist grabbed him by the collar and slammed him against the wall.

"Your anger is understandable," Dr. Barry said, his voice cold and emotionless. "But ultimately misguided. You cannot hope to defeat me—not with brute force, at least."

"Enough!" Agent Simmons barked, drawing his weapon and training it on Dr. Barry, who was still gripping Bruce. Blood spurted from Bruce's nose.

"Enough, you say?" Dr. Barry replied, his gaze flicking between Bruce and the gun pointed at his chest. "You'll shoot me? I doubt it. You need me alive, if only to find out what other secrets I might possess."

"Try me," Simmons dared, his finger tightening on the trigger.

"Agent Simmons, wait," Nina ordered, her voice calm but firm. "He's right. We can't risk killing him, not yet."

"Fine," Simmons grumbled, lowering his weapon. "But if he so much as twitches wrong, I won't hesitate to put a bullet in him."

"Understood," Nina said, her eyes locked on Dr. Barry. "Now, let him go." She nodded at Bruce.

"Very well," Dr. Barry released his grip on Bruce's collar. As Bruce crumpled to the floor, gasping for breath, Dr. Barry straightened and smoothed his hair back into place. "I trust I've made my point?"

"Your point?" Bruce coughed, glaring up at the alien. "All you've proven is that you're a monster." He wiped the blood from his nose onto his trousers.

"Perhaps," Dr. Barry conceded, unfazed by the insult, "but I am also the only one who can help you understand the true nature of the threat you face. And whether you like it or not, I believe that makes me a valuable asset to your cause."

Julia laughed. "Please, you have no allegiance to anything or anyone other than yourself and your precious science."

Barry shrugged off the remark.

"I say we tie him up," said Bruce. "And shut him up!"

"Good idea," agreed Alex.

Dr. Barry made no effort to fight back as they trussed and gagged him and stuffed him in a locker.

"I don't like it," replied Bruce "That was too easy."

"I know what you mean," Agent Simmons checked his watch, "but the clock's ticking and we've got to keep moving. The more time we spend inside, the more chance of being caught." He stood near the lab's exit. "Let's not forget, we still have a job to do here."

CHAPTER 8

Minutes later, following Zachary's guidance, the Reptilian command center's entrance loomed before them. Pulsating violet light cast unearthly shadows on Bruce's face. He blinked away the sweat that threatened to blur his vision as he exchanged a tense nod with Nina, Julia, and Alex. Jack's lifeless body, which they'd pushed along on the gurney, was a constant reminder of the stakes each of them faced.

"Be ready for anything," Bruce whispered above the hum of the unfamiliar machinery that surrounded them. The team braced themselves, hands gripping their weapons tightly, eyes scanning ahead for potential threats.

"Let's do this," Nina said.

They pushed the gurney into the command center, their senses on full alert as they took in the bewildering alien environment and advanced technology.

"Stay close," Agent Simmons instructed, his voice calm but firm. "We need to neutralize them before they realize what's happening."

Inside the command center, a pair of Reptilians in human form hunched over a console, eyes focused, their fingers tapping rapidly across the glowing surface. They were so engrossed in their tasks that they didn't even notice the humans invading their space.

"Julia, you know what to do," Bruce whispered, his heart pounding in his chest. He pulled his own Taser from his belt. "I'll take the one on the left."

"Got it," she replied, her hazel eyes narrowing in focus.

"Now!" Bruce fired.

Julia stepped forward, her Taser crackling with energy. In one swift movement, she sent a powerful surge of electricity toward her unsuspecting target.

Both barbs hit their targets. The two Reptilians convulsed violently—their forms shifting back and forth between human and Reptilian appearance—before collapsing to the ground unconscious in their Reptilian bodies.

Bruce holstered his now-useless Taser. It carried only a single charge.

"Nice work, you two," Nina said. "Now let's secure the area."

"Wait!" Agent Simmons commanded, his eyes locked on something across the room. "There's one more."

A final alien stood at the far end of the command center, its Reptilian eyes widening in alarm as it gaped at them in wonder. Bruce tensed, readying himself for a fight, but Nina was quicker.

"Stop!" she shouted, brandishing her weapon. "Don't move, or I'll shoot."

The Reptilian hesitated, its gaze darting between Nina and its fallen comrades. Its hand gripped a white gun-like object with a green knobby tip. A weapon? Or merely a useless tool?

Sensing their advantage, Bruce stepped forward. "Drop your weapon," he demanded, his eyes never leaving the alien. The Reptilian complied, its hands trembling as it released the strange device. It clattered to the ground.

"Good," Bruce said, nodding to Agent Simmons, who quickly moved to restrain the Reptilian with plastic cuffs. He gagged the alien and hid him behind a bank of computers.

"That'll keep it from warning the others," Simmons said.

"Everyone okay?" Bruce asked once the area was secure, his heart still racing from the adrenaline surge.

"Fine," Julia replied, rubbing her hands together to dissipate her nervous energy. "But we need to move. They'll know something's wrong soon enough."

"Right," Bruce agreed, exchanging a glance with Nina. "Let's do what we came for and get out of here."

Bruce scanned the command center, taking note of its layout. The room was circular, with control panels lining the walls and a large holographic display at its center. He motioned for Julia to push the gurney carrying Jack's body to a concealed spot behind some dark metal equipment.

"Alex, can you make sense of any of these controls?" he asked, his voice low and urgent.

"Working on it," Agent Simmons replied, his eyes scanning one of the panels. "It's similar to the tech we discovered in the ship that came down near Roswell, but more advanced."

"Take your time," Nina joked, eyes flashing with impatience. "It's not like we've got an army of aliens breathing down our necks."

"We need to find this alien crystal and get out before some Reptilian hits the alarm." Bruce looked hastily around the chamber. But how to figure out what they were looking for? Everything in the room appeared alien!

"Found it!" Julia exclaimed suddenly. She pointed to a small pedestal near a holographic display. Atop the pedestal sat a glowing crystal, pulsating with energy. It was completely smooth and its surface glassy, almost watery.

"Holy shit," Nina breathed, her eyes widening in awe. "I think you're right. That's got to be it."

"Let's grab it and go," Bruce urged, his heart pounding in his chest.

"Wait," Agent Simmons cautioned, holding up a hand. "We need to be careful. Remember, it'll burn through human flesh." He extracted a pair of welders' gloves from his backpack. "These should do." He handed them to Bruce. They were aluminized rayon and wool gloves with extended cuffs that reached practically to his elbows. The gloves were rated to withstand temperatures as high as one-thousand degrees Fahrenheit.

Bruce pushed the thick gloves over his hands and approached the pedestal.

"Easy does it," Julia cautioned. Purple light from the crystal washed over her face. "I believe the crystal is powering this entire facility—maybe more. Removing it could cause anything from a minor disruption to a complete system meltdown."

"At the very least, set off a dozen alarms," cautioned Nina.

"Great," Bruce muttered, running a hand through his hair as he pictured an army of bloodthirsty Reptilians descending on them. "So, how do we handle this?"

"Julia, check that console over there and see if you can find a program that controls the crystal. Maybe we can shut it down before moving it," Agent Simmons suggested. "Nina, cover the door. I'll work with Bruce to extract the crystal." He slipped on a pair of welders' gloves himself while Julia hastened to a bank of computer monitors and sat.

"On it," Nina replied, her fingers tightening around her weapon as she moved into position.

"Nothing yet," Julia said. "This could take time."

"Time we don't have," replied Agent Simmons.

"Then let's just do this," Bruce said, turning to face the alien crystal. Heat radiated all around it.

"Right," Agent Simmons agreed solemnly.

"On three," said Bruce. He pressed his hands against the crystal and felt an immediate surge of heat in his fingertips.

They moved in sync, carefully lifting the alien power source from its cradle. The crystal, while no larger than a bowling ball, felt as heavy as a dozen fifteen-pounders and was proving hard to manage, even with Agent Simmons taking half the load.

The instant they succeeded in lifting it from its perch, the ground beneath them shook violently and all the lights dimmed.

"Shit," cursed Alex, struggling to maintain his hold.

"Yeah, that's bound to draw some attention." Bruce said.

"I'm afraid it already did," said Nina.

"What?" Bruce asked.

"We've got company," Nina whispered urgently, her eyes scanning the monitors on the command center console. Bruce felt the hairs on the back of his neck stand up as he saw the increasing heat signatures on the screen. Dozens of Reptilians were closing in on their position.

"Damn it," Julia hissed under her breath. "Nothing!" She slammed a fist against the computer keyboard.

"Alright, listen up," Agent Simmons said, as his arms quaked under the weight of the crystal. "Bruce, you and I will carry the crystal. Julia, you're on point. Nina, watch our backs. We have to move fast, but we can't afford to make any noise. And don't forget about Jack."

"Got it," they each murmured.

"Let's go," Bruce urged, as he and Agent Simmons carefully cradled the crystal between them. Heat from the alien crystal continued to seep through his thick gloves. It was getting hotter and hotter. Soon, he feared it might become unbearable.

The team moved out of the command center, with Julia leading the way and Nina pushing the gurney that carried Jack's lifeless body.

They navigated wordlessly through the caliginous corridors. Survival depended on staying one step ahead of the relentless Reptilians. Capture would lead to enslavement, probably even death. Either way, they'd end up as nothing more than lab specimens to be cruelly dissected and studied by Dr. Barry.

"Turn left here," Julia whispered, her hand motioning towards a branching corridor. They cautiously turned the corner, their eyes constantly scanning for any sign of enemy movement. The silence was deafening, punctuated only by the soft whirring of the wheels on the gurney and their own shallow breaths.

"Stop!" Nina suddenly commanded. "Listen!"

The team froze in their tracks. They heard the unmistakable

sound of approaching footsteps. Bruce's heart raced as they pressed themselves against the cold metallic walls, trying to blend in with the shadows. The sound of steps came closer, then faded.

"We go on one," Nina said.

The others nodded.

"Three... two... one." Nina counted down in a hushed tone. As soon as she reached 'one,' the team darted across the corridor, narrowly avoiding being spotted by a pair of Reptilians in human guise passing by.

"Good call," Bruce whispered to Nina, giving her a nod of appreciation. She simply nodded back and kept moving.

The team continued running, evading and outmaneuvering their pursuers, navigating as swiftly and silently as possible through the alien stronghold. They moved like a well-practiced team despite their lack of training, their actions driven by their mission to sabotage the Reptilian base and stop their sinister plot.

"Up ahead," Julia murmured, pointing towards a set of double doors that led into a large, open chamber. "If I'm right, from this position, we can circle back towards the exit. Zachary, is that correct?" They waited for an answer that never came.

"Grandpa?" Nina asked worriedly into her comm.

"Don't worry, Nina. We may be too deep underground for the signal to get through," Bruce suggested.

"Right," Agent Simmons agreed, his eyes scanning their surroundings for any signs of hidden danger.

"Let's get moving," Nina said. "I don't like this. We're too vulnerable here."

They rolled Jack's gurney through the chamber. Bruce and Alex had set the crystal on the lower level of the gurney. It made the gurney twice as heavy a load but it was far easier than continuing to carry the alien rock in their hands, which had been slowing them down.

"Almost there," Bruce whispered to Jack as much as himself.

"Just a little further." He gripped the handle of the gurney, every muscle in his body tensed and ready to change course for the hundredth time at a moment's notice. The corridor seemed to stretch on forever, the alien tech embedded in its walls serving as a reminder of what they were up against.

"Left," Agent Simmons whispered, pointing to a nearby intersection. Bruce glanced back at Nina, who gave him a quick, encouraging smile.

"Right behind you," Bruce said, his breath coming out in ragged bursts. Together, they turned Jack's gurney down the left passage.

"Stay low," Julia cautioned, her voice hushed and urgent. "I hear more coming."

They crouched down in an alcove, as a group of Reptilians marched past them, hissing in an alien tongue that sent shivers along Bruce's spine. Their malevolent presence turned his blood cold.

"Nice catch, Julia," Nina whispered once the coast was clear. "Come on, we need to keep moving."

"Agreed," Bruce replied, pushing the gurney forward once more. "Let's hope there are no more close calls."

"Zachary, you there?" Agent Simmons asked. He received no reply.

"I'm worried," said Nina.

"We all are," replied Julia, briefly squeezing her friend's hand.

"If I'm correct, we take the next right, then head straight until we reach the central chamber," Agent Simmons said. "From there, we can double back towards the exit."

"Sounds right," Bruce confirmed, a picture of the schematics flashing in his brain. Thoughts of Jack's wife, Carla, and their two young children, suddenly filled him. He also couldn't help wondering if they'd become lost. Simmons didn't sound so sure of himself. And while he'd said it sounded right, he really wasn't so sure...

Were they lost? Were they running in circles?

He paused.

"Come on, Bruce," Nina murmured, sensing his distress. "Can't stop now. We'll make it out of here."

He nodded, drawing strength from her unwavering confidence. Together, they moved in sync, their bodies fluid yet precise as they navigated the maze-like corridors.

"Right turn up ahead," Agent Simmons said. The others followed close behind. But as they rounded the corner, a trio of Reptilians appeared, blocking their intended route.

"Back up! Back up!" Julia shouted, her eyes wide with alarm.

"Move! This way!" Nina urged, guiding them towards an alternative passage as the Reptilians closed in.

They sprinted through the narrow corridor, the sound of pursuit growing louder behind them. Bruce's muscles burned with exertion, but he refused to slow down. To slow down was to die, become a lab specimen in the hands of Dr. Barry.

"We can't keep this up forever," he panted, stealing a glance at Nina. "At least, I know I can't. I'm an architect, not a marathoner. We need a plan—and fast!" They were rats trapped in a maze with no escape.

"Let me think," Nina replied, her brow furrowed in concentration. "There has to be a way to buy us some time..."

"Wait," Agent Simmons interjected, an idea forming in his mind. "I've got it. We split up, lead them in different directions. It'll confuse them and give us a chance to regroup."

"Split up? Is that really a good idea?" Nina asked.

"No, Alex is right. It's the only way. There's three of them and three of us," Bruce replied, feeling a spark of hope. "Nina, Julia, you go left. Alex and I will take Jack and go right. We'll meet back at the central chamber and try to find our way out from there." He frowned as the din of alien voices grew louder. Had more Reptilians joined the hunt?

"Be careful," Nina implored.

"You too," Bruce assured her, reaching out for a brief, reassuring touch of her hand before they parted ways.

Bruce huffed as they weaved through the complex alien architecture, searching for a way to fulfill their plan to sabotage the Reptilian stronghold and then make their escape. All of which seemed impossible now. Their well-thought out plan was in shambles and they were reduced to fleeing for their lives. The gurney bearing the weight of his brother and the crystal moved like a lead sled over coarse gravel as they rushed back to the Reptilian command center.

"Alex," Bruce gasped, sweat dripping from his brow, "there has to be something we can do to cripple their operation. And that might draw their attention away from us. Get them off our backs."

"I know. Let's keep our eyes open," Agent Simmons said, his eyes scanning the banks of advanced computers. "Maybe we'll find something that will help us."

"Right." Bruce shifted Jack's body carefully and began inspecting the computers but it was no use—everything was written in an alien language and indecipherable. He looked but saw nothing familiar. Had their entire operation been useless?

"Over here!" Nina called out from a few feet away as she burst into the room, eyes wide with excitement. "I found something!"

The team hurried over to find Nina standing before a large, glowing panel of controls, its complex design intimidating yet strangely mesmerizing. A silvery image of the Gateway Arch stood in the center. As he watched in amazement, Bruce's eyes followed the path of an alien spacecraft, long and V-shaped, as it passed beneath the Arch and then disappear. Where had it gone? Had no one up in the city seen in?

Wasn't that impossible?

"Maintains a link to the Arch. Let's blow it," Julia snapped, eyes narrowing as she carefully studied the panel. Bruce wondered what she was seeing that he wasn't— because all he saw were alien hieroglyphics and a rainbow of colors. All meaningless.

"On it," Agent Simmons said, shrugging off his backpack and grabbing a packet of plastic explosives. The panel emitted a deep, resonant hum, and the entire room began to vibrate as if the panel knew what they were up to and that it was in danger.

"Will it work?" Bruce asked, anxiety evident in his voice as he watched Agent Simmons at work.

"Only one way to find out," Nina replied, her expression determined. "Remember, we only have five minutes once Simmons sets the charge."

"Ready, everyone?" Simmons hunched over the computerized timer on the explosives.

"Go for it," Bruce said. He gripped the gurney, sensing the Reptilians closing in, their footsteps louder and faster and the buzz of their alien tongue pulsating throughout the room.

Two small beeps and a blinking red light warned that Agent Simmons had started the timer. "Time to move, people!" Simmons whispered, jumping to his feet.

They pressed on, navigating the labyrinthine halls as best they could while struggling to avoid encounters with the hunting Reptilians.

"Wait!" Bruce suddenly exclaimed, grabbing Nina's arm as a group of Reptilians ran past just inches from where they hid behind a stack of rotting crates. The team held their breath, hearts pounding in their chests, their clothing damp with sweat, as the aliens moved on, unaware of their presence. There was still no word from Zachary.

Bruce prayed Zachary hadn't been discovered and captured by the Reptilians. He kept his thoughts to himself for fear of worrying the others, Nina, in particular.

"That was too close," Agent Simmons muttered, wiping sweat from his brow. He glanced at his watch. "Two minutes till detonation."

"Let's keep going," Nina urged, her voice barely a whisper. "We're nearly home free."

The gurney wheels screeched, echoing in the alien corridors. The back left wheel snapped off with a crack that broke the silence.

Bruce's grip slipped on the handles, his palms wet with perspiration. "Can't keep this up," he panted. "We've got to ditch the gurney."

"Are you sure?" Nina's concern pierced through her hushed tone.

"It's busted. There's no other option." Bruce hoisted Jack onto his back, muscles straining. "Let's go!"

"What about the crystal?" Agent Simmons said.

"We leave it behind," Nina said.

"But—" began Agent Simmons.

"We have no choice. It's Jack or the crystal."

Agent Simmons swore but relented.

They ran. Each step thudded with urgency, sweat dripping down their frightened faces. Sounds of the Reptilians grew louder, closer. Bruce concentrated on his breathing, Jack's cold corpse jostling his shoulder, straining his back muscles.

"Left, now!" Simmons barked, leading the team through another branch of the cave.

"Are we close?" Bruce asked, feeling himself slowing and on the verge of collapse.

"Almost," Nina replied, squeezing his hand for reassurance. "Hang in there."

"Got you!" Zachary's voice suddenly rang in their ears.

Bruce smiled, and felt a surge of new strength. "Zachary, you old fool!"

"Yes, it's me! Steady on!" urged the professor.

"Wait," Julia froze, motioning them to halt. Reptilian guards scuttled by, talking rapidly.

"Damn it," Bruce thought, back pressed against a wall, struggling to balance Jack's body. "We can't keep this up. We'll never make it out."

"Go!" Simmons urged as the guards vanished from sight.

"Up ahead," Nina pointed, "I see a light up ahead...and stars. That's got to be an exit!"

"Finally," Bruce breathed, relief washing over him. But his relief was short-lived.

"Simmons!" Julia cried out, her voice a mixture of terror and disbelief.

Bruce turned to see Agent Simmons ensnared in the grasp of a pair of Reptilian guards. He fought with all his strength but they were too powerful even for him. The agent's eyes met Bruce's, silently urging them to continue without him.

Bruce started to lower Jack's body to the ground, determined to help Agent Simmons.

"No, run, goddammit!" Simmons shouted, struggling against his captors. "Run!"

"Simmons!" Bruce yelled, torn between saving his comrade and completing their mission.

ꞏ⅂ᴲ⋊ⴀⵑⴸⱯⴸ 9

Bruce sprinted down the tight corridor, Nina and Julia hot on his heels. Their steps echoed off the metal-paneled walls, mixing with the distant sound of alarms blaring and the buzz of Reptilians chasing them through their underground base. Agent Simmons' order to run still rang in their ears, a chilling reminder of the life-and-death danger they all faced.

Leaving Simmons behind had been no easy choice.

"Here." Nina pulled Bruce and Julia into a secluded corner. They huddled together, their faces illuminated only by the faint glow of an emergency light, backs pressed against the wall, catching their breath, and exchanging panicked glances.

"Despite what he said, we can't leave Simmons behind," Nina said.

"Agreed," said Julia.

Bruce nodded. "Yeah, we need to help him." His thoughts turned to Jack's lifeless body. A painful lump formed in his throat. During their escape, they'd hidden his body in a nearby storage room, intending to return for him later. "How did this go so wrong?" He frowned at his watch. "The explosives were supposed to detonate minutes ago."

Nina's eyes flickered with fear and frustration. "The Reptilians must have discovered and diffused them or found a way to contain the explosion somehow. Face it, our plan failed." She cursed. "And now Simmons has been captured."

"Damn it," Bruce muttered, his fists clenching at his sides. He felt responsible for the precarious situation they found themselves in. The thought of losing a member of their team was unbearable. "Why did we even think we could pull this off!? The whole thing was crazy. We'd need a fucking army to beat these bastards."

Nina bit her lip, her eyes filled with determination. "I know. But the army isn't coming, remember? It's up to us. We can't just rush into this. We need a plan, if we want any chance to succeed and not end up like Simmons."

"What about Jack?" asked Bruce. He couldn't bear the thought of his brother's corpse being left behind.

"We'll come back for him as soon as we can, I promise. First things first," Nina replied. "Okay, Bruce?"

Bruce hesitated only for a moment. "Okay."

The three exchanged hurried whispers, struggling to formulate a strategy to rescue Agent Simmons from the clutches of the aliens. They dismissed one plan after the other, either because it was too unlikely to succeed or simply too dangerous to attempt. They were all feeling the viselike pressure of the mission as it seemed to be unraveling before their very eyes.

"Hey," Julia's voice came from around the corner, startling both Bruce and Nina. They had not realized she'd moved away.

"Julia... what are you doing there?" Bruce asked, tensing up momentarily before remembering she was one of the few allies they had in this alien-infested stronghold.

"Let me create a diversion," Julia offered, her tone resolute.

"A diversion? How?" asked Bruce.

"Use myself as bait."

"What? Never!" Bruce said. "Not after what happened to Alex."

"Trust me, Bruce. I'll be extra careful."

"I don't like it," agreed Nina.

Julia pressed on. "I have an idea. If I'm right, I can create...chaos in another section of the base. That should give you two enough time to find Agent Simmons and effect a rescue."

"I don't know..." Bruce hesitated. "Sounds crazy, if you—."

"Are you sure you want to do this, Julia?" Nina interrupted.

"Positive. Trust me, I know what I'm doing," Julia replied.

"How will we even know if you've managed?" Bruce wanted to know. The comms seemed iffy at best and they hadn't heard from Zachary since his last message.

"If I succeed, the Reptilians will be racing to the other end of the base," Julia said, confidently. "Now, go. We don't have much time."

Bruce and Nina exchanged a look.

"Fine," Bruce said. Oddly, he found himself trusting Julia without exactly knowing why. The slightest misstep could lead to capture, torture, or worse. But Alex's fate, and possibly the fate of the entire human race, hung in the balance. Sometimes you had to act on faith. And pray that you make it out alive.

With a final nod to Julia, Bruce and Nina slipped into the shadows as she ran in the opposite direction. Bruce and Nina tiptoed cautiously, their footsteps barely sounding on the cold, dirt-packed floor. Visions of the horrors Agent Simmons might be subjected to fueled their determination to rescue him in time.

"Stick close," Bruce whispered. He took Nina's hand. "I don't want to lose you next."

As they rounded yet another curve, a distant, muffled alarm pierced the stillness. Julia's diversion had begun. They exchanged a glance, thankful for her resourcefulness but aware that their time was limited.

"It's go time," Nina murmured. "And be ready to shoot. We need to find Simmons as fast as possible."

"Trust me," Bruce replied, his jaw clenched with resolve. "We will." But he didn't half-believe his own words.

The two continued to move stealthily through the underground corridors, cautiously poking their noses into every room. The convoluted layout of the stronghold played tricks on their minds. Sometimes, Bruce was sure they'd been literally running in circles.

"Which way?" Nina looked back at Bruce. They faced two

diverging passages.

"Let's try down that way," Bruce replied, gesturing towards the narrow passage to their right. He couldn't shake the nagging feeling that time was running out, that every second they spent navigating the base put Simmons in greater danger…if he wasn't dead already.

Suddenly, they heard muffled voices up ahead—the buzzing language of nearby Reptilians. Bruce held up a hand, signaling for Nina to stop.

"Over there," he whispered, pointing towards an open doorway from which the voices emanated. They crept closer, careful not to make a sound, and peered inside.

There, within the sterile confines of Dr. Barry's lab, lay Agent Simmons. Strapped to an examination table, he appeared unconscious, his muscular form dwarfed by the sinister-looking equipment surrounding him. Two Reptilian guards stood watch, while Dr. Barry, his black hair gleaming under the harsh LED lights, prepared a syringe filled with an unknown drug.

"Simmons." Nina's voice trembled. "We have to do something." Nina reached out and grasped Bruce's hand, her fingers intertwining with his. Their eyes locked for a brief moment, silently communicating their shared resolve.

"Agreed," Bruce said, his brow furrowing as he weighed their options. "But we can't just barge in. We need to be smart about this." The logical thinker within him battled against the mounting urgency of the situation and his desire to run inside.

"We could lure one of them out," Nina suggested, her eyes darting between the Reptilians and Dr. Barry. "Then overpower them and use their weapon to take out the other one."

"Maybe." Bruce considered the idea. It was risky and they couldn't afford any mistakes, not with Simmons' life on the line.

"You have a better idea?"

"Give me a moment," Bruce replied, racking his brain for a better plan. "Ready?" he whispered after a moment.

"Ready for what?"

He leaned forward and kissed her on the lips. "Plan B," Bruce replied with a smile.

"Plan B?" Nina traced her lips with her fingertips. Had he really just kissed her? At a time like this? It caught her off guard and threw her off balance. "What the hell was plan A?"

"I couldn't think of one, so I decided to go straight to plan B." His eyes sparkled mischievously.

"Which is?"

Bruce sucked in a breath and tensed his muscles. "This!" he shouted. He ran full speed into Dr. Barry's lab.

"Bruce! What the hell?" Nina froze in shock then rushed in after him. This wasn't a plan, this was suicide!

Their sudden entrance caught the Reptilian guards and Dr. Barry by surprise. An unnatural blue light bathed the lab, casting running shadows on the walls.

"What! How did you get in here?" Dr. Barry stammered, the syringe clattering to the floor and shattering as he recoiled in astonishment.

"Step away from him!" Bruce commanded, his voice steady despite the pounding of his heart.

"Or what?" one of the Reptilians snarled, taking a menacing step forward.

"Or we'll make sure you regret it," Nina shot back, her gaze never leaving the creature's calculating eyes.

"Your threats are meaningless," the second Reptilian barked.

"Get them out of here," Dr. Barry ordered, his face flushed with anger. "I won't have my work disrupted by these...humans."

As the Reptilians moved toward Bruce and Nina, Bruce knew he needed to act fast. He scanned the room for any potential weapons or means of escape. It wasn't fair, he thought bitterly. They had come so far, only to be thwarted by these monstrous beings.

Nina drew a small device from her pocket. With the press of a button, it emitted a high-pitched whine that had the Reptilians recoiling in pain, hands clamped over their ears.

"Now, that's what I call plan B!" Bruce shouted. Seizing the opportunity, Bruce lunged at Dr. Barry, knocking the Grey alien to the ground.

Nina darted towards Agent Simmons. But just as she reached for his restraints, the Reptilians recovered quicker than she anticipated. The first guard lunged at her while the second blocked Bruce's attempt to reach them.

Nina grappled with the guard while desperately trying to free Simmons. Just as she loosened one strap, a powerful shove sent her sprawling across the cold floor. Before she could recover, the second guard seized Bruce and slammed him into a wall. Despite their desperate struggles, they were vastly overpowered and quickly restrained.

"Enough," Dr. Barry snapped, dusting himself off as he rose to his feet. "You humans always think you can play hero." He cast an icy glance at Bruce and Nina who were forcibly held by the guards. "Dispose of them. I will extract their souls at a later date."

Before anyone could react, a thunderous crash emanated from the opposite end of the lab. All eyes turned to see Julia bulldoze her way through the entrance, her eyes ablaze with fury. "Leave them alone!"

Time seemed to stand still as Julia hurled something small and metallic at the Reptilians. A blinding flash erupted as an electromagnetic pulse detonated, plunging the lab into darkness and chaos. Every Reptilian in the room staggered. Dr. Barry slumped to the ground.

"Run!" Julia's voice rose above the din.

Bruce ran to the examination table and savagely cut Agent Simmons' bonds with his knife.

"Thanks," muttered the agent.

"You're okay!" Bruce took Alex's hand and helped him off the table.

"Yeah, barely." Alex rubbed his wrists. "Thanks." He struggled to his feet. Around them, the Reptilians were struggling to their feet too, recovering from the EMP. "We'd better do like Julia said and get the hell out of here!"

Bruce turned to collect Nina, but she was already at his side, lips set in a determined line and eyes filled with purpose. With surprising strength, Julia grabbed Alex and helped the weakened agent walk.

Behind them, the lab remained shrouded in darkness. The only sound that reached their ears now was the disorienting whir of machinery short-circuiting and the distant cussing of Dr. Barry.

Quickly scanning their surroundings, Bruce led them down a flight of stairs. They proceeded through a series of twisting tunnels that ended abruptly in a desolate cavernous expanse that housed an alien spaceship—just like the one Bruce had watched fly through the Gateway Arch and disappear earlier. Bruce stopped and stared at the thing. The sight was as scary as it was awe-inspiring.

"It's really something, isn't it?" Julia appeared at his side and dropped her hand on his shoulder.

Bruce nodded. "I've never seen anything like it..."

"Man, how I'd love to hot wire that thing and take it for a spin," Alex said.

"I feel the same way," said Bruce. "Wonder what kind of power she's got?"

"And how fast she'll go," replied Alex.

"Men," joked Nina. "If it isn't cars, it's spaceships. Now, if you two don't mind, let's get Jack and get our asses out of here!"

"This way," Julia said, moving swiftly around the nose of the alien spacecraft.

Bruce gazed up again at the alien spaceship towering above them.

It was an impressive piece of alien technology, nothing Man had so far created came anywhere near to this. Its color ranged from silver to black and seemed to shift in the light. Strange symbols and markings tattooed its surface, giving it an otherworldly appearance. And otherworldly it was…

Shaped like a giant saucer, long, thin appendages extended from its sides, giving the impression of outstretched arms ready to take flight at any moment. Glowing ports lined the center but revealed no activity within, only darkness. The ship seemed almost alive, pulsing with a power that Bruce could feel radiating from the ship. It was both a terrifying and a fascinating thing to behold.

"This way." Julia led them up a stairway. "I found this earlier. I don't believe they come this way much." She pushed away a cobweb with her hand, proving her point.

Several minutes later, they found Jack's lifeless body where they had hidden it earlier. Bruce was relieved to find that he'd been undisturbed. The sight of his brother's broken form sent a fresh wave of grief washing over him, but he fought to keep it in check, focusing on the task at hand.

"Help me carry him?" Bruce said. He was exhausted and his muscles ached.

Nina jumped in. "Of course."

"Thanks." They carefully lifted Jack's body between them. "Which way now, Julia?"

"Follow me," Julia urged, her eyes darting nervously down the hallway. "I discovered another exit this way. It's a bit further from the van but at least it will get us out of here."

"Right behind you," said Alex. He took up the rear and held his firearm at the ready.

Two minutes later, Julia led them up three narrow metal steps. The door creaked loudly as she shouldered it open, the metal groaning in protest. The sound of their footsteps set off tiny alarms in the otherwise quiet alley, as they tramped through the accumulated mounds of trash. In the distance, a dog barked and a car engine rumbled to life before fading away.

Bruce and Nina struggled with Jack's body, clambering with difficulty over piles of loose debris. They turned the corner of the crumbling facade of a warehouse. A crisp, cool breeze greeted them, carrying the faint scent of distant factories and exhaust. Amongst the trash, a lingering smell of rot and decay mixed with the faint whiff of urine and alcohol.

"I see the van!" Julia cried.

"Where?" asked Nina.

"A hundred yards that way! Come one!" Julia surged forward.

Bruce and Nina did their best to keep up.

"You okay, Alex?" Bruce huffed. "Alex?" He looked behind him and froze.

Alex was gone!

CHAPTER 10

Darkness pressed in around them. Zachary's voice pierced through the night, his eyes wide and anxious as he stood by the van, gripping the open door for support. "Where's Simmons?" he asked urgently.

Bruce's jaw tightened as he struggled to lift Jack's limp body into the back of the van. The weight of his brother's lifeless form bore down on him, both physically and emotionally. "Can't talk about it now, Zachary!" he snapped, trying to focus on the task at hand. "We need to get out of here!"

Nina nodded in agreement, her gaze darting around the desolate urban landscape as if expecting some new danger to materialize at any moment. Her hand hovered near her holster, ready to defend against any threat. "The Reptilians could be closing in, Grandpa."

Zachary's eyes widened as he registered the gravity of the situation. He quickly moved to help Bruce secure Jack's body in the rear of the van. The sound of his brother's body hitting the cold metal floor sent a chill down Bruce's spine, but he pushed aside his emotions. There would be time for grief later. For now, the goal was to survive. He carefully laid a dark wool blanket over Jack's body, a small gesture of respect as well as protection.

"Julia, secure the gear, please," Nina instructed, while she helped Bruce in back.

"Yes," Julia replied. She scooped up what was left of their equipment from the ground and stowed it in the van.

As the last of their gear was tossed into the van, Bruce slammed shut the heavy rear doors, the sound reverberating through the stillness of the night. He couldn't shake the unsettling feeling that they were being watched, that the Reptilians were lurking just beyond the shadows, preparing to strike again. And that spacecraft he'd seen! What hope did humanity have against technology like that? It was like something out of a sci-fi nightmare.

"Everyone in, now!" Bruce urged. They clambered quickly into the van. Zachary climbed into the driver seat.

"Go, go, go!" Nina said as she plopped herself down in the front passenger seat and strapped herself in.

Zachary wasted no time in starting the engine, its roar cutting through the night.

The van lurched forward. Bruce allowed himself a moment to breathe, his thoughts swirling. What had become of Agent Simmons? Had they left him behind to face the enemy alone? Or worse, had he remained behind on purpose? Had he been lying to them all along? Tricking them? Was he truly one of them?

For now, those questions would have to remain unasked and unanswered, locked away in the recesses of his mind as they focused on escape and the journey back to the farmhouse.

The van's tires squealed as they tore down the street, its engine growling like a wounded beast. The darkness outside was ominous. Inside, the atmosphere was grim and silent, each passenger lost in their own private thoughts.

The professor finally broke the silence. "What happened back there?" Zachary wanted to know as he raced up the onramp and merged onto the highway.

"Lots," said Bruce. "And none of it good. We lost Alex."

"How?"

"We don't know, Grandpa," answered Nina, more sharply than she'd intended. "Sorry. One minute he was there with us, the next thing we knew he was gone."

"You think they captured him?" Zachary's eyes met Bruce's in the rearview mirror.

"Either that or he was working with them," Bruce decided to say.

"No, I don't believe it. Why would he do that?" Zachary replied. "Besides, he led us to their base."

"Maybe hoping we'd be captured?" suggested Nina.

Bruce rubbed his temples. "I just don't know… We did see him strapped in Dr. Barry's lab. A captive."

"That could have been staged for our benefit," Nina replied.

Had they been duped by one of their own? Or had Simmons fallen into Reptilian hands?

A sudden flicker of light in the sky behind them interrupted their theorizing. Bruce turned sharply, and saw a silent spacecraft zip overhead—a fast-moving blip against a backdrop of stars that then vanished into the night as if it had never been there.

"A Reptilian ship…" Julia whispered, her voice barely more than a breath as she stared up at the now-vacant sky.

Bruce turned his back on the spectacle and asked Julia. "Anything on Simmons?"

"No." Julia's fingers danced across the keyboard of her laptop, each keystroke an urgent rhythm punctuating the tension inside the van. She scanned the screen with laser focus, searching for some signal indicating where Alex might be and where the Reptilians might be taking him. Each of them had carried an electronic tracking device. His didn't appear to be functioning. "I'm getting nothing." She slammed the cover of the laptop down. "It's no use, I'm afraid."

"What about the crystal?" Zachary asked. "Did you get it?"

"No, Grandpa. We weren't able to sabotage the base either." Nina explained what had happened. It all seemed like a horrible joke. Nothing had gone right.

The van's headlights cut through the darkness like a knife as they approached Zachary's remote farmhouse, the weathered exterior a welcome sight. Bruce wondered how much longer their safe haven would remain secure.

"Wait here," Bruce instructed, as Zachary brought the van to a halt. "I'll go in first, make sure it's clear."

Nina nodded reluctantly, Julia simply stared at her laptop screen on the backseat, lost in her research. Bruce stepped out of the van. Unused to such intense physical activity, he felt stiff and his muscles ached. Nina rolled down her window and handed him the keys to the house. He jiggled the keys in the palm of his hand, studied the farmhouse a long moment, before cautiously making his way towards the front door.

He rested his hand on the pistol tucked into his waistband. As he reached the door, he hesitated for a moment, listening intently for any signs of movement within. Hearing nothing, he carefully pushed the door open, tensed and ready for action.

The familiar sights and smells of the cabin greeted him as he swept his gaze over the space. Lit only by the weak rays of the rising sun, he searched for any evidence of uninvited guests. Everything appeared unchanged and in its place. There were no signs of Reptilians or any other unwanted visitors.

"Clear!" he called out to the others, exhaling a sigh of relief. Nina and Julia exited the van, each carrying their own burdens and concerns as they made their way inside.

Once they had all entered the cabin, the door shut behind them with a heavy thud, and an oppressive silence settled over the room. Each of them found a place to sit, exhaustion and mental fatigue rendering them mute as they sank into their private thoughts.

Bruce couldn't stop replaying the events of the past few hours in his mind, nor stop wondering what had become of Agent Simmons. Was he a traitor? Or just another casualty of this war they were fighting? He glanced over at Nina. Her haunted expression seemed to mirror his own inner turmoil. "Hey," he whispered, reaching out to gently squeeze her hand. "We're safe for now."

"Yeah," she managed to smile weakly, her grip on his hand tightening as if clinging to some elusive hope.

Across the room, Julia focused on her laptop keyboard. What she hoped to find, he had no idea. But the woman never gave up.

"Your grandpa, he's alright?" Bruce asked Nina.

Nina nodded. "Tired, but okay."

Bruce glanced over at Zachary who sat in his favorite armchair, his gaze vacant and distant. But he was safe, they were all safe for now, and that was what mattered.

"What now?" Nina said.

"We recharge, regroup, and plan our next move," Bruce said. He looked around at each of them—a group of ordinary people thrust into an extraordinary situation. And yet, despite the odds stacked against them, they had managed to survive…so far. But merely surviving wasn't enough. They needed to win this war against the Reptilians and stop their impending invasion.

"But first," Bruce said, "we get a few hours' sleep." They'd been running on adrenaline for too long, their bodies pushed to their limits. "We're going to need some rest if we're going to be any use in fighting the Reptilians."

"Bruce is right," Zachary said, his voice weary but firm. "Tomorrow is another day. Sleep now."

"But not all at once," cautioned Bruce. "One of us should keep watch at all times while the others sleep."

"You're right," said Nina, glancing through the curtains out into the empty yard. "We're sitting ducks here."

"But at least we'll see any strangers coming," Bruce said. "Go ahead. Get some sleep. I'll take the first watch." He yawned loudly.

"What about you?" Nina asked.

"I'll be fine."

"Okay, but I'll relieve you in…" she glanced at her watch. "Two hours."

They agreed on a rotating watch schedule, with each of them taking turns to monitor outside for any sign of danger. Zachary bid everyone goodnight and slowly climbed up the wooden staircase to his bedroom while Nina and Julia took up residence in the downstairs guest room, neither wanting to be alone.

Bruce pulled a chair to the window and settled himself with his gun on the table beside him. He had told everyone to keep their phones within reach in case something happened. Left alone in the living room, he peered out into the darkness that stretched beyond the farmhouse's front yard. It was a peaceful scene, starkly juxtaposed against the turmoil brewing like a witch's cauldron, both out there and within him. Jack remained lying inside the back of the van. As soon as possible, he intended to give him a proper burial.

His eyelids fluttered and sleep threatened. Every creak of the old wood-framed house sent a jolt of adrenaline through him—startling him awake again. His fingers felt for the reassuring presence of the handgun as he continually scanned the darkness for any sign of movement.

Sometime later, fatigue won the battle and he drifted into an uneasy sleep. A hand on his cheek woke him. His eyes shot open and he automatically reached for his weapon.

"Bruce."

"Nina!" He blinked several times.

"Shh." Nina settled on the rug beside him. "You okay?"

"Yeah," he rubbed his stubbled chin. "Some lookout I make."

"You're only human," Nina said with a grin.

He drew in the scent of her soap, a calming blend of earth and spice that reminded him of open fields and summer rain. For a moment, he allowed himself to get lost in it, to drown out the memories of the recent horrors and the dread of those yet to come.

Nina gently took his hand and squeezed it, a wordless gesture that said so much. He felt an unspoken bond growing between them, an inexplicable connection that both scared and reassured him.

He leaned forward and they kissed.

It was brief, a mere brushing of lips that conveyed so much more than mere words could express—shared fears, mutual respect, and an unspoken promise that they would face whatever came next together. Bruce pulled away first, his eyes holding hers for a moment longer before he cleared his throat.

"I should... I need to go check on Jack," he said suddenly.

Nina nodded, understanding shining in her eyes. "Mind if I come with you?"

"Please do."

They left the warm confines of the farmhouse, stepping out into the early morning chill. The van sat some distance away, shrouded in a gray mist that lay low over the ground. They had covered it with a tarp in hopes to conceal it.

"Bruce," Nina said, her voice barely a whisper, "look." She pointed across the valley.

He blinked against the sleep tugging at his eyelids, straining to see what had caught Nina's attention. And then he saw it—a strange, faint red-and-purple glow coming from the woods bordering Zachary's property. His breath hitched in his throat as he reached for his gun, then remembered he'd left it sitting on the table inside the house. As they watched, the light faded and disappeared. A minute later, it was back.

"What is that?" Bruce whispered.

"I don't know," Nina answered, her gaze still fixed on the spot where they had seen the glow. "Could be nothing, just a trick of the light, weather conditions... Or it could be them."

"Should we wake the others?"

"Not yet," Nina replied. "Let's go check it out first. Quietly."

Bruce nodded, curiosity pushing back his fatigue as they moved toward the source of the strange light. The grassy earth under their feet was dew-drenched, slippery, and icy cold. A chill seeped through their shoes and made them shiver.

The journey to the woods was eerily silent, save for the crunch of their footsteps and the occasional rustling from small animals startled from their sleep or activity.

As they reached the edge of the woods, they slowed their steps. Crouching behind a tree, they each peered through the trees. The deep forest loomed ominously ahead, a dark maw ready to swallow them whole.

"Let's split up," Nina suggested in a whisper. "We'll cover more ground."

"No, absolutely not" Bruce insisted, shaking his head. "We stick together, remember?"

She nodded, pressing a finger to her lips in a universal signal for silence. Then, taking a collective breath, they moved slowly forward into the woods. The wind rustled through the leaves overhead. Goosebumps prickled up on Bruce's arms despite the thick flannel shirt he wore.

They threaded their way deeper and deeper into the woods, twigs snapping under their feet and leaves rustling around them as they went. They moved cautiously, eyes peeled for any sign of movement or change in the landscape. Suddenly, Nina stopped so abruptly that Bruce collided against her. "Sorry."

"Shh. Look. There," she whispered, pointing ahead. Bruce squinted at where her finger was directing him. There—just beyond a cluster of trees—stood the source of the strange light. It was a spacecraft, the spitting image of the one they'd seen in the underground Reptilian base, a blue aura ebbed and flowed around it.

An alien spaceship right across the fence beyond the edge of Zachary's woods!

"Reptilian?" he asked.

"Probably, although I suppose it could belong to the Greys," Nina replied. "Either way, it's not a welcome sight."

"No, it sure as hell isn't. We need to get back to the house," Bruce said.

"Back? No, we should…" Nina started before stopping herself, her gaze fixed on the spaceship.

"No, we shouldn't." Bruce hissed.

Nina gripped his hand tightly, her fingers trembling. He could feel the tension radiating off her, a mirror reflection of his own.

"Nina, we need to get out of here," Bruce whispered urgently. "We need to tell the others."

"You're right."

Before they could make their move, an ominous sound caught their attention. A low hum, a vibration that seemed to resonate through the air and seep into their marrow. It was unlike anything Bruce had ever heard before—ethereal yet terrifyingly alien.

A second, smaller spacecraft landed. Bruce could barely believe his eyes. Suddenly, a small figure, with smooth, grey skin and a hairless head, emerged from the spacecraft. Its eyes were large and black. As the strange being slipped through a glowing ring at the entrance, it transformed itself into a tall human with short black hair. A halo of light spilling from the opening of the spaceship further revealed thin-rimmed glasses on an unsmiling face.

Bruce's heart dropped. "Dr. Charles Barry," he uttered, feeling like he'd been punched in the gut. "Alive and well."

"And in our backyard," Nina said.

ᒷᔑᔑ 𝖈🜂ᑐ⼃ᑎᗇ Ⅱ

The heavy wooden door of the farmhouse creaked open. Bruce and Nina stepped inside, their faces etched with concern. Flickering logs in the fireplace filled the room with welcome warmth and light. They shrugged off their coats.

"Where is everyone?" Bruce asked.

"Somebody's awake," Nina whispered, her voice echoing in the quiet space as she wiped her muddy boots on the mat inside the door. "I smell coffee."

"You're right." Bruce's nostrils flared greedily as he took in the familiar aroma.

As they made their way further into the farmhouse, they heard the soft sounds of movement, shuffling feet, tinkling glasses, coming from the kitchen. At the sound of their voices, Zachary and Julia emerged from the kitchen entrance, wearing matching expressions of surprise and relief.

"Where have you two been?" asked Julia. She glanced between them and noticed the bags under their eyes and the dirt, leaves and debris on their clothes. Julia herself had borrowed a pair of olive-green sweats from Nina. "We've been worried sick."

Bruce recounted their encounter in the woods. "Nina and I noticed a light out there, to the west, across the fence. We went to check it out."

"And?" Zachary asked. He wore a heavy blue velour robe over black pajamas. A pair of suede slippers covered his feet.

"We found a spacecraft," Bruce said, his words coming out in clipped sentences as if they were reluctant to leave his lips. "Like the one we saw earlier. Like the one I saw on the monitor too."

"And we saw Dr. Barry," Nina added. "He emerged from the spaceship."

Zachary and Julia gasped.

"Dr. Barry?" Zachary said. Lines of fatigue battled with age lines across his tired face. "Are you sure it was him?"

"Positive," Nina replied.

"Did he see you?" wondered Zachary.

"No, I don't think so," answered Bruce.

"But why is he here?" Julia asked, her brow furrowed in thought.

"I don't know but whatever that sadistic Grey's up to, it can't be good. We need to find out what his plan is and we need to do it soon," Bruce said.

They settled around the kitchen table with coffee and toast, although nobody had much of an appetite. Crumbs lay scattered on the tablecloth amidst crumpled napkins and half-empty cups of coffee. The group sat slumped in their chairs, saying little.

"Grandpa, what is it?" Nina asked suddenly. "What's wrong?"

Zachary had barely said a word as the others talked, hypothesizing about this new development, the disappearance and apparent capture of Alex Simmons, and what they'd seen inside the downtown Reptilian command center.

"Nothing, Nina. It's just…"

"Just what?"

"I knew about the Reptilian presence nearby. The old MacGregor Mine is over there, in those hills, near the creek. In its time, it was quite an extensive operation. All played out now. Has been for ages. The mine intercepts an ancient system of caverns."

"You knew and you didn't say anything?" Nina's eyes grew wide.

"I didn't want you to worry needlessly."

Nina sighed and hugged her grandfather.

"So tell us about it now," Bruce urged.

"When I was younger, about your age, Bruce," he began, his voice soft and reflective, "I encountered the Reptilians for the first time. It was in woods very much like those," he pointed in the vague direction of the farmhouse's window. "A spacecraft landed right there and out they came, creatures the likes of which I'd never seen and had barely imagined. The beings that emerged were intimidating and seemed to be searching for something."

"Grandpa, you should have told me," said Nina.

Zachary's next words were barely above a whisper, filled with a heavy regret that hung in the silent room. "I tried to communicate with them. They took me captive instead. They brought me to their ship and kept me for days. Weeks maybe, I never could figure out exactly how long I'd been…gone."

"What happened, Zachary?" Bruce asked.

"I don't know. I've tried and tried to remember." Zachary clutched his head. "But I just can't… Perhaps I am not meant to." He pulled himself to his feet and tottered to the kitchen sink with his empty cup. "You know, when I was working at the university, I had a colleague, Mark Stafford. We both specialized in extraterrestrial studies. But as you can imagine, we held vastly different viewpoints— me acknowledging their existence and him fervently denying it.

"Stafford was the poster boy for conventional science," continued Zachary, his voice barely above a whisper. "He was charismatic, assertive, and highly influential among our peers, as well as within the local government."

"I don't understand. You've never mentioned him before, Grandpa."

"He is not someone I like to remember." Zachary cleared his throat. "Stafford began to take interest in politics himself. Before long, he'd left academia for the political life. He's Chief of Staff for the Mayor of St. Louis now. And soon after his entering politics, I found myself being forced to retire, ridiculed and belittled by my peers. Called a pseudoscientist, a fool!" Zachary frowned. "My work was discredited, ensuring no one would believe me when I tried to warn them about the invasion by the Reptilians."

"Stafford's doing?" Bruce asked.

"Yes, he wanted me out. Probably because I was too close to the truth and stood in his way. A truth he wanted the world to deny. That's when I came here." The old man's face was a map of past battles and present woes, etched with lines of age and stress. "And I have been keeping an eye on that stronghold for years now," Zachary started, his voice barely above a whisper. "I knew about this property from my research and suspected the Reptilians had an installation out here in that cavern.

"This farm has proven to be the perfect location to monitor their activities discreetly. Stafford has visited many times."

"Maybe Stafford was behind your abduction," suggested Julia.

"Quite possibly," Zachary agreed.

"Stafford," grunted Bruce. He'd met the "man" once at a public function and had thought there was something odd about the man. Now he knew what that something was—he wasn't a man at all. He/it was a Reptilian!

"He also implemented the arrangement by which corpses were transferred from the morgue to Dr. Barry for use in his experiments. And," Zachary said, "I've heard stories of harvesting souls, and more."

"Harvesting souls?" Bruce clenched his fists. "How many of them are there? How deep does their infiltration go? How many people are working for them? How many people are under their control?"

"Impossible to say," Zachary admitted, his expression grim. "But I'm certain Mr. Stafford's influence extends far beyond St. Louis. He's merely the tip of a very large, very dangerous iceberg."

"Then we need to stop him, stop them," Bruce said.

Zachary looked at him with a mix of admiration and sadness. "I know, my boy. But we must tread carefully. The Reptilians are quite cunning and, as I've said, they have very powerful human allies."

"I'll scout out the alien encampment, see what I can uncover," Bruce said suddenly climbing to his feet.

"*We* will scout out the alien camp," Nina corrected.

"We?"

"You don't think I'm going to let you have all the fun, do you?"

"Are you sure that's wise?" Zachary asked. "It's dangerous, alone or together. We saw what happened the last time."

Bruce locked eyes with his new friend. "We have no other choice, Zachary. If we're to stand any chance against them, we need to know what size force they have and what they're planning next."

Nina rose from her seat. "Don't worry, we'll be careful, Grandpa, and we'll stick together."

"Very well," Zachary acquiesced, his hands trembling ever so slightly. "Julia and I will remain here, continue our research. Come, all of you. I've a map in the study. I'll show you the lay of the land."

After Zachary's briefing, Bruce excused himself.

"Where are you going?" Nina asked, following him through the farmhouse.

"To bury Jack."

"You want some help? Shall I come?"

Bruce steeled his jaw. "No, I need to do this alone."

Nina leaned close and kissed Bruce on the cheek. "I understand." She opened the door for him and he stepped outside.

Bruce opened the back of the van and said a silent prayer for his brother. After making preparations, he held his breath, his eyes scanning the nearby woods across the way, their depths now foreboding and full of menace. He looked down at the makeshift stretcher at his feet, Jack's lifeless body covered by a shroud. With a grim resolve, he lifted the stretcher and headed towards the opposite side of the woods. Zachary had told him there was an old cemetery belonging to the original homesteaders dating back to the late 1800s.

Hours later, Bruce was deep in the woods, his hands coated with dirt, and sweat trickling down his forehead. He dug a simple grave, a resting place for Jack beneath the sheltering branches of an ancient oak tree. He gently placed Jack's body into the grave, then filled it again with earth, trying to ignore the unsettling silence of the surrounding forest.

With his task done, Bruce knelt by the gravesite for what felt like an eternity. He whispered words into the wind. The wind carried his words away, silent promises and regrets. His brother would like it here. One day, when the time was right, he'd bring Carla here. She'd like that. Maybe the children too—when they were old enough to understand what had happened.

Bruce stood and brushed himself off. It was time to get back to the others.

It was now late afternoon. Bruce and Nina prepared, packing water, weapons, and binoculars. Julia kissed them both at the door and handed them a pair of walkie-talkies. "Keep them with you and on at all times. Call at the first sign of trouble." They promised they would.

Leaving the safety of the farmhouse, they skirted the woods, hoping it would provide some cover from prying alien eyes.

"Keep low and stay quiet," Bruce murmured, his breaths shallow and measured as they approached the alien site. "Don't get too close. Remember, we're here to observe, not engage."

Nina nodded, her auburn hair sticking to her sweat-dampened forehead. She moved with a feline grace, her every step calculated and precise as a chess move.

As they neared the old MacGregor Mine, they caught the dissonant symphony of machinery. Peering through the foliage, they beheld a sight both fascinating and frightening. Reptilians in their true form, surrounded by an array of bizarre instruments and devices. An abandoned narrow-track rail line disappeared into the opening of the mine shaft. It would have been used in its day to carry down mine workers, and haul up their hard-earned ore.

There was no sign of the spaceship they'd seen earlier, nor of Dr. Barry. Julia had shown them a screenshot of Mark Stafford so they'd know him if they saw him. They didn't.

"Look at them," Nina whispered as they huddled in a clump of bushes on a small rise looking down on the half-hidden entrance to the cavern. "They're hardly bothering to hide anymore."

"Who is there to see them?" Bruce never imagined he would be facing extraterrestrial enemies, and the reality was more chilling than any nightmare he could have conjured. He felt Nina's heart beat as she pressed up against his side.

As they continued to watch, Bruce found himself grappling with conflicting emotions—the desire to protect those he loved and the burning need to destroy his enemy. Could he succeed at both?

Only time would tell…and the clock was ticking.

ᴴᴱ꒐꒫Tᴵᴬᴷᴺ 12

A mask of darkness enveloped the narrow cavern entrance, swallowing Bruce and Nina as they crept inside. Damp air clung to their skin, sending shivers down their spines. Their footsteps echoed off the frigid rocky walls and they feared being discovered.

"Stay close, Nina," Bruce whispered. He felt responsible for her safety, compelled by a sense of duty—and something more he couldn't quite define.

"Right behind you," Nina replied, as she scanned their surroundings.

Glowing bioluminescent fungi cast a low light across the cavern walls, illuminating intricate alien structures that seemed to defy the very laws of physics. Bruce marveled at the advanced craftsmanship, his architect's mind reeling with questions about the materials and techniques used by these extraterrestrial beings.

"Look at this," Nina whispered. Her hand hovered an inch above a large and smooth metallic object. Its surface appeared to respond, rippling like water, in response to her presence. "This is it. It must be!"

"What?"

"Element 115, moscovium! I can't believe we're actually seeing some…in a stable form."

"Yeah," replied Bruce, unable to take his eyes off the stuff. He reached out his hand, his curiosity outweighing his caution.

"Careful!" warned Nina, swatting his hand away. "It could be highly radioactive…or worse."

"Sorry. This technology is far beyond anything I've ever seen." As an architect, he imagined the incredible uses to which such a material could be put.

"It's too bad the Reptilians seem determined to subjugate or destroy us. Imagine what we could learn from them," Nina mused.

"Yeah, both the good and the bad," whispered Bruce. "Right now, I'm more concerned about staying alive long enough to share what we find with the others," Bruce reminded her, his senses on high alert.

As they ventured further into the alien camp, the shadows seemed to be watching them, shifting and twisting with every step they took. Suddenly, Bruce spotted a group of Reptilian guards patrolling the area.

"Hide!" he whispered urgently, grabbing Nina's arm and pulling her behind a stack of metal lockers. They pressed their backs against the cold metal, praying they wouldn't be discovered.

"Think they're looking for us?" Nina asked.

"Could be," Bruce replied. "Or maybe they're just doing their rounds. Either way, we can't move until they pass."

They held their collective breath, watching as the Reptilian guards marched past within a foot of their hiding place. The Reptilians paused and seemed to taste the air with their tongues. Almost as if they could smell or taste a human presence nearby. Then they moved on.

"Okay," he murmured once the guards were out of sight, "let's keep moving."

The cavern sloped downward. Strange structures fascinated them as they wound their way deeper.

"Look at this," Nina whispered. She gestured towards a panel hidden in the wall, its surface covered in alien symbols. "I wonder what it controls."

Bruce approached the panel cautiously, trying and failing to decipher the intricate design. He traced a light finger over the strange symbols. But it was too alien and absolutely hopeless.

"Can you make anything out?" Nina asked, her eyes wide with curiosity.

"Not a damn thing," Bruce replied, hesitating for a moment before pressing one of the symbols. To his surprise, a holographic map sprang to life before them, displaying the layout of the cavern. "Maybe it's like a mall directory. All that's missing is the *You Are Here* flag."

"Amazing," Nina marveled, examining the map closely.

As Bruce continued to study the panel, Nina investigated the artifacts scattered throughout the area. Her fingers danced over alien items whose uses were unknown to her. She pocketed several that were small enough to slip into her pockets.

"Find anything interesting?" Bruce asked, glancing over at her.

"Perhaps," Nina answered. "But it will take time to analyze these items properly. As I've said, people often discuss ancient alien civilizations in the context of theories that suggest extraterrestrial beings visited Earth in the distant past and influenced human history. Proponents argue that certain ancient structures, artifacts, and texts, such as the pyramids of Egypt, the Nazca lines in Peru, and ancient religious manuscripts, show evidence of advanced technology or knowledge that ancient humans could not have possessed. Pieces to a giant puzzle. And now, we have proof."

"If you told me any of that before, I would have just smiled and thought sure, but now… It looks like anything is possible," Bruce said. He pulled his eyes away from the tilting holographic image. "Right now, we'd better keep moving."

The corridor narrowed and the ceiling fell until they were forced to bend forward to keep from banging their heads on the hard rock surrounding them.

Bruce whispered to Nina, "I hear something." A faint hum coming from somewhere ahead of them.

Nina nodded, her fingers gripping a small device she had found among the alien artifacts. It pulsed with a faint blue glow, its purpose completely unknown but oddly it provided her some semblance of comfort.

"Finally," Bruce said suddenly, stopping in front of a nondescript door. "What have we got here?" He reached out and pushed it open, revealing a room bathed in a cold, sterile light. Monitors lined the walls, displaying surveillance footage from various locations around St. Louis and other major US cities.

"They're watching us," Nina breathed, as she took in the scope of the Reptilians' surveillance network.

"Seems like they're keeping tabs on us, alright," Bruce observed. That was an uncomfortable thought. But it did explain a lot, like how they knew about Jack and what he had found and had been up to before they'd murdered him.

A dizzying array of technology filled the room, all of it beyond their understanding. Alien script danced across many of the monitors while others displayed imagery so clear it was uncanny. They hovered over one that showcased a rambling farmhouse and barn.

"That's..." Bruce muttered, squinting at the screen. He swallowed hard, feeling an icy finger trace down his spine.

"Grandpa's house," finished Nina.

Shaking himself from the unsettling thought, Bruce scanned the room. There were chairs, empty and scattered, as if left in haste or during some commotion. Several monitors flickered with static while others displayed clear images of city streets and residential areas. A few displayed what appeared to be captured human faces, their features twisted in fear and confusion.

Nina moved towards one of the desks, her fingers hovering above an array of alien symbols etched into the surface.

"Better not touch anything," Bruce warned, his gaze darting from screen to screen. The potential for triggering an alarm or worse was too great.

Abruptly, an alien symbol popped up on one of the other screens. Nina rushed towards it, taking in the flood of information, trying and failing to decode the stream of symbols.

"Any idea what this means?" Bruce asked her.

"None. Maybe Julia can tell us." Nina grabbed her walkie-talkie.

"Are you sure you should chance it? They could be monitoring the airwaves."

Nina reclipped her walkie-talkie back to her belt. "Right."

A bass hum rose in the room. The lights dimmed for a moment before returning to their original luminosity. The monitors flickered, the surveillance images blurring and then sharpening again. Bruce shot a worried glance at Nina, who was frozen in place, her eyes locked on the monitor. To their shock, the central monitor now displayed their faces, mirroring their every move and emotion.

They'd been detected!

"Footsteps," Bruce whispered, his gaze darting to the doorway.

The echo of heavy boots hitting metal reverberated through the room, each thud like a drumroll announcing the impending doom. They scrambled for a hiding place.

A Reptilian guard, humanoid in appearance but with cold, Reptilian eyes and a cruel twist to his mouth, sauntered into the room. His gaze immediately swept over the monitors, his fingers playing over the alien console as he inspected it.

Bruce and Nina held their breaths from behind one of the larger screens. Every muscle in their bodies tensed as they watched the Reptilian's reflection in the monitor's surface.

"This is too close for comfort," Bruce mouthed to Nina, who nodded in agreement. Her fingers tightened around the strange device she had found earlier.

The Reptilian continued to prowl around the room, his eyes narrowed as he scrutinized each monitor. He paused when he came to the one displaying their images. A low growl rumbled from his throat as his gaze fixed on the screen, his Reptilian eyes glinting dangerously.

All of a sudden, the guard's head snapped up. His nostrils flared as if sniffing the air. Nina and Bruce exchanged a look of terror before quickly retreating further into the shadows. Bruce pressed his hand against Nina's mouth to suppress any sound. The room filled with a tense silence, save for the soft hum of alien machines and the distant echo of footsteps outside. The Reptilian began to pace, his unnatural movements patterned, as if he was conducting a search grid. His boots tapped against the metal floor—an ominous rhythm that reverberated in Bruce's chest. He squeezed Nina's shoulder reassuringly, his gaze never leaving the guard.

The Reptilian turned and approached their hiding spot. His cold Reptilian eyes scanned the area, seeming to look through the screen and into their hiding place. The guard's hand rested on a lethal-looking weapon. Bruce felt a bead of sweat trickle down his temple and sting his eye.

For what felt like an eternity, they remained frozen. The alien took a step closer to their hiding place, and Bruce could hear Nina's quickened breaths as the Reptilian's gaze traveled close to their location.

Unexpectedly, the alien device in Nina's hands whirred to life—painfully luminous waves pulsating outwards from it. She cried out in surprise and hurled it at the Reptilian. Blinding light filled the room. The Reptilian guard cried out, shielding his eyes against the unexpected onslaught of brightness.

Seizing the moment, Bruce surged forward from behind the screen. He collided forcefully with the Reptilian. The impact knocked both of them to the ground, but Bruce was quicker to recover. He grappled with the disoriented guard, landing a few hasty punches before wrestling the alien's weapon from its grip. It was an odd, angular device, but Bruce figured out the trigger mechanism quickly enough. He fired it at the Reptilian just as it started to recover.

A brilliant beam of searing energy shot forth, hitting the guard square in the chest. The Reptilian collapsed to the ground, motionless and its body returned to its original Reptilian form.

Bruce turned back to Nina, who was picking herself up from where she'd thrown herself to avoid the blinding light. She looked shaken but unharmed. Her eyes widened when she saw the downed

Reptilian.

"Bruce," she breathed, staring at him with a mixture of relief, awe, and concern. "I didn't know you had it in you."

"Neither did I," he admitted, pushing a shaky hand through his hair. "Come on, we need to get out of here before more of them come to see what's going on." He raced off in the direction he hoped was the exit. And there it was, just ahead! "We're going to make it," he called back to Nina, his voice echoing through the tunnel.

But as they neared the tunnel's exit, a wall of yellow energy flickered into existence, blocking their way. Bruce skidded to a halt, inches from the radiant barrier. Touching it could result in instant death. He hastily grabbed his water bottle from his pack and lobbed it at the wall of energy. The bottle burst, the water evaporated and the plastic melted away.

"Nina!" He reached out just in time to pull her back before she crashed into him and the deadly wall of energy ahead. Her eyes widened with fear.

Twisting around, he saw a group of Reptilian guards closing in on them.

"Trapped," he muttered under his breath, feeling a cold sense of despair creep up his spine.

Nina looked around frantically for some kind of escape route, but there were none. "Bruce..." she began, but he cut her off.

"We're not done yet," he said grimly, his fingers tightening on the alien weapon still in his hand. He turned to face their pursuers, tense but ready. "Stay behind me."

Nina pressed herself against the cave's wall, and watched as Bruce prepared to confront the Reptilians. "Be ready to run," he hollered over his shoulder, before charging at the Reptilian guards. He fired the alien weapon as he ran, a streak of bright energy lighting up the tunnel as it collided with the nearest Reptilian.

Bruce moved swiftly, using his surprise attack to his advantage.

Another Reptilian fell under the onslaught of energy beams from his weapon. The remaining Reptilians recoiled, momentarily disoriented and at a loss what to do.

Taking advantage of their momentary confusion, Nina dashed towards a narrow crevice in the stone that she had noticed earlier. Behind her, Bruce continued firing at their pursuers.

"I've found something!" she called out to Bruce. "Come on!" She waved and disappeared into the slim fissure just as a wave of energy burst from one of the Reptilian's weapons hit Bruce squarely in the right shoulder. He grunted as pain exploded through his body, his vision swimming.

"Bruce!" Nina's scream echoed through the cavern.

With Nina's anguished cry ringing in his ears, Bruce fired a last blind shot in the direction of the enemy and staggered backward towards the crevice.

"Nina?" His voice was rough, strained with pain.

"I'm here, Bruce," Nina replied, her hand reaching out from within the shadowy crevice to grip his. She pulled him forward into the narrow opening in the rock just as another blast of energy struck the spot where he'd been standing mere moments before.

The fissure was dark and cold. Smaller than they'd hoped, but it would keep them hidden, at least for now. They heard the angry shouts of Reptilians echoing through the cavern outside.

"Nina..." His voice trailed off as he slumped onto the hard ground, his fingers loosening their grip on his weapon. His entire right arm tingled, the pain more intense than anything he'd ever felt in his life.

Nina cradled Bruce in her arms, her fingers trembling as she felt for a pulse. She found one—weak but steady, a small spark of hope amidst their desperate circumstances. "You're going to be okay," she said shakily, more to herself than to him. "We're going to get out of this."

In the cavern beyond their cramped refuge, the Reptilians prowled menacingly. Every so often they fired a blast of energy at the crevice, each one making Nina's heart leap into her throat.

"Arm's getting better," he said, giving it a shake. "At least, I can move it."

"Thank god." She hugged him fiercely.

"The question is," Bruce said, looking around, "where are we?" He scooped up the Reptilian's weapon which he'd commandeered earlier knowing it could come in handy.

"I have no idea. Just a tiny natural passage intersecting with one of the mine shafts. At least they don't seem to be following us." She helped Bruce to his feet. "Can you move?"

"Yeah." His knees wobbled and he took a tentative step. "Yeah, let's go." They held hands and moved forward in the darkness.

Five minutes later, Nina slammed to a halt. "Look," she said, as she pointed to a faint outline of a door hidden within the cavern wall. It was almost invisible, blending nearly seamlessly with the rock, but there it stood. She ran her fingers along its edges and the door slid open.

"Let's see what's behind door number one," Bruce said, trying to inject some levity into the tense situation. Entering the chamber, their eyes widened in shock at the sight that greeted them. Rows upon rows of cryogenic coffins filled the room, each containing a human corpse—men, women, and children alike. The air within the chamber felt colder, heavier, and the very atmosphere was suffused with the stench of the innocent lives lost to Dr. Barry's sinister experiments.

"God, it's... horrific," Nina choked out, tears welling up in her eyes as she took in the gruesome scene.

"Look," Bruce said softly, his voice quivering with rage as he pointed to the far side of the chamber, where Dr. Barry and Mr. Stafford stood, their faces betraying no emotion as they surveyed their macabre handiwork.

Dr. Barry's cold, unfeeling eyes locked onto Bruce's gaze, sending a shiver down his spine.

"Ah, Ms. Lind and Mr. Finger," Dr. Barry said, smirking. "I see you've decided to join your friend."

"Friend?" Bruce seethed, his anger barely contained.

"Agent Simmons, of course. Such a stubborn man. I look forward to exploring what makes him tick. I can conduct my research and the Reptilians get another valuable soul. As I've explained, the Reptilians can't wait to use Earth as a large farm of souls. And to make use of its resources." As he talked, he walked over to a vertical glass-fronted coffin. Agent Simmons stared out at them.

"Is he...?" began Nina.

"Dead?" Dr. Barry's eyes danced with delight. "No, no. Much more useful alive. When I am done with him, the Reptilians can do as they wish. I'm arranging to have him transported up to my shipboard lab." He turned to Mr. Stafford. The Reptilian leader was speaking rapidly into a communication device strapped to his wrist. "A bit too much...commotion going on here on Earth at the moment for my taste. Quite distracting."

Bruce tapped Nina on the shoulder. "I think we should continue this conversation another time..." He pointed at Stafford who was moving quickly away.

Dr. Barry smiled. "I'm afraid your time grows short." He looked over his shoulder. "I believe you may want to leave before Stafford gets back with his reinforcements. He's neither a patient nor a pacific creature. Not like myself."

"You're warning us?" Bruce said. "Why?"

"Why? Because, as I said to you before, I'm a scientist. I do not share the Reptilians' thirst for dominating worlds. I thirst only for knowledge." Dr. Barry paused before continuing. "Besides, I'm afraid my...dance card is full for now. I'm sure we'll be seeing one another again." The Grey rubbed his hands together. "Yes, I'm certain we shall.

I look forward to getting my hands on the two of you."

A loud buzz caused all three of them to turn and gape at a large opening on the far side of the chamber. Reptilians were spilling out.

"That way!" Dr. Barry urged, pointing towards a narrow and steep metal stairs anchored to the stone.

"How do we know we can trust you?" demanded Bruce.

"What choice do you have, human?" Dr. Barry replied.

"Come on, Bruce," Nina urged. "He's right, what choice do we have?"

"I suppose…"

Nina turned to Dr. Barry. "You won't get away with what you're doing!"

"Come on," Bruce growled urgently to Nina, grabbing her hand and pulling towards the staircase. "We need to get out of here, now."

"Fine," Nina said, her jaw set with determination as she followed him.

They sped as quickly as they could up the metal steps which carried them several stories upward. All the while, Bruce couldn't shake the images of those cryogenic coffins from his mind.

The stairs ended at a small bare landing of packed earth. A flickering red sign, the shape of an unfamiliar alien symbol, greeted them. Instinctively, Bruce veered towards it, pulling Nina along with him. At the end of the pathway, a rusty-looking door creaked open to reveal yet another narrow flight of stairs leading further upward.

"Up!" he commanded, and they pounded up the steps, the echoes of their pursuers growing louder behind them. They ascended what seemed like a dozen floors before finally reaching the top landing. A circular metal hatch loomed above them.

Bruce pushed against it, his shoulders straining with effort. It moved stubbornly at first, but then suddenly gave way to the outsider world. Fresh air rushed in as they scrambled out of the hatch. They landed in a dense thicket high atop a hill from which he caught sight of the farmhouse in the distance. From their vantage point, they watched Reptilians swarming out of hidden entrances all over the hill blanketing the cavern.

They were trapped. All they could do was hide…and wait.

CHAPTER 13

Bruce and Nina stumbled into the farmhouse around midnight. The pair were exhausted from their reconnaissance of the cavern and the hours they'd spent afterward stuck hiding atop that hill while waiting for all the commotion to die down.

Once confident it was safe to descend, they followed a circuitous route down, struggling over the uneven ground in the darkness. They were cold and their clothes were damp with sweat. Dirt clung to them.

"Is that you?" Julia's voice cut through the silence, startling them both.

That was when Bruce noticed her sitting silently in a tall wingback chair near a smoldering fire. Her hands clutched the chair's upholstered arms. The flickering flames cast shadows across the walls and the scent of burning pine filled the air. The warm glow illuminated Julia's worried face, her eyes filled with concern. He felt a pang of guilt. They'd been gone for hours with no word. "Sorry, we wanted to communicate but were afraid using the radios would give our position away."

"I understand. I'm just glad you're both alright."

"Everything okay, here? Where's Grandpa?" Nina asked, struggling out of her shoes, and wriggling her stockinged feet in front of the fire.

Bruce removed his shoes and stretched before collapsing to the floor. His shoulder stung a bit from when he'd been shot earlier. Still, he considered himself lucky. If that had been a bullet…well, he didn't care to dwell on that. But it made him realize even more strongly just how dangerous a game they were playing.

Scratch that, this was no game.

"Sleeping," Julia replied.

"Good for him," Nina answered, her voice rough from exhaustion. She collapsed into a chair next to Julia, rubbing her temples. "We found something, Julia."

Julia stared at them expectantly, wringing her hands. Bruce knew she must be desperate to hear what they'd discovered. With a heavy sigh, he took a seat opposite them and began to explain. "We managed to infiltrate the facility."

"And we found Alex," added Nina.

Julia stiffened. "Is he alright? Where is he?"

Bruce shrugged and scrubbed his hands over his face. "Still back there, I'm afraid. He's in some kind of stasis along with a bunch of other humans. Dr. Barry says he's going to send him up to his ship in the morning."

"Dr. Barry's here?" Julia rose and paced in front of the fire. Her feet seemed barely to touch the floor. "You say Dr. Barry said he intends to take the humans up to his ship? You're sure that's what he said?"

"Yes, I'm sure." Nina waved at Bruce. "We both heard him. What's up, Julia? What's the matter?"

"Yeah," Bruce pulled himself to his knees. "What aren't you telling us?"

"Well…" Julia came to a stop in front of the fireplace. She grabbed the iron poker from the rack and jabbed it around, sending sparks and ash into the air. She stared into the flames as if they held the answer to their predicament, her eyes flickering with an emotion that seemed far older than her years. The silence hung heavy in the room, almost tangible, as Bruce and Nina braced themselves for what she was about to reveal.

"Alright," Julia finally said, her voice firm as she turned to face them. "We don't have much time and I don't have any other choice."

"Julia," began Nina. "Please, whatever it is, just spill it. You're scaring me."

Julia clutched her hands. "There's something I need to tell you both." She locked her eyes on them. "And I need you to listen."

"Of course," Nina and Bruce agreed.

"I am not human," Julia began. "I am one of the Annunaki."

"You-You're from Nibiru?" Nina asked, incredulous. "Seriously, Julia, this is no time to joke!"

"I do not joke," Julia said. "As you surmised, we have been visiting Earth for millennia, guiding humanity's development in subtle ways. And, a very long time ago, in maybe not so subtle ways."

"You're really an Annunaki?" Bruce's mouth dried up. Poor Jack. If he was alive, he'd be elated to meet her.

"Yes."

Bruce and Nina exchanged glances, disbelief evident in their eyes.

Julia continued, her words becoming more urgent as the truth tumbled from her lips. "I didn't want to deceive you," she explained. "But my duty to the Annunaki demanded it. We are never to reveal ourselves to you. However," she began pacing once more, "the stakes are higher than you can possibly imagine."

"Higher?" Bruce said. "We're facing an alien invasion! How much higher can it get?"

"Much higher, and much sooner," Julia replied, unwaveringly. "The Reptilians will arrive tomorrow via a portal they've created—"

"The Arch?" interjected Bruce.

"Yes, the Gateway Arch. As you have learned, the Reptilians wish to claim Earth for its resources and its people. This is why they allow you humans to even still exist here. You are a resource to be plundered, while you are also something of an inconvenience to their plans."

"Wait," Nina interrupted. "You said tomorrow? Then that means we're too late…we've lost before it's even begun."

Bruce reached out and clasped Nina's hand in his.

"Enslavement is only the beginning," Julia confirmed grimly. "The Reptilians are a ruthless race, hell-bent on conquest and domination. They won't stop until they've drained this world dry."

As her words echoed around the room, the fire seemed to grow more restless, its flames reaching hungrily toward the heavens as if seeking escape from a dire future.

"Julia," Bruce asked, "how do we stop them?"

"Maybe more to the point, can we stop them?" asked Nina.

"We must find a way. Earth's fate hangs in the balance." Julia started for the front door. "I must go," she announced abruptly.

"What? Why?" demanded Bruce, jumping to his feet.

"I have to communicate with my ship. I need to update them on what's happening here on the ground."

"Wait!" Nina reached out toward her friend. "Julia, we still don't know how to stop them. We need your help."

Julia hesitated in the doorway, her eyes filled with concern. "I know," she said softly, "but I have a duty to my own people as well. I promise, I'll return as soon as I can."

With that, she disappeared into the night, leaving Bruce and Nina alone in the room.

Bruce stared at the now empty doorway, struggling to comprehend what he'd heard and the enormity of what they faced. Alien invasion? Reptilian conquerors? Sure, they'd talked about it but now it was all too real. Tomorrow! It was all too much.

"Bruce, what are we going to do?"

"We fight," he replied, though he wasn't sure how they could possibly stand against such a formidable, and alien, enemy.

"Fight?" Nina echoed, her eyebrows furrowing. "We're just two humans, Bruce, three counting Grandpa. How can we hope to make a difference? And, even if there was time, we'll never get anyone else to believe us, let alone help us."

"We could take them to the cavern, let them see for themselves."

"Like I said, there isn't time. Even if there was, who could we get to believe us enough to even follow us that far? And," her eyes locked on Bruce's, "how could we be sure they weren't Reptilians themselves or humans in league with them?"

"Shit. You're right." It all seemed so futile, so hopeless. Had all of this and Jack's death been for nothing? He pulled back the curtains and stared outside. Julia had disappeared. Where had she gone? "Look, Julia said it herself, the Annunaki have been guiding our development for millennia," Bruce reasoned, trying to reassure himself as much as her. "Maybe they've given us the tools we need to fight back. We just have to figure out what those are."

"Or maybe," Nina countered, her voice tinged with anger, "they've been manipulating us for their own purposes as well, and now we're caught in the middle of some cosmic battle between alien races!"

"Maybe," he conceded. "Listen, whatever happens," he told her, reaching across to take her hand, "we'll face it together. We won't let the Reptilians win—not without a fight. We'll see what Julia has to say when she gets back." He looked at his watch. "I hope she doesn't take long."

"We don't have long," Nina quipped.

"Right. I know she's your friend but do you think we can we really trust her?" Bruce asked.

"Julia did save our lives, Bruce," Nina replied. "And remember, she's been risking her own life to help us. The Annunaki are believed by many to be gods. They have shaped our world, our religions, the Bible, the Koran. In Arabic, Anna means grandmother, and naki means grandfather. And Annunaki translates as 'ancestors.' Did you know the Annunaki are referred to as Anak in the Bible? In Numbers 13:28 in the Scripture, I came across descendants of Anak who were described there as giants.

"Also, the term 'watcher' appears only in the Book of Daniel in the Bible, but is used extensively in the Book of Enoch, a non-canonical book found among the Dead Sea Scrolls, and quoted by both Peter and Jude. Potentially, the Annunaki are fallen angels or watchers. Developing us and keeping an eye on us. The Book of Enoch describes fallen angels that were once good having supposedly fallen for a human woman. However, in the Sumerian cuneiform tablets, they're all gods or beings perceived as superior to humans. All these ancient texts and religious writings are eerily similar. Why would she lie about something like this? Tell me, why? Would a god lie?"

"Maybe if it was convenient or suited their purposes," he snapped. "We know the Reptilians are evil, but now we're supposed to believe there's another alien race, the Annunaki, that's not only benevolent but has also been helping humanity for centuries? It sounds too good to be true. And you know the saying, 'if it sounds too good to be true, it probably isn't true.' What if Julia is lying? She lied to you about who and what she really is, remember?"

Nina crossed her arms over her chest, her eyes flashing angrily. "So what do you suggest we do then? Do we just sit back and wait for the Reptilians to arrive and destroy everything, including us?"

"Of course not!" Bruce shouted. "But we can't afford to just sit around waiting for Julia and then blindly follow her lead either, can we? We need a plan of our own, something concrete to protect ourselves and Earth."

"Like what?" she challenged, stepping closer to him. "You don't have all the answers, Bruce. None of us do."

"Exactly," he snapped. "That's why we can't simply rely on the word of an alien we barely know. There has to be something else, some other way to fight back."

"Then tell me what that is, dammit!" Nina shouted. "You tell me how we're supposed to save Earth when we're up against creatures far more advanced than us!" She threw her arms in the air.

Bruce clenched his fists. "I don't know."

"Then stop doubting Julia!" Nina yelled. "She's our best chance at survival, whether you like it or not!" She poked him in the chest. "You don't know shit about the Annunaki, and how they made us what we are today!"

"Maybe she is our best chance," Bruce conceded, his jaw set. "But

I still say we can't afford to blindly trust everything she says. We have to be prepared for any possibility—even the ones we don't want to consider."

Nina's shoulders shook. He knew they couldn't continue like this. Every moment spent arguing was a moment wasted.

"Listen, Nina," Bruce said, "I... I'm sorry, okay? I know we can't afford to be at odds right now. We're on the same side."

Nina exhaled slowly, her tense posture softening. "You're right, Bruce." She turned back to face him, her eyes red. "Let's not fight. If anything, it only makes us weaker."

"Agreed," Bruce replied, nodding solemnly. "And I suppose I should trust Julia—as hard as that is for me. I'll try to keep an open mind about her and the intentions of the Annunaki."

"Thank you," Nina whispered. "I know it's difficult but you don't know her like I do. I believe in my heart that she truly does want to help us."

Bruce pulled Nina in his arms and she collapsed against his chest. They shared a searing kiss. The room seemed to hold its breath as their kiss deepened, their lips moving hungrily, exploring and savoring each other amid the uncertainty that shrouded their future.

"God, Nina," Bruce said, his voice ragged with emotion. "I never thought I'd feel like this..."

"Me neither," she admitted.

"Are you scared?" he asked, his thumb gently brushing away a tear that had escaped down her cheek.

"Terrified," she confessed.

"Me, too." As they pulled apart, their breaths mingled. "So we wait for Julia to come back." He prayed it would be soon.

"We wait for Julia."

Outside, the wind howled mournfully through the trees.

CHAPTER 14

The door to the farmhouse flew open, slamming into the wall and startling Bruce and Nina as they huddled on the sofa trying and failing to come up with a plan that stood any chance at all of success. Bruce looked up.

Julia stood in the doorway, her face drawn. "Good," she gasped, catching her breath as if she'd just run a full marathon. "You're both awake."

"Impossible to sleep," Bruce said, rubbing his eyes.

Nina nodded agreement. "Glad you're back, Julia. Where've you been? What's happening?"

"All in good time. I need something to drink. Follow me to the kitchen. I'll explain." Julia poured herself a large glass of water from the tap and drank quickly. They gathered around the kitchen table. "I just returned from a meeting on board our ship."

"You mentioned a ship before," Bruce said. "You mean an Annunaki spaceship?"

"Yes, the ship here now is called the Cali," Julia explained. "We've been in orbit around your planet for some time."

"How is that possible?" Bruce asked.

"And why haven't we detected your ship?" Nina added.

"Our technology allows us to do things you humans can only imagine," Julia said. "There's no time to explain all that now, even if I wanted to. We have to act now. Enlil, captain of the Cali, confirms a Reptilian invasion is imminent. His crew have been tracking the Reptilian fleet's approach. "

"Damn it," Nina muttered.

"How many?" asked Bruce.

"More than fifty ships," Julia said, not even attempting to sugarcoat the situation.

"Fifty..." Bruce and Nina exchanged worried glances. Every minute, the threat was becoming bigger and more real. "Please, tell us you got some good news up there," he said, looking towards the heavens. "Anything that could help us stop them? Are the Annunaki willing to join us?"

Julia hesitated, her gaze flickering between him and Nina. She seemed to be weighing her words carefully, as if unsure how much to reveal. "No, not directly. Sorry."

"We're fucked!" Bruce swore as his fist slammed into the table.

"I did manage to get some valuable information," Julia continued, her voice low and guarded. "But we need to move quickly. We don't have much time."

"Tell us everything," Nina urged. "We can handle it."

"Alright," Julia agreed. "Understand, we can't stop the Reptilians, not completely. Not at this time. There are far too many of them and too few of us. Plus, they've embedded themselves here on Earth too deeply."

"I don't think I like the way this is going," muttered Bruce.

Julia patted his hand. "All is not lost. We can thwart this invasion, here and now. This won't stop them from continuing with their overall plans, but it may be a way to slow them down."

"Then maybe we can raise some support here on Earth," Nina said.

"If we can ever get anyone to believe us," cut in Bruce.

"For now, you'll have to believe me, trust me." Julia spread her arms and looked at them both.

"Of course," Nina said first.

Bruce nodded. "Tell us what to do."

"Good. Now, let me explain. We don't have a moment to lose." Julia rose and paced back and forth. "Where do I begin... Alright, while the Annunaki won't send troops, Enlil has agreed to support you in the effort to stop the Reptilians. The Cali has many assets. They will provide us with advanced weaponry and technology."

"Not that I'm not grateful for any support," Bruce began, choosing his words carefully for fear of insulting Julia, "but why are they doing this? Why help us at all?"

"Because we do not wish to see the Reptilians destroy your planet and its resources."

"And its people?" Bruce asked.

Julia smiled. "Them too."

Bruce and Nina exchanged glances.

"Thank you, Julia," Bruce murmured. "We appreciate any help we can get."

"We are happy we can be of assistance," Julia replied, offering a small, determined smile. "There is much that I can tell you about the Annunaki and our interest in your world and its people. We can talk about this further when the time is right."

"I can't wait to hear," Nina said, eyeing her friend. "There's a lot more to you than I ever imagined. I've been intrigued by the Anunnaki and their involvement with us forever! Tell me, did you tinker with our DNA as primates? Oh, I can't wait to hear some stories!"

Bruce interrupted. "Julia," he began, "Nina and I saw something back in the alien control center we forgot to mention earlier... We saw surveillance footage of this farmhouse. The Reptilians know we're here."

Julia's eyes widened with alarm. He'd never seen her look so frightened. The sense of unease that had been gnawing at him intensified, threatening to overwhelm him.

"Damn," Julia cursed under her breath, her fists clenching at her sides. She muttered in some sort of ancient Hebrew-sounding dialect, then cut back to English. "All the more reason to act now. We don't know when they might choose to strike at us."

"Agreed," said Bruce.

"We've got a lot to do, and not much time to do it. Where's

Zachary?"

"Sleeping," replied Nina.

"We'd better wake him," Julia said.

"Right," Bruce said. "We need to get him up to speed." There was no sheltering the elderly scientist from this, not with the Reptilians watching them. Besides, they couldn't leave Zachary alone in the farmhouse. He could be captured or killed. He'd be safer with them, wherever they went.

They made their way to Zachary's room, the floorboards creaking beneath their feet. Bruce hesitated for a moment outside the door before rapping softly on the wood.

"Zachary?" he called out. "We've got news. You need to wake up."

"Grandpa?" Nina pressed her ear to the door. "You awake?"

They heard a grunt and the door swung open to reveal a bleary-eyed Zachary, clad in his pajamas, his unkempt gray hair sticking up at odd angles. He squinted at them, clearly disoriented by their intrusion.

"Wha—" he began, yawning widely. "What's going on?"

"Sorry to wake you," Bruce said. "But there's been a development."

"The Reptilians are on to us. They're monitoring the farmhouse," blurted Nina.

Zachary's eyes widened as he absorbed this information, his sleepiness evaporating in an instant. "We must leave here!"

"Slow down, Grandpa!" urged Nina. "We have to move carefully."

"Right," Zachary gulped. "It won't do to do anything rash."

"Let me show you what the Annunaki have provided for us," Julia said, moving through the farmhouse with the others on her tail.

Zachary looked at his granddaughter. "The Annunaki?"

Nina filled him in on Julia's revelation about her true identity and that there were Annunaki orbiting Earth, and that they had offered to help them against the impending arrival of a heavily-armed Reptilian invasion fleet.

Zachary staggered under the news. "Well, I never…"

Julia went outside and returned moments later with a bulging nylon pack. She set it down on the rug in front of the hearth. "Everything we need is in here." She untied the bag. "We'll use the cover of darkness to sneak into the cavern. Once there, we'll disrupt their operations and cripple their command structure. Enlil and his crew will be monitoring from the Cali and provide assistance as needed." She reiterated that this did not include use of Annunaki fighters. "He and members of his strategy team will be in constant contact with me.

"Now, pay careful attention." Julia pulled out a weapon like nothing Bruce had ever seen before. Its gray-blue shape was both familiar and foreign, with sleek lines and sharp edges. She pulled more weapons from her pack and explained the uses of one after the other of the unfamiliar new weapons. Bruce made an effort to memorize every detail as he watched her expertly handle each alien device.

"Focus your energy on this point," Julia said, her fingers brushing against a seemingly innocuous spot on one of the weapons. "The weapon will respond to your intent and fire accordingly. It's a bit like Bluetooth, only with your brain enhanced with AI protocols."

Bruce nodded, although he didn't begin to understand a thing she said. After instructing Nina and Bruce on each weapon's use, she watched them practice with a critical eye as she put them through their paces.

"Good. Once we're inside the cavern," Julia said, "our first goal is to disable their communications array. This includes destroying the crystal. That will sever ties with the Gateway Arch. With the Arch disabled, the invading fleet will not be able to enter."

"Got it," Bruce replied.

"Be prepared for anything. We don't know the full extent of their defenses. Annunaki intelligence is limited regarding the interior of the cavern."

They gathered up their things. It was 3 a.m. Time to go.

As the team gathered at the back door, a sudden explosion rocked the farmhouse, shattering windows and throwing them off their feet. The force of the blast sent debris flying through the air, and the once-secure walls cracked and crumbled around them. Timbers burst into flames.

"Get down!" Bruce shouted, shielding his face from the onslaught of shattered glass and splintered wood.

"Reptilians!" Nina cried out, her eyes wide with terror as she spotted Mr. Stafford and his forces advancing on their position.

"Stay together!" Julia ordered, her voice rising above the cacophony of destruction. "We'll have to fight our way out!"

Bruce scrambled to his feet, gripping his new alien weapon tightly, prepared to face the Reptilians head-on. A storm of gunfire erupted and broken glass rained down upon the team. They scrambled once more for cover. Bruce felt the reassuring heft of his weapon in his hands, a comfort that was swiftly melting. He saw Nina and Zachary pinned down behind an overturned table.

"Stay down," Bruce urged.

"Probably using Earth weapons here to avoid leaving evidence of their presence," Zachary noted as bullets buzzed overhead.

"Julia!" Bruce lifted his head, searching frantically for their Annunaki ally amid the chaos. But she was nowhere to be seen.

"Get down, Bruce!" Nina screamed as another round of gunfire erupted around them.

"Where's Julia?" he demanded.

"I don't know! She was just here!" Nina replied, struggling to remember how to use the strange weapon in her hand. "Damn, give me an old-fashioned shotgun any day!"

Bruce managed to let off a shot, sending a white hot streak from the tip of his weapon. He succeeded only in putting a fresh hole in the already half-wrecked and crumbling ceiling. "Shit!"

"Keep your heads down," Zachary warned.

"Nina," began Bruce. "I'm going to lay down some fire. I want you and Zachary to make a run for it and—"

"And leave you here?" Nina cried. "Not a chance!"

"It's our only chance. If we all get killed, that's the end of everything!"

"But Bruce—"

Before she could continue, Reptilian forces swarmed the room, seizing Bruce, Nina and Zachary. Their hands were bound tightly behind their backs with elastic bands that constricted their wrists painfully with every movement.

Out of the smoky haze and rising flames of the burning farmhouse, the cold eyes of Mr. Stafford appeared. "Pathetic humans," he sneered. "Did you really think you could stop us?"

"Damn you," Bruce spat. "You won't win. There are others who will fight against you."

"Ah, yes, your precious Annunaki friend," Mr. Stafford said, an unsettling grin spreading across his face. "I have plans for her."

"Leave her alone!" Nina shouted, struggling against her bonds.

"Silence!" Mr. Stafford hissed, backhanding Nina across the face. Nina reeled.

Bruce seethed with rage, wishing desperately that he could break free and protect her.

"And you, my old friend," Stafford said to Zachary. "So good to see you again."

"You'll never win, Stafford!" vowed the old professor.

"Ah, but I already have. Take them away," he ordered with a wave of his hand.

As they were dragged from the farmhouse, Bruce felt the crushing weight of failure.

"Where are they taking us?" Nina whispered to Bruce as they were led away from the burning farmhouse.

"I don't know," he said. "To one of their ships maybe." The bigger question was what would Stafford and his Reptilians do to them or with them once they got to whatever their ultimate destination might be. But he refrained from saying so because the answer wasn't pretty.

"Do you think Julia managed to get away?" Zachary scanned the dark fields surrounding his home.

"I hope so," whispered Nina. Her being free might be their only hope.

They were herded into an ominous-looking black armored vehicle. They were thrust into the rear and the door slammed shut behind them. The vehicle rumbled to life and shook beneath them, its oppressive confines hot and suffocating as they were transported across the uneven ground.

Bruce clenched his jaw, his hands bound tightly behind him, struggling to figure a way out and coming up with nothing.

"Any ideas?" Nina whispered, seated shoulder to shoulder with her grandfather on one of the two hard metal benches in the rear.

"Working on it," Bruce whispered, as he spun through various possible escape scenarios. But his hands were tied…literally.

"They're probably taking us to the cavern first," Nina said. There was no seeing out the blacked out windows.

"I believe you are correct," said Zachary.

But from there? Where? Up to one of the Reptilian ships? Or straight into the hands of Dr. Barry?

Bruce weighed the possible outcomes—none of them good—trying to prepare himself for what may come. Would they be tortured? Imprisoned? Killed? And where was Julia? Was she safe, or had she too been captured?

"Wait," Bruce said. "Julia mentioned that she was in constant communication with the Annunaki ship. That means they must know what's happened. Maybe they're planning a rescue mission."

"I don't know. I hope you're right," Nina replied. "But you heard Julia, she said they refused to supply personnel."

"Yeah," Bruce sighed as the vehicle bounced along a dirt track.

"I hate to say it," began Nina, "but we don't even know if Julia is alive."

"And if she's dead, communication with the Cali might have been severed," said Zachary.

"Exactly."

Several heart-stopping moments later, the vehicle came to a jarring halt. The back doors swung open, revealing Mr. Stafford bathed in the jaundiced glow of the cavern's low hanging lights.

"Out," he ordered and his Reptilian underlings yanked them from the vehicle, their grips harsh and unyielding.

They found themselves in an unfamiliar cavernous space, a sprawling complex with limestone tunnels flying off in every direction. Glistening stalactites dripped from the ceiling. A state-of-the-art control center hummed with an energy totally alien to its natural surroundings. An incongruity that was at once breath-taking and terrifying.

Screens flickered with alien symbols, along with images of maps of many of the major cities across the globe, surveillance feeds, and other things that Bruce couldn't begin to comprehend.

Stafford led them towards a glass-walled room at its epicenter. The space buzzed with activity as Reptilians worked behind complex consoles, madly typing at holographic controls.

"Impressive, isn't it?" Stafford said to Zachary. "You were right all along."

"Being right doesn't always bring satisfaction," Zachary muttered bitterly.

Stafford chuckled, a cold, desolate sound that echoed long after it had ended. "That's true," he admitted, walking ahead to open a set of massive double doors. "But it does bring...clarification."

They were led through the doors into a strange room that was as stark and sterile as the control center was chaotic. The walls were an unnerving white that reflected the cold light from above and the floor was made of some sort of glass-like substance that gave off an unsettling luminescence.

At the center of the room stood Dr. Barry. "Ah, Mr. Finger, Ms. Lind. Welcome back. And hello to you, sir," the Grey said, turning his attention to Zachary. "A pleasure to meet you. Mr. Stafford has told me so much about you. You've quite the reputation."

Dr. Barry paused and tapped his index finger against his cheek. "I do hope we live up to your...expectations."

CHAPTER 15

"I will be taking you up to my ship shortly," Dr. Barry said coolly. "You'll make excellent subjects for my experiments."

"I'd rather die first," Zachary spat in defiance, "than become one of your experiments!"

Dr. Barry stopped at the door and turned around. "Dead or alive... One way or another, I will have my way with you, Professor." The alien looked at the three of them. "With all of you."

They all knew what the doctor meant by "experiments." Fear gnawed at Nina's insides as she realized they were completely at the Grey's mercy.

Dr. Barry smirked before sauntering out of the room, leaving them under the watchful gaze of the Reptilian soldiers standing outside the solid steel door.

"Don't worry. We'll find a way out of this," Bruce said, although he didn't have a clue how. But there was one thing he could do. He discreetly shifted in his seat. "Can you reach my pocket?" he asked Nina.

"I think so," she said, sliding closer.

"Good, front right. I've got a pocketknife the guards missed. See if you can get your fingers on it."

"Right." Nina pushed against Bruce and managed to get her fingers inside his pocket. She felt the knife and slowly pulled it free. Moving carefully, she managed to open the blade. "Got it!"

"Great." Bruce glanced nervously at the door, then scooted closer to her. She skillfully sliced through the elastic bands with the sharp blade. Once freed, he returned the favor and cut her bindings, before untying Zachary. "God, this is bad," he muttered. He stood and rubbed his wrists as he looked around the cell, assessing their options.

"It could hardly be worse," Zachary agreed. "And we still don't know what's happened to Julia—not to mention our Annunaki allies up in orbit."

"Who knows?" Nina whispered, her eyes shining with unshed tears. "If Julia didn't manage to escape back at the farmhouse, she could have been captured or be dead by now." Would the Annunaki still provide support? Would they even know what was happening down here?

"Let's hope she managed to get away," Bruce added, trying to sound optimistic but failing miserably. They all knew the odds were stacked against finding Julia alive. "Harsh as this may sound, we can't afford to dwell on Julia's fate. We need to focus on our own survival."

"We can't let Barry take us to his ship," Nina declared. "We need to find a way out of here, and fast."

"Before they come back for us," added Zachary.

"Agreed," Bruce said.

They scanned the chamber for any potential weaknesses they could exploit.

"There must be something we can use to our advantage," Zachary said. "But I don't see what."

Nina banged the side of her fist against the damp, cold wall. "Solid rock.

"Maybe a loose stone or a weak spot in the wall? Another fissure?" Bruce suggested. He joined her in the search. "Zachary, keep your eye on the door. If you see the handle turn, warn us."

"Yes, Bruce." Zachary turned and stared at the closed door.

Their desperate search was interrupted by the sudden sound of approaching footsteps. All three froze in place, exchanging panicked glances as the steps grew louder.

"Quick!" Bruce whispered, grabbing the discarded elastic bands that had bound their hands moments before. "Pretend we're still tied up!" They scrambled back to their original positions, hastily draping the broken bands over their wrists, trying to make it look convincing.

The door opened, revealing one of the Reptilian guards. The alien trooper surveyed the room with unblinking eyes, its gaze lingering on each of the prisoners before finally settling on Nina.

"Your presence is required," it rasped, stepping towards her.

"W-What for?" Nina stammered.

"Dr. Barry has requested you," the guard replied, reaching for her arm. A wave of terror washed over her, but she fought to keep her expression neutral, knowing that any sign of resistance could spell disaster for all of them.

"Fine," she said, allowing the guard to pull her to her feet, all the while keeping her hands hidden behind her back.

"Nina, no!" shouted Zachary, leaping to his feet. The guard cuffed him and he crumpled to the ground.

"Grandpa!" Nina dove for Zachary but the guard wrapped its hand around her neck and pulled her back. A second and a third guard filled the doorway. Bruce knew there was nothing he could do for the moment so he held back.

"Be careful," Bruce murmured, as the guard led Nina away. When the door slammed shut, he dropped the pretense of being bound and helped Zachary to his feet. "Zachary, are you okay?"

The old man rubbed his swollen cheek. "Yes, I'll be okay. But Nina—"

"Shh, I know. We'll get Nina but first we have to get out of here."

"Of course," Zachary murmured, joining Bruce in the far corner of the cell. "But how?"

"I don't know."

"The thought of Dr. Barry getting his hands on her…" Zachary left the remainder of his words unsaid. "Where do we start, Bruce?"

"First, we need to figure out where we are in relation to the surface," Bruce said, scanning the walls of the cell. His architect's mind attempted to visualize the layout of the alien base. "If we can determine our position, we'll at least know which way is out. I think—"

"Wait," Zachary whispered, interrupting Bruce's train of thought. "Look at that." He pointed to a faint outline on the rough stone wall where it met the floor.

"Nice eye, Zachary! That could be an old ventilation shaft," Bruce breathed, his pulse quickening with hope. "From the days when this was a working ore mine."

Zachary moved closer. "And if we can find a way to open it, we might be able to crawl up to the surface."

"Or at least to another part of the cave system," Bruce added. "It's risky, but it looks like our only shot." He looked at Zachary, seeking confirmation that they were on the same page.

"Then we take it," Zachary said, determination sparking in his eyes. "We can't just sit here and wait for the Reptilians to take us too."

"Alright," Bruce nodded, steeling himself for what lay ahead. "Let's see if we can find a way to pry this open without attracting attention."

Using his knife, they set to work quietly and quickly, their movements punctuated by the occasional grunt or a strained breath. Nina's absence weighed heavily on both of them. Minutes later, his knife reduced to broken bits of metal, they'd come up with nothing more than a thick strand of wire. Bruce's eyes darted from one potential tool to another. They considered their limited options. The faint sounds of Reptilian footsteps passing outside served as a constant reminder of the danger they were in.

"Here," Zachary whispered, handing Bruce a small, jagged piece of tough metal bracket he had found in a corner. "Think you can use this?"

"Maybe," Bruce said, taking it from the professor and turning it over in his hand, feeling the sharp edges dig into his palm. He glanced at Zachary, who was gripping the wire they'd dug up earlier. "Zachary, can you twist that wire around the edge here? Through this hole? We might be able to create some leverage."

Zachary nodded, his hands shaking slightly as he did as Bruce asked. He maneuvered the wire around the edge of the ventilation shaft. Together, they pulled with all their strength, muscles straining and sweat dripping down their faces. Pain shot through their hands and it began to look like nothing was going to happen. Then, with a groan of metal, the panel budged ever so slightly.

"Keep going!" Zachary urged. The sound of footsteps grew louder, and he cast a nervous glance toward the door. "We don't have much time."

Finally, with one last heave, the panel gave way, revealing a dark, narrow passage hidden beneath layers of dust and cobwebs. Without hesitation, they scrambled inside, the tight confines of the shaft pressing against their bodies as they crawled along on their elbows and knees.

Bruce led the way. "Follow me and try not to talk." They went along for several minutes, bodies aching. A sudden drop forced them to slide down a steep incline, their hands scraped raw by the rough surface.

"Are we going the right way?" Zachary whispered, speaking for the first time since their escape.

"No idea," Bruce confessed. He swallowed hard. "All we can do is keep moving."

They continued their slow, cautious journey through the oppressive darkness. The air grew stifling and thick with dust. Each breath became a struggle, and they could feel the tons of earth above them, threatening to crush them at any moment.

"Wait," Bruce hissed suddenly, freezing in place. The faint sound of voices echoed through the shaft, barely discernible but unmistakable.

"Reptilians?" Zachary asked.

Bruce nodded and held his finger to his lips. They pressed themselves against the walls of the shaft, praying they wouldn't be discovered as a beam of light shot out from their left and angled around inside. Had their guards noticed they'd escaped? Were they being hunted?

The Reptilian voices faded away, leaving them in tense silence once more. "Let's keep going," Bruce whispered, knowing that their window of opportunity was rapidly closing. "We need to figure out where Dr. Barry is. You heard the guard, wherever the good doctor is, that's where we'll find Nina."

"Yes, good thinking," said Zachary.

They pressed forward. The tight passage seemed to stretch on forever, filled with dust and shadows that played tricks on their strained eyes. As they crawled over the rough earth, Zachary's breathing came out in more and more labored bursts.

"Are you alright?" Bruce asked, glancing back at the older man.

"I've been better," he joked weakly, wiping sweat from his forehead. "But I'm holding up. Let's keep going."

Bruce nodded, offering a small smile of encouragement before turning back to the task at hand. He was worried about Nina, Julia and now Zachary as well. Forcing these grim thoughts away, he pressed on, knowing that their only hope was to stay one step ahead of their enemy.

After what felt like hours, they finally emerged from the ventilation shaft into a large open space that took their breath away. They'd stumbled into a vast cavern with an intricate network of tunnels leading off in every direction, like spokes of a wheel. Stalactites hung from the ceiling like icicles, shimmering with moisture. He found it all eerily beautiful yet unsettlingly alien.

Bruce glanced at Zachary, who shared his sense of awe. "Where do we go from here?"

"Stick to the shadows and look for signs?" Zachary suggested.

"Sure, sounds as good as anything I can come up with," replied Bruce.

Their ears picked up distant sounds as they cautiously explored—

the rumble of machinery, the murmur of voices. Was Nina somewhere nearby? Julia?

The deeper they ventured, the more uneasy Bruce became.

"Wait!" Zachary suddenly held up his hand, eyes narrowing.

In the distance, a flicker of light appeared. A flashlight?

Bruce pressed himself against the tunnel wall, pulling Zachary back with him. He dared to peek around the corner and saw yet another vast cavern filled with blinking lights and strange devices. Figures in dark uniforms moved between them, some in human guise, some Reptilian.

"There." Bruce pointed towards the center of the activity. Dr. Charles Barry stood hunched over a console displaying the city of St. Louis. Two Reptilians flanked him. They appeared to be fully engaged in an animated discussion.

"Now what?" Zachary whispered back.

"We need to move closer," Bruce replied. "Maybe they'll say something that will give us a clue as to where we might find Nina…and Julia."

They moved silently, hugging the cavern walls and ducking behind thick stalagmites. Bruce focused on Dr. Barry, on the way he gestured as he spoke, on the way the Reptilians listened with their heads tilted slightly to one side—a sign of respect or agreement, maybe?

They dropped to their bellies and crawled forward. Bruce's nose twitched as the smell of damp earth mixed with a strange metallic scent hit his nostrils. He prayed he wouldn't sneeze and pushed the thought from his mind.

Stafford stormed in and approached Dr. Barry. Inching closer, he strained to listen in on the conversation.

"The Reptilian fleet will be here any moment," Stafford told him.

"So soon? Then I need to get my specimens loaded immediately," Dr. Barry replied.

"That's your business," Stafford snapped and departed as quickly as he'd come.

Bruce's heart hammered in his chest as he glanced at Zachary. They had to act fast.

Suddenly, from one of the side tunnels, came a faint whimpering sound, quickly stifled. Bruce cocked his ears. Could it be Nina? He looked at Zachary and motioned towards the noise.

"We need a distraction," Bruce said. "Here's what I'm thinking—" But before he could finish his sentence, Zachary was off and running towards Dr. Barry and the Reptilians!

ꞋꞀƎꓘꟼꓔꞮꓥꞀ 16

Nina stood defiantly between two uniformed Reptilian guards. Their eyes conveyed a malevolence that she didn't mind admitting unnerved her. She clenched her fists at her sides as she steadied herself for whatever was to come.

"Ah, Miss Lind," Dr. Barry drawled as he entered the room, his voice dripping with condescension. The Grey scientist carried himself with an unmistakable air of superiority. "I've been looking forward to some one-on-one time with you. I am certain our little chat will be quite stimulating…for me, at least.

"Dismissed," Dr. Barry said without even glancing at the Reptilian guards, who obediently stole out of the room like weightless wraiths. The heavy steel door slammed shut behind them, sealing Nina inside with the alien scientist.

"Please, take a seat," Dr. Barry gestured toward a metal chair in the center of the room.

Nina hesitated for a moment, weighing her options. But she knew better than to defy him outright—at least not yet. She had nothing to gain. Keeping her wary gaze locked on him, she crossed the room and sat down, her back straight and shoulders squared.

"Comfortable?" Dr. Barry asked mockingly, folding his arms across his chest.

"Very. Just like home," Nina retorted. She refused to let the Grey see her fear, even though it churned deep within her like a tropical storm. "Not that you give a damn."

"Quite right," he admitted. "You see, Miss Lind, you and your friends have been quite the thorn in our sides. Your persistence and curiosity have proven rather inconvenient. I do not like disruptions and delays. I work best in a quiet and predictable environment."

"Boo-hoo," Nina said. "So sorry to have inconvenienced you."

"Don't get too cocky," Dr. Barry replied smoothly, his gaze never leaving hers. "I'm sure you're smart enough to know you and your friends are doomed. As is the Earth."

"This isn't over yet."

"It is as far as you and your friends are concerned. Soon, you will join me in my spacecraft. It may not be as spacious as this, but I've quite a nice lab there as well. It will do. And we'll be far out of harm's way when the battle between you Earthlings and the Reptilians begins. A battle you are fated to lose, I might add."

Nina scoffed, refusing to let him intimidate her. "I wouldn't be so sure about that. We'll never submit to the Reptilians."

"That's where you're wrong," Dr. Barry said. "Humanity's downfall has always been its arrogance—the belief that you are the center of the universe. The truth is, you're nothing more than pawns in a greater game, and other, more advanced beings, hold the power to control your every move. You were made to be slaves by one, farmed for souls by another. And then you, mere primates, managed to develop nuclear bombs. A long way from poking ant hills with sticks you have come, but the end is near."

"Enough!" Nina snapped. "Where's Julia? What have you done with her?"

"Julia?" Dr. Barry raised an eyebrow. "I'm afraid I have no idea who you're talking about."

"The…woman who was with us at the farmhouse when we were attacked."

"Inconsequential, I'm sure." Dr. Barry said with a toss of the hand. "One more human more or less makes no difference to me."

"Julia is not inconsequential." Nina gritted her teeth.

Dr. Barry leaned back, crossing his arms over his chest, an air of detached amusement playing across his features. "As I said, I know nothing about this woman you call Julia, nor her whereabouts. Nor do I care. My focus is on my work alone."

Nina fought to keep her emotions in check, knowing that revealing Julia's true identity and the Annunaki's involvement would only put her in jeopardy—and maybe jeopardize everything. "No matter what you do, you can't break us. We'll find a way to stop you."

"Such determination," Dr. Barry mused. "It's almost... endearing. But I assure you, your attempts to defy the Reptilians will only hasten your own demise. Pity, I could learn more from you alive than dead, but if you insist on being uncooperative, dead it shall have to be."

The Grey turned away from her, signaling his disinterest in further conversation. Nina struggled to quiet the storm of emotions within her. She couldn't let Dr. Barry see how much his words affected her—doing so would be giving him the very power he clearly sought.

As she watched Dr. Barry's back, she thought hard. "Dr. Barry," she began, "you may think you have the upper hand here, but don't underestimate me or my friends."

"I know all about your friends, Miss Lind," Dr. Barry said as he turned to face her. "And frankly, none of you stand a chance against the Reptilians."

"You may be right...to a degree," she conceded. "Perhaps we can't stop you alone. But the human race has always found a way to rise above adversity. We adapt, we grow. We build alliances. Maybe we'll even find allies who share our cause."

"Your faith in your species is admirable, but misguided," Dr. Barry replied, his tone dismissive. "And childish. You're like ants trying to comprehend the stars."

"Ants?" Nina shot back. "You see us as insignificant because you're too arrogant to consider the possibility that you might be wrong about us."

Dr. Barry took a step toward her, his eyes cold and calculating. "Do you know what I see when I look at you, Miss Lind? A desperate, frightened creature clinging to hope."

"Then you're not looking closely enough," Nina said. "Because I intend to use everything I know to bring you down."

"You know, Miss Lind," he began, circling her like a predator stalking its prey, "as much as I've enjoyed our little tête-à-tête, I believe it's time for me to let you in on a secret or two."

"Why should I care about anything you have to say?"

"Because," Dr. Barry replied, pausing behind her, his voice a hot whisper in her ear, "it concerns your kind's fate—not just here on Earth, but on other worlds as well. Trust me, I've travelled the galaxy. I've been places, seen things."

Her pulse quickened, but she refused to show any sign of weakness. She glared in defiance. Trusting this alien was the last thing she'd ever do. Still, she found herself saying, "What are you talking about?"

"Ah, now that would be telling," Dr. Barry said, moving away from her and leaning against a nearby table, his fingers tapping an erratic rhythm. "But let's just say that the Reptilians have plans far grander, far more impressive than simply conquering this insignificant little planet of yours."

"Is that supposed to scare me?" Nina shot back.

"Scare you?" Dr. Barry laughed, but there was no geniality in the sound. "No, my dear, I expect you're far too stubborn for that. But perhaps it will give you something to think about while you're rotting away in a cell with all your other little lab-rat friends. Here's another tidbit for you. What if Greys such as myself are actually humans from the future? Plot twist. Primates to Neanderthals and Denisovans. Now slowly morphing into smaller less-physical beings. Sex, emotion, and race become meaningless. Escape a planet before a cataclysm. AI slowly guiding your own demise."

"You think you're invincible," she said, "but you're not. You may be powerful, but you're still just flesh and blood—or whatever the hell it is that runs through your veins."

"Your point?" Dr. Barry asked, his patience clearly wearing thin.

"Everyone has a breaking point," Nina replied. "And I will find yours."

"Is that a threat, Miss Lind?" Barry laughed. "How quaint."

"Call it a promise."

Dr. Barry's eyes narrowed, his lips pressed into a grim line. But before he could respond, Nina made her move, launching herself at the door in a desperate bid for freedom.

"Stop her!" Dr. Barry barked, but Nina was already out in the corridor, sprinting past the startled guards outside and running for her life.

Heart pounding against her chest, every nerve ending screamed for her to keep moving, to put as much distance between herself and Dr. Barry as possible.

"Turn left!" a voice shouted in her mind.

Nina about jumped out of her skin.

The voice shouted adamantly once more. "Left! Turn left!"

That was Julia's voice!

Nina obeyed and turned without question. Her Annunaki friend was alive! And guiding her through the Reptilian compound and to safety.

"Stop!" Dr. Barry's voice echoed from somewhere behind her, sending a shiver up Nina's spine. She knew she couldn't outrun him forever.

"Julia," she thought desperately, "I need a place to hide."

"Understood," Julia replied telepathically. "There's a small alcove up ahead on your right. Hide there, quickly!"

Nina skidded around the next corner and squeezed herself into the tiny space, pressing her body against the cold stone wall even as she fought to catch her breath. She heard angry footsteps approaching—Dr. Barry and the Reptilians coming for her, no doubt. She held her breath, praying they wouldn't find her.

"Find her!" Dr. Barry snapped, his voice ice-cold and dripping with menace. "She can't have gone far. And remember, I want her alive, you clumsy oafs. She's far more valuable to me that way."

As the footsteps grew louder, Nina examined her surroundings, searching for anything that might aid her in her escape. There! A loose panel on the wall, just within reach. With trembling fingers, she pried it open, revealing a mess of wires and circuits.

"Julia, can you see this? What is it?" she asked silently, praying for a miracle, and waiting tensely while Julia seemed to see the exposed panel through her eyes.

"Circuit panel. Maybe you can use it," Julia replied. "Now, listen and do exactly as I say!"

Nina's hands flew over the wires, guided by Julia's telepathically transmitted instructions, until her fingers found the wire she sought—a thin red strand that carried power to a nearby room filled with cryolockers awaiting transport up to Dr. Barry's orbiting ship.

"Pull it!" Julia urged. "That should cut power to this section, which should in turn set off an alarm."

"Right, here goes." Nina yanked the wire free, plunging the hallway into darkness. A half-second later, a shrill alarm rang out, piercing her eardrums.

"Go now!" Julia commanded, and Nina sprinted from her hiding place, running blindly through the pitch-black corridor. She heard Dr. Barry's enraged shouts behind her, but she didn't dare look back. She had to keep moving, had to find a way out.

But in the darkness, she stumbled, tripping over an unseen crate and crashing to the floor. Pain exploded through her elbows and chest. She scrambled to her feet, knowing that if she stopped now, all would be lost.

"Enough!" Dr. Barry's voice boomed through the darkness, and an unseen force slammed into Nina, pinning her helplessly against the wall. The lights flickered back on, revealing the furious Grey standing before her, his alien eyes burning with rage.

"Did you really think you could escape me?" Dr. Barry sneered, summoning the Reptilians guards with a wave of his hand. They appeared instantly, grabbing Nina roughly by the arms.

"Bring her with me. Secure her in one of the empty cryolockers," Dr. Barry ordered coldly. "Let's see how resourceful she is when she's frozen solid."

As the guards tossed her into the freezing confines of the cryolocker, Nina's last thoughts were of her grandfather, Bruce, Alex, and Julia, even as the cold began to claim her body.

CHAPTER 17

Bruce crouched behind a cluster of jagged stalagmites. Through the small gaps between the glistening rocks, he stared in jaw-dropping shock at the scene unfolding before him. Zachary, fueled by desperation to protect his granddaughter, charged forward with a primal scream towards Dr. Barry and his Reptilian soldiers.

But it was all for nothing. Within seconds, he was captured and subdued, his arms pinned painfully behind him and forced to his knees by the merciless grip of his captors.

"Is this your idea of a rescue mission?" Dr. Barry sneered. "Pathetic." Dozens of cryolocker storage containers and body bags occupied the cavernous space, making it appear smaller than it was. "I may have to reconsider my assessment of you, Professor. I seem to have overestimated your intelligence. You may not be as smart, for a human, as I had believed."

His words stung like acid and Zachary clenched his jaws in frustration. He couldn't let this pompous alien get under his skin, no matter how much it bruised his ego to be looked down upon by someone like Dr. Barry. "I've been insulted by better than you!"

Bruce admired Zachary's unwavering bravery in the face of death. Brave but stupid.

"Tell me, old man," Dr. Barry growled, circling Zachary. "How did you manage to escape your cell?"

"I'll tell you nothing. Where's my granddaughter? Where's Nina? What have you done to her?"

Dr. Barry came closer, until their faces were mere inches apart. "You bore me." He paused for dramatic effect before continuing in a low, menacing tone. "Where is the other human? The one called Bruce?"

Zachary's lips twisted into a small, defiant smile. "He's out of your reach. Where is my granddaughter?"

"You really want to know?" Dr. Barry shrugged. "So be it." The Grey pointed towards one of the sleek, futuristic cryolockers leaning up against the walls, their surfaces emitting a soft blue glow. "Place him inside…next to his granddaughter," he instructed firmly. The empty cryolocker stood tall and imposing, an upright metal coffin watching over the room.

Bruce's breath caught in his throat as he watched Zachary being violently hurled into the cryolocker adjacent to the one holding Nina. Through the cryolocker's transparent window, he saw her face contorted, a frozen mask exhibiting a mix of anger and fear. Helplessness consumed him as he stood frozen, unable to intervene. Rushing to their aid would only result in his own capture, leaving them both at the mercy of their captors.

"Go and check the cell for the human called Bruce," Dr. Barry ordered two of the Reptilians. "If he isn't there, search the entire area. I want him brought to me. Alive! These humans do intrigue me."

As the Reptilians hurried away, Bruce moved silently closer.

Dr. Barry's voice rang through the cavern as he barked orders at the remaining Reptilian subordinates. "Secure everything for transfer to the ship—and do it quickly! I want the Linds and Agent Simmons taken there with the rest of my human guinea pigs."

Barry's hard eyes gleamed with cruel anticipation. "Once onboard, awaken the Linds but maintain your guard. They're valuable specimens for my experiments, and too long in stasis may do injury to their brains. As for Agent Simmons," Dr. Barry said coldly, "he can remain in stasis. He's served his purpose."

Bruce's blood boiled as he watched Dr. Barry. If only he could get to Zachary, Alex, and Nina before they were carried into space, but how? He glanced around, searching for any opportunity that might present itself.

"Get moving, you useless creatures!" Dr. Barry snarled, stalking towards the exit of the cavern. The Reptilian workers immediately sprang into action, transporting cryolockers and body bags with unnerving efficiency.

As soon as Dr. Barry was out of sight, Bruce seized his chance. Staying low and quiet, he crept ever closer to the cryolockers. When the last Reptilian departed and the chamber stood empty, Bruce ran to the cryolocker with Nina inside. He detected a flicker of movement. So she wasn't completely immobile. Did she recognize him? He tapped the window. Nina screamed. He could barely hear her voice, weak and desperate.

"Stay calm, Nina. I'm going to get you out of there," Bruce whispered urgently, his hands fumbling feverishly on the clasps holding the locker shut. At last, the cryolocker hissed open, and Nina stumbled out, gasping for air. She locked her eyes onto Bruce's, gratitude and relief momentarily overshadowing her fear and fatigue.

"Thank you, Bruce," she choked out, throwing herself into his arms. "I could hardly breathe. I thought I'd die in there!" She pulled free. "We need to free Grandpa and Alex! Quick, before they return!"

"Right." Bruce agreed, scanning the room. His heart clenched at the sight of the ashen corpses in the other cryolockers, victims of Dr. Barry's twisted experiments. There was nothing they could do for them now, but as Bruce raced to free Zachary from the cryolocker next to Nina's, he vowed silently that their deaths would not be in vain.

Zachary tumbled out and wiped his sweaty brow. "Damn, thanks, Bruce."

"You're lucky I didn't leave you to your fate, old man," Bruce teased with a smile. "That was a pretty dumb stunt you pulled!"

Zachary colored. "Yes, sorry about that. I don't know what came over me."

Bruce grinned. "No apology necessary. What came over you was a deep and profound love for your granddaughter." He glanced at Nina. "And I know that feeling…"

172

"Simmons is here," Nina said, pointing to a cryolocker slightly apart from the others. Bruce approached it. Simmons face was still but held some color. Hopefully, that was a good sign. Most of the others were gray and clearly dead. "Come on, Simmons," he muttered as he fiddled with the alien mechanisms. "Time to wake up and help us take down these assholes."

With a final click, the cryolocker sprang open, revealing Alex's limp form. As if sensing his freedom, the agent stirred, his eyes fluttering open. Disoriented, he stared blankly at Bruce, Zachary, and Nina before recognition dawned. "Wha... What happened?" he rasped, struggling to stay on his feet. Nina and Bruce helped steady him. "Where am I? How did you...?"

"We'll explain later, Alex," Nina interrupted, her voice firm but gentle. "We need to get moving before they find us."

"They?"

"We're in a cavern near Zachary's farm. It's a major Reptilian base. Like Nina said, we'll fill in the details later," Bruce said quickly—if they lived to tell the tale.

"Right," Simmons agreed. "What's the plan?"

"First things first, we get out of here. We're too exposed like this and they'll be coming back for the rest of these any minute now," Bruce said, pointing to the remaining cryolockers and body bags.

"Which way?" Nina asked, looking in every direction.

"This way. Come on," Bruce led them back to the natural passage he'd squeezed through earlier.

As the foursome made their way through the narrow passage, they took turns filling Alex in on the impending Reptilian attack on Earth—and their plans to thwart it, with the help of the Annunaki.

"The Annunaki?" Alex asked, bewildered.

Nina explained. "Yes, the Annunaki," she confirmed. "They're a third race of extraterrestrials, aside from the Greys and Reptilians, who have an interest in and have been visiting Earth for millennia. Unlike the Greys who seem totally ambivalent and only interested in their research, the Annunaki have shown a willingness to aid against the Reptilian invasion."

Simmons paused in his steps to say, "I've heard stories of the Annunaki and their involvement with potential evolution, but what the hell!? And how do you know all this?"

"Julia is one of them," Bruce said.

"Julia? An Annunaki!?" Simmons blinked. "I'll be damned. I knew there was something about her, something special…but I'd never have guessed there was something that special! Say, where is she?"

"We do not know," said Zachary.

"We don't even know if she's alive or dead," added Bruce.

"Oh…" Alex slumped.

"Bruce, I haven't had time to tell you," Nina began.

"What is it?"

"Julia's alive. At least, I believe she's alive."

"What are you talking about?" asked Zachary. "Are you certain?"

"Well…I think so. I mean, she talked to me."

"She talked to you?"

"In my head." Nina tapped the side of her skull. "I heard her. She helped me when I was in trouble.."

"Nina, I'm sorry," Bruce said, taking her hand, "but are you sure you weren't, you know, hallucinating? Only imagining that you heard Julia?"

"No, I mean, I don't think so. I don't know."

"Can you hear her now?" Bruce asked carefully. "Is she talking to you?" He shot a worried glance at Zachary who merely shrugged.

"No," Nina admitted.

"Okay. Let's say she is alive and can communicate via ESP or something. And let's hope she contacts you again, because without her help, and the help of Enlil and his crew aboard their ship, I don't think we stand much chance of living, let alone thwarting a Reptilian battle fleet."

"Bruce is right," Alex said. "We can't rely solely on these... Annunaki to save us. We need our own plan."

"Any ideas?" Zachary was the first to ask.

"I'm starting to remember some things from when they brought me here. I think I know where they stashed our weapons," Alex replied.

"Good," Nina murmured. "We're going to need them."

They followed Agent Simmons through a series of dark passages until they reached a small unguarded room, illuminated by a single LED bulb. A cache of weapons lay inside, hidden beneath a tattered oilcloth.

"Our weapons!" Bruce said, thrilled to be reunited with the weaponry Julia had given them.

"Take whatever you can carry," Simmons instructed. "And be quick about it. We don't have much time."

Bruce grabbed a handgun, checking its chamber for ammunition before sliding it into his waistband.

Nina and Zachary also armed themselves, their faces showing determination as they prepared to confront the aliens.

"Ready?" Agent Simmons asked quietly, his hands filled with guns and explosives stuffed inside his shirt and under his belt as his eyes scanned the group. The man looked ready to battle the world.

"Ready," they chorused in unison, the word echoing like a promise through the air.

"Time to go reptile hunting," Alex said, raising his weapon.

"We need to work our way to the entrance and then—"

"Shh," Nina hushed Bruce. "I think... I think I can hear Julia."

"Inside your head?" Zachary asked, his brow furrowed with concern for his granddaughter.

"Yes." Nina nodded, her gaze locked on some invisible point in the distance. "She's guiding us to the command-and-control center. This way." She gestured down a tunnel branching to the left. The group followed her lead without hesitation.

As he crept forward, Bruce wondered whether Julia's Annunaki powers would be enough to help them put an end to the Reptilian invasion.

"Stop!" Nina hissed, her hand shooting out to stop Bruce and the others in their tracks. "Reptilian patrol. Everybody keep still."

They held their breaths as the footsteps of the approaching guards echoed through the corridor. Bruce silently prayed that their newfound ally could somehow keep them hidden from the Reptilians' watchful eyes.

"Move, now!" Nina urged. They slipped away just in time, narrowly avoiding detection.

"That was close," Simmons muttered, wiping sweat from his brow. "You okay, Zachary?" The old professor was doubled over, hands on his knees, and breathing hard.

"Yes, yes. Merely catching my breath." Zachary forced a smile.

"Julia says we're almost there," Nina told them. "She says that if we can destroy their command center, we will cripple their entire operation and disable the Arch. Put a stop to the invasion."

As they continued onward, Nina spoke up. "Julia says it's just up ahead. They rounded another blind corner. As they approached a gap in the cavern wall, the now-familiar buzz of Reptilian voices met them.

Bruce swallowed hard, his fingers tightening around the grip of his weapon. He had a feeling that whatever happened next would change his life forever…would change all their lives.

ᴄʜᴀᴘᴛᴇʀ 18

Frustratingly, Nina had received no further word from Julia or the Annunaki in orbit.

They stood alone.

"Check your weapons, everybody. By the sounds of it, we're getting closer." Moving quickly, Alex deftly loaded his weapon. "We don't know how many of these Reptiles we'll be facing."

"Grandpa," Nina whispered to Zachary, her eyes filled with concern, "are you sure you're up for this? It could get dangerous. You could wait. We can find someplace safe for you to remain until—"

"Nonsense." Zachary waved aside her concerns. "My dear, I've spent my entire life preparing for this moment. Don't take it away from me."

Nina smiled. "I wouldn't dream of it, Grandpa." She wrapped her arms around him.

Bruce admired both Nina and her grandfather and the close bond they shared. He felt a pang of longing for the connection he and Jack had shared, a connection, which, for all their brotherly bickering, had been priceless.

"Alright, everyone ready?" Bruce asked, checking his gear one last time. Everyone nodded, and without another word, they continued deeper into the cavern towards the command-and-control center.

Bruce stole a look at Nina, her hair bundled in a ponytail. He couldn't deny his attraction to her. He wondered if she felt as strongly about him as he did about her? Maybe, when this was all over, he'd find out. Right now, they had a mission to complete…and maybe their deaths to meet.

Bruce sensed a metallic odor mingling with the acrid scent of sweat and an otherworldly smell that he surmised might be the alien scent of the Reptilians.

Agent Simmons took point, his eyes scanning the darkness for any signs of Reptilians. "Stay low," he cautioned, signaling to the group as they carefully moved forward, avoiding any loose rocks that might betray their presence. "These Reptilians have keen senses."

"Remember," Zachary said softly, "the crystal and transmission lines are our main objectives."

"Don't I know it," Bruce replied, thinking about Carla and her children back in the city and all the other innocents whose lives were at stake. The fate of St. Louis, and perhaps entire world, rested on their shoulders.

"I wonder how much further?" Nina asked. No one answered because no one knew.

As they advanced further through the tunnels, they seemed to shift before Bruce's very eyes. He felt like he was a character in an all-too-real-looking science fiction novel. The passage veered sharply to the left.

"Wait," Alex said, raising his weapon. "I hear something."

Bruce heard it too, a dull hum coming from ahead, growing in both volume and intensity. The group froze, their eyes searching the darkness around them.

"Something's coming," Nina mouthed. She frantically gestured towards an approaching light source that, as it came closer, revealed what was actually dozens of individual lights.

Bruce knew they were too exposed. There were too many of them to fight. They didn't stand a chance. His gaze locked with Nina's as if they shared the same thought. There was only one option.

"Run!" Bruce whispered sharply. He grabbed Nina's arm and sprinted down the cavern's side tunnel. The others followed close behind. They ducked under jagged stalactites and skidded clumsily around sharp corners. Behind them, the hum turned into a roar as a dozen or more armed Reptilians flooded into the main cavern.

Zachary came to a stop. "Need to catch my breath a moment."

"No time!" Bruce grasped Zachary's arm, supporting his weight as they pressed on.

"Here," Nina said, suddenly veering to the right. She pointed towards a shadowy tunnel that deviated from the main path. The smaller, winding tunnel swallowed them in an icy darkness. The only sounds that filled the tunnel was the sound of their ragged breathing.

Eventually, they emerged into an expansive chamber bathed in a sickly green glow emanating from some weird luminescent crystals embedded in the rock formations. The foreign, almost spectral light cast an otherworldly aura over the room, and illuminated an intricate network of pipes and conduits running up the walls and disappearing into the ceiling. At the center of it all sat a complex mass of pulsating machinery. Bruce found it almost beautiful in a strange sort of way.

"This is it," Nina breathed, her gaze fixed on the alien machines. "The command-and-control center."

Bruce turned his eyes away from the spectacle and scanned the room for threats. To his relief, there were no Reptilian guards in sight—they seemed to have lost them, at least for now. Yet he knew this was probably only the calm before the storm.

Alex immediately went into action, moving towards one of the control panels embedded into the cavern wall with Zachary following him. Nina stayed by Bruce's side, her eyes never leaving the machine, as if hypnotized.

"Let's do this," Bruce said, his voice echoing in the vast chamber. He unzipped his backpack, revealing an assortment of explosives. "Give me a hand."

"Sorry." Nina pulled her eyes away and rushed to assist him in setting up the explosives around the room, affixing them to key points on the transmission lines.

Alex and Zachary examined the control panels. Zachary's eyes shone brightly in the eerie green light as he fiddled with an array of switches and buttons, muttering softly under his breath,

"Unbelievable...the technology is far beyond anything I've seen."

"Can you disable it?" Simmons asked.

"Maybe so," Zachary replied, although he didn't sound very confident. "It may take some time though."

"Time is a commodity we don't have, Zachary," Simmons replied.

"I am aware of that, Alex," Zachary retorted, his eyes never leaving the panel. "Now, if you could stop bothering me, I might be able to work faster."

Bruce smiled to himself as he caught their exchange. This was not the first time he had seen Zachary stand up for himself. The scientist was a tough old bird.

"Nina, Bruce," Alex called out across the cavern, "we've got company."

Bruce turned and caught sight of a group of armed Reptilians pouring out of one of the tunnels. Time seemed to slow down.

"We need to buy some time." Bruce drew his weapon. "Keep trying," he instructed Zachary. He positioned himself between the elder scientist and the oncoming Reptilians. His weapon was up and firing. The cavern erupted with deafening noise and searing blue laser lights illuminated the combatants. The sounds of commotion and weapons echoed off the walls.

"Bruce!" Nina shouted.

Nina's warning drew his attention just in time to see her fire at a Reptilian who had broken away from the rest and was charging towards him. The alien fell to its knees before collapsing onto its face, its strange skin smoking where the deadly beam of Nina's laser had pierced it.

"Thank you," Bruce managed to say before turning back to take out another Reptilian trying to flank them. Out of the corner of his eye, Bruce saw Alex take a hit to his left shoulder. He merely grunted and continued firing, dispatching two more Reptilians in the blink of an eye.

"Look, there's Dr. Barry!" Alex shouted. He aimed at the Grey on the opposite side of the cavern, several Reptilians flanked him. Alex's shots missed and Dr. Barry took cover. His bodyguards returned fire.

Meanwhile, Zachary worked furiously on the panel. Despite the chaos around him, he seemed to maintain an uncanny calmness. "I may have it!" he shouted above the cacophony of gunfire and alien weaponry.

The Reptilian forces appeared to be dwindling. They'd managed to hold them back, but their ammo was running dangerously low.

"The explosives! Now!" Bruce shouted above the din of combat. He scrambled for the plastic explosives in his pack.

"But I think I can—" argued Zachary.

"No, Zachary. It's too late for that!" Bruce yelled.

"Time to go, Grandpa!" Nina grabbed Zachary and dragged him along with her. The older man clung to her arm for dear life.

Suddenly, a deafening explosion drowned out all other sounds. Bruce felt a heat wave rush past them as he dived into the tunnel entrance behind Nina and Zachary. Alex came last, his body thrown forward by the shockwave.

"Zachary! Nina!" Bruce shouted. "Alex!" He stumbled blindly through the chaos and found Zachary lying on the ground a few meters away. The old man was alive but visibly shaken. Bruce leaned over him, checking for any serious injuries. "You okay?" he panted, offering his hand to the scientist.

Zachary nodded, taking his hand and pulling himself up with a grimace. "I'll live. But I can't say the same for their equipment."

Bruce let out a breathless chuckle, relief washing over him. It seemed they had succeeded, at least for now. His gaze darted around the tunnel in search of Nina.

"Nina!" he called out, his eyes finally landing on her prone figure. She lay sprawled near the entrance of the tunnel, unmoving. Fear gripped him as he rushed to her side. "Nina." He knelt and checked her pulse. It was steady but weak.

Zachary and Alex joined him and together they managed to bring Nina back to consciousness. Her eyes fluttered open and she attempted to sit up, wincing as she did so.

"Easy does it," cautioned Bruce.

"I'm okay," Nina said, holding herself up with her arms. "Did we do it?"

Bruce scrambled back and peered into the wrecked command-and-control center. Reptilians rushed around with fire extinguishers, putting out a half-dozen blazes. In the middle of all the smoke and fire, the main crystal appeared unharmed and pulsated with unfathomable energy.

Bruce cursed. Most of the aliens were busy with damage control. This was his opportunity. Looking quickly around, he noticed one last pack of explosives. He picked it up carefully.

"Bruce," Nina began, "what are you thinking?"

"Cover me!" he shouted, sprinting towards the crystal with all the speed he could muster.

"Go, Bruce! We've got your back!" Alex called out.

Bruce weaved through the chaos, dodging blasts of energy and piles of burning debris. *Almost there...* he thought, his eyes locked onto his target, the massive crystal and the intricate network of transmission lines vibrating with alien energy and snaking away from it, and disappearing into the rock.

But just as his fingers brushed against the cool, smooth surface of the crystal, a guttural buzz echoed throughout the cavern. Bruce's blood ran cold as he turned to see a fresh wave of reinforcements pouring in between himself and his escape route, their eyes glowing with murderous intent.

"Damn it!" Bruce cursed under his breath. The explosives in his hand felt suddenly heavier, as if mocking him for his audacity.

"Stand down, human!" one of the newcomers ordered, waving an alien rifle menacingly. "Or die."

"Never," Bruce spat back, defiance burning in his chest. He couldn't—wouldn't—give up now. He turned his attention to the crystal and lifted the explosives.

"Then you shall die!" the Reptilian snarled, raising its weapon to strike him down.

Bruce braced himself for the inevitable. He might die but he'd destroy the crystal.

Zachary, though spent and breathless from overexertion, noticed Bruce's plight. A flash of inspiration darted through his weary eyes, and he scrambled towards a nearby pile of rubble. With a makeshift fuse and a few choice chemicals, he crafted a crude explosive device.

"Stay low!" Zachary yelled. He began counting down as the fuse smoldered. "Get ready!" he warned his companions just before hurling the bomb towards their Reptilian adversaries. The bomb arced through the air. An instant later, an explosion rattled the cavern, a deafening boom echoing off its walls. The Reptilian guards staggered, disoriented by the blast—and for a fleeting moment, the tide of battle shifted in the humans' favor.

"Move, Bruce, now!" Nina screamed, her voice straining against the ringing in her ears.

Bruce ran. Black smoke and debris clouded the air, threatening to choke him as he dashed blindly through the haze. He felt the heat from the blast singe his exposed skin, but there was no time to worry about that now. He had to reach the others before the guards regained their senses.

"Are you alright?" Nina gasped, as Bruce skidded to a halt beside her.

"Been better," he replied tersely. "But I failed."

"You tried," Alex said. "That's all any of us can do. Now we need to get out of here. Zachary's little distraction won't hold them for long."

As if on cue, the Reptilian guards began to shake off their

disorientation, the sound of their angry buzzing filling the mine. Bruce glanced back at the crystal and attached transmission lines, still pulsing with deadly potential. Regret gnawed at him—he had come so close…

"Let's move!" Alex barked, leading the retreat deeper into the mine.

"Where did Barry go?" Nina asked, her eyes scanning the dimly lit surroundings for any sign of the treacherous Grey.

"Looks like he took advantage of the chaos," Bruce muttered. "He's probably halfway to his spaceship by now."

"Damn him," Alex swore in disgust. He'd come close to becoming one of the doctor's gruesome experiments himself. "We'll deal with him later." Or so he hoped. "For now, we need to focus on getting out of here and coming up with a plan B."

"We have to alert the people of St. Louis," Bruce said. "We can't let them destroy the city."

But it was too late. A distant rumble suddenly echoed through the tunnels, reverberating off the walls and causing the ground beneath their feet to lurch and tremble. The team exchanged alarmed glances, instinctively bracing against the tremors.

"Look!" Zachary pointed towards a nearby set of undamaged monitors displaying live footage of the carnage unfolding in St. Louis. Massive Reptilian spaceships, dark and menacing, soared through the sky, raining down destruction upon the city. Thousands of people ran around in terror. Flames danced amidst the ruins, casting an ominous glow across the desolate landscape.

"Didn't think we'd get a front-row seat to the destruction," Nina murmured. "It's already happening. St. Louis is under attack."

"May the gods help us," Bruce whispered. His heart sank as he took in the devastation wrought by the invaders.

"I assume by gods, you mean the Annunaki, right, Bruce?" Zachary said.

"Yeah, I suppose I do."

"Right, let's keep moving," Nina urged. "We've got to help them."

"Agreed," Bruce said. "We can't give up now."

As they turned to continue their retreat, a chilling voice cut through the darkness, paralyzing them with dread.

"Leaving so soon?" The cold, mocking tone belonged to none other than Mr. Stafford—the earthside leader of the Reptilians. A thick group of armed Reptilians flanked him, with the muzzles of their alien weapons pointed at them. They quickly cut off all avenues of escape.

"Seems like our little game of cat and mouse has come to an end," Stafford said triumphantly, eyes glittering with malice. "You've been quite the thorns in our side. But you'll soon learn that we are not to be trifled with."

ᛁᛖᚲᛰᛏᛁᚾᛒᛃ 19

High above, a gargantuan starship came into view over the city of St. Louis—at least, for those humans who weren't too busy fleeing for their lives from the invaders to see it.

From his vantage in the sky, Enlil, captain of the Annunaki vessel, looked down on the city below him, and at the wide Mississippi, with solemn eyes. Enlil was one of the old ones. The Mesopotamians had named a god after him, the god they associated with earth, air, wind and storms. He was also the first chief deity of the Sumerian pantheon, and sometimes referred to as Nunamnir in their religious texts.

The Akkadians, Babylonians, Assyrians, and Hurrians later worshipped him as well. Enlil had personally overseen the construction of the ancient Ekur temple, located in the city of Nippur. The temple was regarded as the "mooring-rope" between Heaven and Earth. Now, in the city below, Enlil observed the explosions of conflict and the tiny fleeing forms of humans desperately trying to escape the mayhem. His heart went out to them.

"Prepare for deployment," he ordered his crew in their strange, musical language. He could not stand by while innocent beings were slaughtered.

***

The interior of the MacGregor Mine reverberated with the sounds of battle in the sky outside as Stafford, identifiable by his human clothes although he was no longer in human guise, aimed a plasma-pulse rifle at Nina, Bruce, Zachary, and Alex. Bruce had seen these alien weapons in action—they were rapid-firing and deadly. The Reptilian's cold unearthly eyes betrayed no emotion, but his voice seemed to hold a tinge of regret.

"As much as he wishes to have you all alive, Dr. Barry will have to accept your deaths," Stafford said, his gaze sweeping over their haggard faces. "You've become too much of a nuisance. I promised Barry I'd keep you alive, but circumstances have changed. The doctor will have to make do with whatever remains of you that he can scrape off the floor."

The four stood rooted in place, facing death. Bruce clenched his fists, his mind searching for a way out, while Nina stared down Stafford defiantly and stood between the alien and her grandfather, whom Alex was propping up by the elbow.

"As I've heard in your films," Stafford asked, his fingers poised on the trigger, "any last words?"

"Go to hell," Nina spat, her eyes blazing with venom.

"Typical human response," he replied. "Tell me, does it make you feel better to curse me out? Frankly, I don't know what Dr. Barry sees in you. You humans are nothing more than semi-sentient creatures, useful as beasts and for the harvesting of your souls, nothing more."

Bruce pulled Nina closer as Stafford narrowed his eyes and took aim. As he squeezed the trigger, an explosion ripped through the air, an intense bright white light filling the chamber like a tidal wave. The force knocked them all off their feet, their surroundings blurred by the blinding illumination. As the light dimmed to normal, Bruce scrambled to his feet, coughing up dust. Nina and Alex were helping Zachary.

Bruce rubbed the dirt from his stinging eyes, trying to make sense of the new figure standing before them. "Julia?" Bruce managed to gasp, recognizing the long red hair and hazel eyes. "How did you get here?"

"And what was that explosion?" Nina asked.

"I detonated a star-flare," Julia explained. "They are small weapons but not lethal. I couldn't risk doing anything further. Anything more powerful might have brought the mine down on you."

"Is Stafford dead?" Alex wanted to know.

"Unfortunately, no. The star-flare will only have stunned him. He's fled, but he'll be back with reinforcements. The Reptilians are openly attacking St. Louis and the military bases across the state. The Americans are fighting back but taking heavy losses."

"Yeah, we saw on the monitor," Bruce replied. "But what about our military? Surely, they can do something—"

"The Reptilians had the element of surprise," Julia interrupted, her face illuminated in the flickering glow of the mineshaft. "That and their advanced technology makes them no match for your military. They were not prepared for this kind of assault."

"And some of our military may be under the control of the Reptilians," added Zachary.

"Yes, that may be so," agreed Julia.

"Then what do we do?" Nina asked, a sense of desperation coloring her words.

"We fight," Julia replied.

"We'll do what we can," began Zachary, "but there are so many of them, and so few of us…"

"We won't last long," agreed Alex.

"But you are not alone, you have an ally," Julia said. "Come, follow me."

Julia led them quickly out of the old mine to the surface. The surrounding woods were filled with Reptilians warships and transports. More Reptilians raced in all directions on the ground hauling gear to and fro. On seeing the team emerge from the depths of the mine, two nearby Reptilians dropped their gear, took aim and fired at them.

Julia waved her hands and, in an instant, a force field shimmered into being around her and the cluster of humans behind her. The incoming plasma bolts scattered harmlessly. "Look to the sky," Julia said, raising her hand to the sky. "It is Enlil. He's come."

At that moment, a new rush of noise filled the air—the whir of powerful engines. Bruce looked upwards to see an enormous shadow looming over them. He shielded his eyes from the blinding lights emanating from the craft as it descended towards them.

The ship landed with a gentle thud, and several figures emerged—tall, humanoid, glowing softly with an aura that made them seem ethereal, godlike. Standing at their forefront was a being of commanding presence.

"Behold Enlil, captain of the Annunaki ship," Julia said.

Enlil's gaze swept over them, taking in their ragged state. "We have come to aid you," the alien announced, his voice resonating throughout the clearing. He was a tall figure. His skin had a bluish tinge and appeared almost translucent. His piercing blue eyes were undoubtedly alien yet held a warmth that eased their fear. "Julia, I didn't think we'd meet again so soon."

"Just soon enough, Enlil," said Julia. "Thank you for coming. Enlil, these are my friends," Julia motioned at Nina, Bruce, Alex and Zachary. "Everyone, this is Enlil of Nibiru. He captains the Cali."

Nina, flabbergasted, gasped. "Member of the triad of gods? God of the atmosphere?" She was standing before the creator of so-called Heaven and Earth. The superior being who wished to people the Earth with sentient creatures. To do so, he'd molded primates as easily as humans mold clay. Then, using his own blood, gave humans life and intellect. All her and her grandfather's theories, come true before their eyes!

Enlil nodded humbly. "The Reptilian forces converging on this location are stronger than anticipated. We must move quickly to the ship...or, as early humans called it, our wheel in the sky."

With Enlil leading the way, Bruce and the others hurried aboard without a second thought. The spacecraft soared into the air even as they were strapping themselves into seats. Nina and Bruce looked around in confusion. Bruce's mouth hung open in stunned silence. If Jack could see him now!

Zachary seemed the least perturbed, chuckling quietly under his breath. "I always knew it would come to this," he murmured while the Annunaki crew hurried to their stations. Overhead, the sound of the ship's engines had grown into a powerful thrumming that reverberated through the hull.

Enlil called up a holo-map of St. Louis overhead, where they saw St. Louis alight with flashes from Reptilian ships in combat with US military fighter jets. The human pilots were battling bravely, their aircraft darting like tiny birds against the monstrous alien ships. But for every hit that the human side managed to land, the Reptilian ships retaliated with twice the force, and one by one, human aircrafts were sent spiraling down in smoky trails.

"Can't you do something?" begged Bruce, looking to Julia and Enlil. "You have this massive ship…"

"We are doing what we can," Enlil answered calmly, pushing a few buttons on a panel. "We are sending our troops, such as we have, to aid your forces on the ground. Meanwhile, we have got to neutralize Stafford."

Enlil turned towards Alex who was standing at attention, his well-trained eyes following the flight patterns of the Reptilian ships on the holographic display. "I command a survey ship, not a battleship. Agent Simmons, I need your advice on the best way to infiltrate their vessels. Do you have any intel that could assist us?"

Alex took a moment, assessing the situation in front of him through narrowed eyes. He'd been independently studying the Reptilians for months and, in addition to his security training, he was a trained aeronautical engineer. "Their hull's weakest point is likely beneath the engine thrusters." He pointed at the holographic image of a Reptilian ship. "If we can hit them there with enough force, it should breach their shields."

"Yes," Enlil nodded. "That matches with what we know of their ships' design and the information our scanners reveal. But it is always good to have another set of eyes on the matter, human ones, in this case." He thanked Alex before swiftly relaying orders to his crew in the Annunaki language.

With the advanced intelligence and technology the Annunaki possessed, Nina wondered if Enlil had only asked the agent's advice as a courtesy, but said nothing. She watched as Annunaki soldiers lined up, readying themselves for deployment. Turning to Julia, she said, "I thought you Annunaki were only going to provide logistical support? No troops. Not that I'm complaining!" she hastened to add.

"Enlil has decided that the time has come to reveal ourselves," Julia explained. "And rightly so. Earth doesn't stand a chance of defeating the Reptilians on their own."

Nina agreed wholeheartedly and said so.

An Annunaki officer hurried to Enlil's side and whispered in their alien tongue. The expression on the captain's face grew dark. "I have just received troubling news," he said. "Intel suggests that the capital ship under the command of Stafford is preparing to make use of their energy cannon. If it is deployed, St. Louis and its environs will be leveled in minutes."

"What is this energy cannon?" Bruce asked.

"A weapon powerful enough to destroy entire cities. Much like your nuclear weapons," Julia replied softly. "But on an infinitely greater scale."

"We Annunaki have been watching Earth's nuclear tests and bases since your initial experiments," added Enlil.

Bruce nodded. That would explain why so many alien sightings occurred around military installations, especially nuclear capable ones. Jack had told him there had been dozens, maybe hundreds of sightings, after the first atomic bombs were dropped over Hiroshima and Nagasaki. Once again, his brother had been right.

"Of course, your nuclear weapons are mere flyswatters compared to the energy cannons," added Enlil. "Such a weapon can pulverize an area in the range of fifty of your square miles."

The team stood in stunned silence as the gravity of Enlil's words sank in. An energy cannon powerful enough to level an entire city in one devastating blow? Millions of lives would be lost. The images of their city being reduced to rubble was too horrifying to comprehend.

"We cannot let that happen," Bruce said fiercely. He looked around the room at the faces of his friends and allies. "We have to stop him."

Enlil nodded. "Agreed. We must prevent this catastrophe." He instructed his officers to strategize an assault plan to take on and destroy or disable the energy cannon. Meanwhile, the others prepared themselves for the battle of their lives. The ship boiled with activity, the atmosphere tense.

"Crew of Cali," Enlil announced through the ship's comm, "we are about to embark upon an operation that could potentially decide the fate of this planet and its inhabitants. We must succeed at all costs. Even the cost of our own lives."

As he finished his speech, Zachary nudged Bruce gently. "Never thought I'd see the day when I'd be on board an Annunaki wheel in the sky preparing for battle against a Reptilian invasion," he mused, his eyes darting across the unfamiliar controls filling the Annunaki helm room. "As deadly serious as it is, I must say I find the entire thing fascinating. Simply fascinating."

Bruce noted the glint of excitement that lit his old eyes. That was Zachary, forever the enthusiastic scholar, even in the face of life-threatening danger.

As if on cue, an officer raced into the room, skidding to a halt in front of Enlil and handing him a tablet with a grim expression on his face. Enlil's eyes scanned the screen before he let out a sharp breath and looked up at the other occupants of the room.

"Stafford has detected us. Sensors reveal he's turning the energy cannon towards the Cali." His voice was steady, but something in his gaze made Bruce's stomach drop.

"Can we evade?" Alex asked.

Enlil shook his head grimly. "Not in time. Our only chance is to disable that cannon before it can build up its store of energy to fire on us."

"Maybe if we get closer—" began Bruce.

"Closer?" Nina snapped. "Won't that just get us killed faster?"

"No." Bruce pointed at the monitors. "Look at all those other Reptilian battleships." A ring of smaller Reptilian battleships circled the capital ship. "If we can get the Cali in closer, might they not be too close to fire on us, Enlil?"

Enlil thought a moment then smiled. "Yes, good thinking, Bruce." Enlil gave a sharp nod. "We have our mission, everyone," he announced. The starship buzzed with heightened intensity as the spaceship was programmed to accelerate toward the very thing that was determined to kill them. Orders were quickly relayed and Annunaki obediently rushed to carry them out, every member of the crew busy preparing for their designated role in the impending confrontation.

"I hope somebody here has a plan," Nina said, looking around the comm, "for what to do if the first part of this crazy plan works!"

Bruce shared a glance with Agent Simmons before replying—the two of them had been whispering back and forth. "Not much of one," he admitted grimly. "I guess we'll have to improvise, right, Enlil?"

"At the very least," answered Enlil, stoically, "we shall ram them."

And they all knew what that meant to everyone onboard the Cali…

As Enlil's commanding voice echoed around the ship, there was a moment of silence before the Annunaki ship's engine suddenly hummed and shook as its advanced magnetic propulsion system kicked in. Within seconds, they were rocketing at high speed toward their deadly objective. The sheer velocity pressed everyone into their seats as they sped towards the much larger Reptilian warship.

In the distance, they could see the Reptilian ship, its general structure somehow eerily similar to that of a giant serpent. Enlil pointed out the energy cannon, pulsating with an ominous glow. As they watched, it began to spark with increasing intensity.

"That means it's nearly ready to fire," explained Julia.

Sweating profusely, Bruce grabbed Nina's hand tightly. Their eyes met. Nina gave him a weak smile—death would soon be upon them. They shared a brief kiss. A sudden jerk snapped them back into focus as Enlil skillfully maneuvered the ship closer to their enemy's vessel.

"Prepare for battle!" The Annunaki captain's voice boomed through the starship. Annunaki soldiers stood ready at their stations, tense and ready for battle. "How long before the force field is operable?"

"Working on it, Enlil!" shouted a crewman.

Julia explained to Bruce and the others that the force fields drew energy from the engines and required some minutes to build to full strength.

Suddenly, the spaceship shook, the lights flickering as a low groan filled the room. They were being attacked!

"We've been hit!" an officer yelled through the cacophony of high-pitched alarms blaring across the spaceship.

An unexpected and unwelcome voice burst through the Cali's intercom. It was Stafford. His cold, omnipresent voice made the hairs on the back of Bruce's neck bristle.

"Surrender now and I shall spare your ship and your city," Stafford taunted. "Make your choice: ensure complete annihilation, or surrender and live."

"Never!" Nina spat, her knuckles white around the armrest of her seat.

"Your threats are empty," Enlil retorted defiantly. "We will not be intimidated by your brutish tactics. The Annunaki stand with Earth. And we shall not fall."

Stafford's laughter echoed through the comm system. "We'll see about that," the Reptilian sneered, his voice falling silent as an explosion rocked the Cali once more.

The attack further galvanized the Annunaki crew. They adjusted their course, skillfully maneuvering their ship through the onslaught of laser fire, aiming for the pulsating heart of the Reptilian warship—the energy cannon.

The spaceship shook violently as another explosion rocked them off course. The alarms grew more urgent and deafening, adding to the chaos as crew members scrambled to regain control of their starship— a craft built for exploration, not war.

Stafford's voice crackled over their comm once more. "You should have stayed out of this, Enlil," he seethed. "Your interference will be your downfall."

As his sinister words echoed around them, a surge of power hummed through the starship. Bruce felt the floor of the Cali vibrating beneath his feet. An eruption of blinding light filled the ship's front viewscreen as the energy cannon's beam shot straight towards them.

"Brace for impact!" Enlil ordered, but he was already too late. The beam struck the Cali ship with a colossal force, throwing everyone off their feet as the Cali spun out of control.

"Enlil!" Bruce called out, his voice drowned out by the deafening alarms and the groaning of the ship's hull. He pulled himself up, senses overwhelmed with the tang of burning circuitry. Nina lay unconscious beside him, a thin trail of blood shone on her forehead under the emergency lights. Zachary hovered over her providing succor.

"We've lost primary control," Enlil spat through gritted teeth, struggling to bring the ship back on course. "Backup systems are failing."

Alex helped Bruce to his feet before rushing over to Julia who lay sprawled on the floor. He held a hand to her pulse. She was alive but unconscious.

"Keep her steady," Enlil commanded. "Reroute power to the defense systems."

In a desperate play, the Annunaki worked furiously on the failing systems. The ship quaked violently under the barrage of attacks. From the corner of his eye, Bruce watched Alex Simmons lift Julia onto a makeshift stretcher. The sight of her and Nina hurt tugged at his heart, but he pushed his concerns aside and focused on the task at hand.

Staying alive and thwarting the Reptilian attack.

Enlil let out a triumphant yell. "Got it! Shields are back online!"

In that moment, the ship steadied, a force field surrounding them just in time as another blast from the Reptilian warship hurtled toward them. The cannon's energy dispersed around their shield, illuminating their ship with a pulsating glow of resistance.

Stafford's voice once again came through the comm. "You're only prolonging the inevitable!"

Ignoring Stafford's bravado, Bruce turned to Enlil. "What's next?"

"We counterattack," Enlil stated, with resolve.

ᴧᴇᴋᴆᴛᴧᴧ 20

Darkness enveloped the cockpit of the space pod, pierced only by a kaleidoscope of flashing lights and the glow from the console. Enlil had instructed the pod to be disguised as one of over hundred ultrasonic magnetically-propelled missiles set to launch all in one giant burst. The starship's computer systems told them there was a good chance that at least a third of the missiles would reach their target, knowing what they did about the enemy's capabilities.

Bruce could only hope and pray as his hands gripped the controls with white-knuckled determination, that they'd be one of the lucky few to survive. If not, at least he'd die knowing he'd died trying to save the Earth. Beside him, Julia kept her eyes fixed on their target, the formidable Reptilian spaceship looming larger with each passing second.

"Port side, incoming fire!" Julia said, her voice taut with urgency.

Bruce yanked the control stick to the right, narrowly avoiding the searing plasma blast that threatened to tear through their hull. The space around them was a cacophony of chaos—smoldering wreckage, desperate radio transmissions, and the relentless barrage of enemy fire. Yet amid the pandemonium, an unbreakable bond of trust had formed between Bruce and Julia as they navigated side-by-side in the cramped quarters of their little pod against impossible odds.

"Almost there," Bruce muttered, sweat dripping from his brow. "We just need to get a little closer."

As they approached the Reptilian spaceship, the true magnitude of their mission weighed heavily upon them. They were all that stood between the Reptilians and humanity's pending destruction. But as Bruce glanced at Julia, he saw the same fierce resolve mirrored in her hazel eyes that burned within him. Together, they had come this far— a St. Louis architect and an Annunaki from Nibiru—and together, they would face Stafford and whatever horrors awaited them.

"Prepare yourself," Julia warned, her slender fingers deftly adjusting the settings on her weapon. "With luck we'll be boarding in under a minute. There's an open docking port on the underbelly of our target. I've set our pod to make entry there. With luck, the Reptilians will not notice our approach." She smiled. "Enlil is keeping them quite occupied."

"Good. I want to take Stafford by surprise," Bruce said. It wasn't merely that he wanted to, it was imperative that they did. Without the element of surprise, they'd likely be killed before stepping foot inside the Reptilian mother ship.

"Ten seconds," announced Julia.

Their tiny pod came in too hard and the entire vehicle shuddered as it contacted the Reptilian spaceship's docking port, metal grinding against metal in a cacophony that reverberated through the small craft and set the pod to dancing. Bruce held on tight as Julia hovered over the control panel trying to keep the pod from crashing into the far wall and killing them both in the process.

The pod bounced, skidded, rolled end over end, then came to a bone-jarring halt. Bruce peered out the portal. They had achieved the first part of their mission. He and Julia stood in the heart of the enemy.

"All secure," Julia announced, as she scanned the various readouts on the control panel.

"Good job," Bruce replied, releasing his grip on his seat and unclipping his straps. "Now comes the hard part." The deadly part.

Julia opened a hidden compartment beneath the console, revealing two sleek, compact weapons. "Take one," she instructed, handing one of the weapons to Bruce. "Remember what I taught you—short, controlled bursts. We don't want to draw attention to ourselves."

"Got it," Bruce said, gripping his weapon hard. The cold metal seemed to pulse with unearthly power.

"Let's move," Julia whispered, leading the way to the airlock. With a hiss, the hatch opened before them, revealing the dark interior of the Reptilian ship. The pair stepped cautiously inside the bay. The sounds of weapons filled the air and shook the ground beneath their feet.

Endless corridors stretched out before them, giving them way too many choices. Reptilian symbols adorned the walls, illuminated by an unsettling, pulsating light that seemed to throb in time with some unseen heartbeat. Fortunately, Julia said she could read the symbols. The air felt heavy with menace, practically suffocating them as they moved deeper into the bowels of the huge enemy vessel.

Julia took the lead, navigating the unfamiliar passageways. Their footsteps were muffled by the soft, almost organic flooring that seemed to squirm uncomfortably beneath their feet.

"Wait," Julia signaled, her hand shooting out to halt Bruce in his tracks. A faint sound echoed through the corridor—an ominous buzzing accompanied by heavy footfalls. Reptilian guards, no doubt patrolling the ship to maintain order during the chaos of battle.

"Down here." Julia pulled Bruce into a narrow alcove as the guards approached. They held their breath as the monstrous forms lumbered past, their cold alien eyes glinting as they passed within inches of their hiding place.

"Let's go," Bruce urged once the guards had moved on. Before long, the corridor gave way to a vast chamber. The command center of the Reptilian spaceship sprawled before them, an intricate network of alien technology that practically screamed its sinister intent. At its epicenter stood Mr. Stafford, his cold eyes fixed on a holographic display that projected the pandemonium of the ongoing battle beyond the ship's skin.

"Stafford—our final obstacle," Julia whispered. The Reptilian leader stood alone on the bridge.

Bruce slowly raised his weapon and took aim. Enlil had explained to him that killing Stafford would likely immobilize the Reptilian forces—for the time being at least—putting an end to the current invasion. "Cut off its head, and the snake dies," Enlil had explained.

Sensing their presence, Stafford turned slowly from the display, his icy gaze falling upon the intruders. A cruel smile twisted his lips as he spoke, his voice dripping with arrogance. "Ah, Bruce and Julia. I must admit, I'm impressed you made it this far."

"It ends here, Stafford," Bruce declared. "We won't let you destroy Earth."

"Destroy?" Stafford feigned offense, raising a hand to his chest. "I prefer to think of it as... reshaping. This world is ripe for change, and we will be the architects of its new era."

"Over our dead bodies," Julia spat, her hazel eyes blazing with defiance.

"An unfortunate, but not unforeseen possibility," Stafford replied, his tone chillingly casual. "And none too soon, I may say. As you see," he drawled, waving at the monitor, "you're too late. Our plan is already in motion. And soon, Earth and all who inhabit it will bow to Reptilian rule."

"Never underestimate the power of the human spirit," Bruce countered, clenching his fists at his sides. He knew the stakes were higher than ever, but he refused to give in to fear.

"Nor the Annunaki," Julia said.

"Human spirit? Such a primitive concept," Stafford sneered. "It's no match for the might of the Reptilian empire."

"Guess we'll have to prove you wrong, won't we?" Julia challenged.

"Very well," Stafford replied, his eyes narrowing. "Let us see if your 'spirit' can withstand the wrath of a Reptilian overlord."

With a swift movement, the alien launched himself at Julia and Bruce. Julia fired off a shot, the energy blaster in her hand spewing forth a concentrated bolt of intense heat. Stafford deflected it with ease, an energy shield around him shimmering into existence just in the nick of time.

Bruce hurled himself at Stafford, his fist making contact with the energy shield. The force recoiled back on him, sending him sprawling backward onto the hard ceramic floor. He grimaced at the pain lancing through his hand but forced himself up to his feet again.

Julia was already on the move, her every action calculated and precise as she weaved around Stafford's deflections and attacks. Despite her agility and quick thinking, Stafford was matching her move for move. It was like watching a deadly dance unfold before him.

"Julia!" Bruce called out, drawing Stafford's attention to him. He gulped and took a step back, leveling the energy weapon at the Reptilian leader. "It's over, Stafford!"

Stafford didn't respond, only smirked at him. The air around the alien began to shimmer, the pulsating energy field seemed to be growing in intensity and size with each passing second. Bruce's gaze sharpened on the apparent source of that power—a glimmering gem embedded in the center of Stafford's chest.

"The core," Julia breathed out beside him as she too realized what they needed to do. "We have to hit the core."

Bruce nodded, gripping the weapon tighter in his hand. His breaths grew shallow as he focused on the pulsating gem, its radiant glow almost blinding him. He felt Julia move closer to him, and found her presence a comforting force beside him.

"Now!" Julia shouted. She and Bruce fired simultaneously. The twin blasts of energy arced through the air and collided with Stafford's energy shield. For a moment, nothing happened—the shield shimmered under the assault, its glow intensifying in sync with the gem at its center.

Bruce frowned and lowered his weapon.

Then, with a sound like shattering glass, Stafford's energy shield cracked and buckled. Their final, desperate attack had struck true. The gem embedded in the Reptilian's chest sparked and fizzled wildly, its once steady pulse now erratic and volatile.

"No!" Stafford roared, his icy composure finally shattered. He clutched at the malfunctioning gem, stumbling back as it sputtered and failed. His cruel eyes were wide with disbelief as he looked up at Bruce and Julia, a hint of fear finally breaking through his arrogant facade. "You... You cannot defeat...me!" the alien growled. But even as he spoke, his body began to convulse violently.

The gem on his chest flickered one last time before detonating in a brilliant display of light and color. A deafening explosion filled the chamber, throwing Bruce and Julia off their feet. The overwhelming brightness quickly faded, replaced with a thick mist that left them temporarily blinded.

When the haze finally cleared, all that remained of Stafford was a charred crater where he'd once stood. The command center was eerily silent now. The only sound they heard was their own labored breathing.

They had done it. Stafford was dead.

"We...we did it," Bruce panted, climbing to his feet and offering Julia a hand up.

She accepted his hand with a tired smile, struggling to steady herself as she rose. "We did," she acknowledged, her voice filled with raw relief. "Look!" she pointed to the holographic display. As soon as their leader had fallen, the Reptilian troops began retreating en masse from both Earth's surface and orbit.

"It's over." Bruce exhaled.

"Yes," Julia murmured. "But this is no time to relax. Now we have to get out of here if we want to live."

"Yeah."

The spaceship began to quake around them as onboard systems started to fail catastrophically. Sparks flew from consoles and smoke filled the corridors, making visibility near impossible. Alarm bells rang shrilly throughout the ship, adding a note of urgency to their escape.

Using the map on Julia's wrist device, they raced through the ship's corridors, praying they would make it out in time. As they neared the docking bay, the floor beneath them lurched violently, and they stumbled.

Bruce caught Julia just before she hit the ground, pulling her close. "Are you okay?" he asked, scanning her face for signs of injury.

"Fine," she gasped out. "Just... run!"

They sprinted the remaining distance to the docking bay, their breaths coming in short, sharp bursts. The ship gave another violent shake, and the walls around them began to crumble. Just as they reached their vessel, a massive explosion rocked the spaceship. The force of it sent them sprawling into the open hatch of their vessel.

With a grunt of effort, Bruce pulled himself up, slammed the hatch shut, and crawled to the cockpit beside Julia. A flurry of flashing lights and beeping alarms lit up the console—warnings of impending destruction. He glanced back at Julia as she gripped the controls.

"Hold on tight!" she said.

Their pod rocked violently as they sped away from the disintegrating Reptilian mother ship, dodging pieces of white-hot wreckage hurtling towards them from every direction.

ᚺᛖᚳᛞᛏᚢᚱ 21

The sun dipped below the horizon, casting long shadows across the ravaged landscape as Bruce, Nina and Zachary trudged quietly toward Zachary's battered farmhouse, an all too vivid reminder of what they'd gone through. The weary trio moved slowly, picking their way through the debris-filled yard.

"Damn," Bruce muttered under his breath, surveying the damage to the former professor's home. The once-picturesque farmhouse lay in ruins, its walls pockmarked with fresh blast marks, and its roof partially caved in. He ran a hand through his hair.

"I-I can't believe it's gone," Zachary responded, his voice laden with sorrow.

"Neither can I," Bruce replied, his eyes scanning the surrounding devastation. "And so many lives lost..." They'd all heard the news reports. Thousands had died in the Reptilian onslaught before the alien invaders had been driven off the planet by the Annunaki and the US military fighting together.

"Indeed," Zachary sighed, his gaze focused on the shattered remains of his research materials. "But we must remember that our sacrifices were not in vain. We've rid our world of the Reptilians, and gained invaluable knowledge about the universe beyond in the process."

Nina laid a hand on Bruce's arm. "You okay?" Her eyes took in the devastation that had once been her grandfather's home.

"Yeah. Just wondering what things are like for everybody back in the city." Did his house yet stand? Were Carla and the kids okay?

Bruce inhaled deeply as he realized the significance of what he and the others had accomplished. They had defeated an alien invasion, but at what cost? His brother Jack's face flashed in his mind, and he felt a pang of guilt and grief for their complicated history. The tension between them had never been resolved, and now it never could be. But at least there would be peace, closure.

"We'll rebuild, Grandpa," Nina promised Zachary. "Not only the farmhouse, but our lives... and this community."

"Yes," Zachary replied. "Thank you. None of this would have been possible without the two of you by my side…believing."

As they surveyed the ruins of the farmhouse, the distant rumble of approaching vehicles caught their attention. A convoy of black SUVs pulled up to the property, tires crunching over the scorched earth. Alex emerged from the lead vehicle, flanked by Julia and a group of stern-faced government officials.

Alex was the first to approach, his hair catching the setting sun's last light, his muscular frame cutting a strong figure against the ruined backdrop. Behind him, Julia stood back in a flowing green dress that fell to her ankles. She shuffled her feet.

"Congratulations," Alex said. He extended his hand towards Bruce. "You did good."

Bruce returned the firm handshake. "We all did."

Alex nodded in agreement before turning to Zachary and Nina. "Your help was invaluable."

Zachary's face lifted at Simmons' words. He knew how much the agent had sacrificed for them, how much he had risked his career and his own life. "We all did what we had to do. You too, Alex." He embraced the agent.

Alex nodded, then gestured towards Julia, who had been silently observing until now. Her expression was serene yet distant, her eyes filled with a universe of knowledge yet unknown by humans.

"I have much to tell," she began softly, stepping forward. "About the Annunaki, our plans for Earth and humanity...but for now it's important that you understand that we are your allies, and we wish to live in peace." Her gaze met each of theirs in turn, her sincerity evident. "I will return. Enlil, too. And there will be others.

"In the meantime, there are many secrets to unveil within reach of your own grasp. We Annunaki are a big part of many mysteries here on Earth. There are stories, even in your Bible, that replicated old Sumerian stories. The Sumerian tablets are a good starting point," Julia continued. "But also, read Ezekiel in the Bible and take care to interpret it correctly. The description of Ezekiel's wheels in the sky comes from a passage in the Bible, specifically the Book of Ezekiel. The passage, found in Ezekiel 1:4-28 and Ezekiel 10:1-22, describes a vision that the prophet Ezekiel had, which includes a complex and symbolic depiction of heavenly beings and chariots.

"In the context of aliens, some individuals have interpreted Ezekiel's vision as a possible encounter with extraterrestrial beings or advanced technology. The description of wheels within wheels, and the beings with four faces—human, lion, ox, and eagle—has led to various interpretations over time, including the possibility of an alien-like spiritual event.

"Furthermore the Book of Ezekiel in the Bible describes a vision that the prophet Ezekiel had of a divine chariot known as the 'Merkabah' or 'chariot of God.' This vision has been often interpreted in various ways, including as a symbolic representation of God's power and presence," Julia continued. "In Ezekiel's vision, he describes seeing four living creatures with human-like forms but with four faces and four wings each. These creatures have the faces of a human, a lion, an ox, and an eagle. They are accompanied by wheels within wheels—as I mentioned—with rims full of eyes, and a platform above them, upon which sits a throne-like structure with the appearance of sapphire."

"Some interpretations suggest that Ezekiel's vision could be metaphorical or symbolic, representing divine beings or even aliens. However, over time, some individuals have interpreted these descriptions as resembling modern depictions of extraterrestrial beings or spacecraft, leading to speculative theories about alien encounters in ancient texts. It's important to note that interpretations of biblical texts, including the Book of Ezekiel, can vary widely depending on religious beliefs, cultural contexts, and individual perspectives.

"These types of stories are abundant and, yet, your government and your religious leaders are hesitant to unveil where your history actually started and what impact we Annunaki had. Yes, we Annunaki had our own selfish motive for creating humans but over the years our quest for survival has changed. Anyway, I am sure I could expand upon this more at a later date. Zachary and Nina actually are aware of a lot of these stories. Maybe it is time for your leaders to listen with more intent to what is laid out right in front of them."

"We will welcome you all," Nina said. "And I will miss you most of all, Julia." The two had become the closest of friends, closer now after all they'd been through together.

"Definitely," said Alex. "I have a hunch our government would love to learn more about that ship of yours, too."

"Perhaps they shall. In the meantime," Julia continued, "I must leave Earth. But know this: when our paths cross again, it will be as friends."

With that, she turned and walked away. The government officials followed her lead and retreated back into the SUVs.

As the convoy drove off, leaving them alone in the fading twilight, Nina squeezed Bruce's hand tightly. "We'll see her again," she said.

Bruce nodded, his eyes lingering on the path Julia had taken. As an architect used to crafting designs with stability and permanence, he now found himself in a world reshaped by realities beyond his comprehension. But he was no longer the man who stood bewildered at the alien skies. He was a survivor, a fighter—a defender of Earth, as crazy and improbable as that once would have sounded. "Let's hope we don't see the Reptilians again anytime soon."

"Yes," said Zachary, gazing up at the sky. "You know, Bruce," he said, laying a gentle hand on the other man's shoulder, "the Sumerian tablets are some of the earliest known written records, dating back to around 3100 BCE. They contain stories and myths that shed light on ancient Sumerian beliefs, including creation, involving gods and the creation of mankind. In Sumerian mythology, the gods played a central role in the creation of humanity. One of the most famous stories is the Epic of Gilgamesh, which includes elements of the creation myth."

"Gilgamesh, right, I've heard of that." Bruce scratched the top of his head, unsure where Zachary was going with all this.

"According to these narratives, the gods created humans to serve them and perform tasks on their behalf," explained Zachary. "In some versions, humans were fashioned from clay mixed with the blood of a slain god. Which can lead others to believe clay is metaphorical for shaping mankind from a bipedal hominid. The gods were often depicted as powerful beings with human-like qualities but possessing supernatural abilities. These creation myths not only explained the origin of humanity but also reinforced the hierarchical structure of Sumerian society, with gods at the top and humans below them. The tablets provide us valuable insights into the religious beliefs and worldview of ancient Sumerians."

Bruce marveled at all he had learned, was learning, and still did not know.

As the first stars twinkled in the sky, they rummaged through the ruins of Zachary's farmhouse. Together, they promised themselves, and each other, that they would rebuild. They would restore their lives and their home from this surreal wreckage.

Underneath the alien constellations, Bruce felt Nina's hand squeeze his own again, her warmth anchoring him amidst all the uncertainty ahead. He returned her grip, looked into her eyes and kissed her lips.

The days that followed were filled with more labor than they had ever known. With their hands and hearts, they cleared away the rubble of the farmhouse, salvaging what little remained of Zachary's research. They worked side by side, their bodies aching with exhaustion but their spirits undeterred. The tension between Bruce and Nina simmered just beneath the surface, the spark of attraction undeniable.

In the meantime, Alex Simmons became a regular visitor, ensuring they had all they needed, from food supplies to construction materials. His stoic demeanor softened somewhat as he worked alongside them, revealing a facet of his personality they hadn't seen before.

One night, after a long day of labor, they all gathered around a makeshift bonfire. The shadow of flames flickered against their weary faces as they reminisced about the journey that had led them there. Bruce found himself laughing, sharing stories of Jack's sarcastic wit that had always brought a smile to his face even in the most absurd situations. With a bittersweet ache, he realized he was honoring his brother, keeping Jack's memory alive in the shared laughter.

Zachary looked over at him, as if reading his mind. "Jack would be proud of you, Bruce."

Bruce nodded, swallowing down the lump in his throat. He felt Nina's hand slip into his own, giving it a reassuring squeeze. Overhead, the stars twinkled like distant galaxies waiting to be discovered— reminding them of the vastness of the universe and their small place within it.

Dawn came with the promise of another day filled with hard work but also with hope. They were survivors, not just of an alien invasion but also of their own broken relationships and pasts. The sun rose on the horizon, its golden rays washing over them like a warm embrace. It was a new day, a new beginning, and although they bore the scars of an unforgettable ordeal, each was ready to embrace it with renewed vigor.

Zachary extended his hands towards the sky, as if greeting an old friend. He closed his eyes, basking in the warmth and the silence that surrounded them. "The universe," he whispered, "is vast, yet here we are... holding on."

Nina chuckled. "Oh, I'm not just holding on, Grandpa. I'm taking charge."

As the days turned into weeks, Zachary led the rebuilding project with unbridled gusto. His age did little to diminish his energy and enthusiasm as he pored over blueprints, debated with Bruce about structural integrity, and directed the reconstruction of his farmhouse like a seasoned foreman.

One afternoon, amid the hammers' clangs and saws' whines, Alex arrived with a parcel. "Delivery from Julia via the agency," he said. "She made me promise to give this to you personally."

Nina and Zachary watched as Bruce tore up the package. "What is this?" he asked, turning the small and feather light silver-and-black device over in the palm of his hand.

"Don't let its size and weight fool you. That compact little thing," explained Alex, "is a communications device capable of near-instant interstellar communication."

Bruce whistled softly. "Sweet." The surface was smooth, devoid of any buttons or screens, yet somehow it was capable of reaching across galaxies? The tiny device reminded him of the strange object Jack had found at the Arch. It was lost forever now, like his brother. Was that what he'd found? An alien communications device? If only Jack had known! He would have gotten such a kick out of it.

"You'll be able to stay in contact with Julia with that," Alex explained.

"And, presumably, Enlil and the others?" Nina chimed in, her green eyes sparkling with curiosity.

"Presumably," said Alex.

Bruce looked at the device in quiet awe. There was something sobering about holding an object that could bridge the gap between Earth and stars they'd only ever dreamed of visiting.

Despite the vast cosmic distance, they would not be alone. They could reach out to Julia, to the Annunaki, whenever they wished. This tiny device symbolized their connection to a far bigger cosmos, filled with allies and adversaries alike. It assured them that their fight had not been in vain.

"Thanks." Bruce pocketed the communicator.

Alex left after lunch just as Jack's widow, Carla, arrived. Bruce introduced his sister-in-law to Zachary and Nina, then escorted her alone to the site of her husband's grave near a mighty oak on the far edge of the farm.

A chill wind whispered through the graveyard, sending shivers along his arms as he and Carla stood before Jack's grave. The headstone loomed like a silent sentinel, bearing the face of their sorrow.

"Jack would've been proud," Bruce murmured, his breath condensing in the cold air. "He played a crucial part in all of this."

Carla's eyes glistened with tears. "If only he could be here..."

Bruce wrapped an arm around her shoulders, offering what comfort he could. "His sacrifice wasn't in vain, Carla. And he will always be here with us."

Carla nodded.

Silence settled over them like a funeral shroud, broken only by the distant calls of crows and bluebirds. Bruce's thoughts churned with memories of Jack and the now insignificant brotherly battles they'd fought.

Despite the chill, a warmth seeped into Bruce's heart. It was a warmth born out of shared pain and shared love. There and then, he made a silent promise to himself and to his brother—he would protect Carla and her children no matter what. Even if it meant standing up against the Reptilians again or some other otherworldly beings.

As weeks turned into months, Zachary's farmhouse started to come back to life. New walls stood tall where once there were ruins. Fresh paint gleamed under the sun's caress. Each brick, each beam echoed with their shared sweat, shared laughter, shared tears. This was not just a house, it was a testament to their resilience and will to survive.

Arch Enemy

One crisp morning, as Bruce stood surveying the almost finished farmhouse, a distant thrum rattled through his bones. A familiar energy pulsed around him, electric and alive. His heart skipped a beat—he knew that thrum.

Looking up, he spotted a silhouette against the bright canvas of the sky, a shape that defied all his architectural knowledge. It was an Annunaki ship, massive and awe-inspiring in its geometric precision and fantastical design—a floating city of lights and motion.

They were back.

Arch Enemy

www.ingramcontent.com/pod-product-compliance
Lightning Source LLC
Chambersburg PA
CBHW050317110726
47899CB00007B/2284